DEAD
SILENT

ROBERT FERRIGNO

DEAD
SILENT

POCKET
BOOKS

LONDON · SYDNEY · NEW YORK · TOKYO · SINGAPORE · TORONTO

First published in Great Britain by Simon & Schuster UK Ltd, 1998
First published by Pocket Books, 1999
An imprint of Simon & Schuster UK Ltd
A Viacom Company

Simon & Schuster UK Ltd
Africa House
64-78 Kingsway
London WC2B 6AH

Simon & Schuster Australia
Sydney

A CIP catalogue record for this book is available
from the British Library.

Book design by Junie Lee

1 3 5 7 9 10 8 6 4 2

0-671-00520-0

Printed and bound in Great Britain by Caledonian International Book
Manufacturing, Glasgow

ACKNOWLEDGMENTS

No writer ever walks alone. My thanks to Ron Hauge for introducing me to the wonderful world of phone pranksters, and to Renée Evans-Hauge for technical advice on the phone system. Peter Barnes of Clatter & Din Inc. patiently walked me through the basics of sound engineering and didn't laugh out loud at my questions. A heartfelt salute to William Ungerman for guidance on proper police procedure and keeping me ballistically accurate. I am indebted to Peter Levine for giving me the benefit of his clear vision. Stacy Creamer, my editor, kept the book in tune and made me look forward to rewrites. I wish to thank Mary Evans, my agent, for her passion and wise counsel.

To Jody

DEAD
SILENT

SHARON LIFTED HER head from the pillow, listening. "There they go again."

Nick had already heard the bed banging against the wall in the guest bedroom directly below them, a rhythmic rocking carried through the ductwork of the quiet house, a bass-beat counterpoint to the whisper of the nearby television. Nick watched Jay Leno's lips move as Alison cried out. He imagined Alison astride Perry, her blond hair flying around her face—

"What is this, the third time today?" Sharon yawned in the flickering video light.

"Who's counting?" said Nick, annoyed at her, angry at himself. It was the fourth time.

"I think it's the third time . . ." said Sharon. She raised herself up on one elbow, the sheet falling from her tiny breasts as she listened, eyes slitted, her expression curious and foxlike. "There was this morning, then again after lunch and now . . ."

"Let's just go to sleep."

"Alison said she thought they would be staying only a few days. Is that what Perry told you?"

"Let's just go to sleep, okay?" said Nick. When he and Perry had driven to the liquor store before dinner, Perry had talked about moving in for a week or so, just before he realized that he had left his wallet back at the house.

"I like Alison," said Sharon. "She's a little flashy, but underneath the makeup she's down-to-earth, and at least she picks up after herself. *Unlike* your old buddy Perry—" She suddenly flicked the TV remote, muting Leno in midmonologue. She cocked her head. "Alison sounds . . . funny. Can you hear her? I don't think she's talking to Perry."

Nick could make out Alison's voice, strangely chirpy now, almost conversational, but not the words. The bed continued its steady rhythm against the wall. Perry was going to have to replaster the damage. Then again, maybe it was Alison who was driving the bed through the wall. Nick shifted, smoothed the sheets, uncomfortable with the image. He felt like he was right in the room with them. It was too crowded. Alison's voice rose slightly and Nick wanted to turn up the sound on the television, drown out the drama from down below . . . but he didn't. He stayed right where he was. Listening.

"There's just the two of them down there, isn't there?" Sharon smiled. Nick could see her thick, dark nipples stiffen. "I don't know if that bed can handle more than the two of them," she teased. "Not the way they go at it."

Nick could see Leno mugging on TV, his bland face grotesque without the sound of laughter to back him up.

"What are they *doing?*" giggled Sharon. She licked her lips. "You're supposed to have the best ears in the business. Can you tell?"

Nick closed his eyes, focused on the buzz of Alison's voice over the creaking of the bed. "I think . . . I think she's talking to somebody on the phone," he said, not understanding.

"We used to play games like that," Sharon said wistfully. "Remember? We couldn't keep away from each other. I called in sick one morning so that we could spend the day in bed. While I was giving instructions to my secretary, you were under the sheets kissing me and I moaned and Michelle asked if I was in pain—"

"I remember."

"It seems like a long time ago," she said.

Nick stared at the ceiling. They both knew she was right.

Sharon reached for the phone on the nightstand.

"What are you doing?" whispered Nick. "They're going to hear you."

She carefully lifted the phone, listening. She raised an eyebrow, then laid the phone on the pillow between them and settled down beside it.

Nick could hear Alison talking, her voice high-pitched and girlish. That wasn't the way she normally talked. The faint rocking of the bed was in stereo now, audible over the phone and through the floor below. He blushed.

Sharon's eyes were bright. He could see a TV commercial reflected in each iris, her gaze boiling with color.

Nick hesitated, finally eased down on the other side of the pillow next to the phone so that he could hear better. His thigh brushed against Sharon's smooth leg.

Alison was complaining to someone about all the homework her geometry teacher had assigned her—Nick looked at Sharon—and she hardly had time for the cheerleading squad. She had almost gone out for practice yesterday without her panties—a giggle from Alison, a nervous laugh from the man she was speaking to. "Wouldn't that have been something when we did our first split leap? Like, embarrass me, royally." The man asked her where she went to high school but Alison laughed then, said, "No way, Jose," and said the reason she was calling a stranger was because she needed to ask some pretty intimate questions and didn't know who else to talk to.

Nick could faintly hear Perry grunt through the receiver. Alison tried to cover the sound by clearing her throat.

"All the girls on the cheerleading squad took a pledge of celebrity . . ." Giggle. "I mean celibacy. But my boyfriend, he's on the football team, and he is such a *total* studmuffin . . . Anyway, my boyfriend says that celibacy doesn't apply to . . . you know"—her voice dropped to a conspiratorial whisper—"oral sex."

"Y-yes . . ." said the man on the other end of the phone, nervous now, "that seems . . . sensible."

Nick and Sharon were cheek to cheek with the telephone receiver, the silent TV flickering through the gray twilight as their breathing deepened. Deepened.

"My problem," continued Alison, "I guess it's a problem, is I'm not really sure, you know, like how to do it right. You know, *it.* This weekend is homecoming and I promised my boyfriend . . . but I'm not sure I really know what to do and I don't want to ask my girlfriends because word would be all over school, and I just thought if I called a man up he would know what to do. You know what to do, right?"

"Well . . . I'm not sure," mumbled the man.

"I'd really appreciate it," said Alison. Her laugh was light and clear. "And I know my boyfriend would, too. So how do you like . . . you know, how do *you* like to be . . . sucked?" Giggle. "This is so weird. I'm usually shy. I guess because I'm lying in the dark here and we don't know each other it's easier to be kind of . . . slutty. So . . . can you give me a little help? Sir? Could you give me some tips?"

Nick became aware that he and Sharon had moved slightly apart, opening up a thin seam of cool air between them as they lay there, eyes closed now, listening.

2

"JAMES DEAN WAS killed in a Porsche just like this," said Alison, lounging in the passenger seat of Nick's battered red Porsche 911. Seven tequila shooters at the record-release party—her voice was still steady but the rest of her was loosening up. She had kicked off her *très* cool, chili-pepper-red Hush Puppies, put one foot up next to the gearbox. Every time he shifted he brushed against her ankle.

"James Dean was driving a silver Porsche Spider, not a 911," Nick corrected her. He was hunched over the steering wheel, trying to see through the beating rain. The summer storm had come on fast, catching him by surprise—black clouds rolled across the night sky, blotting out the moon and stars, bringing sheets of rain the temperature of blood.

"Big deal." Alison's gold lighter flared and the glowing tip of the joint in her mouth was reflected in the windshield. A hot coal in the darkness. Her lips were glistening, pale pink, their fullness outlined with black pencil. The cartography of desire. "September 30, 1956." She inhaled, holding the hit. "Early-morning fog, sun coming up, and our rebel without a cause was DOA."

Nick pushed back his glasses with the tip of his index finger. He had just started wearing glasses, and the thick black frames kept creeping down his nose. Alison said they made him look like Clark Kent. "Nineteen fifty-*five*." He hit his brights, then went back to his low beams as the car splashed down the deserted road that twisted through what was left of the Capistrano Ranch. It was a lousy, potholed shortcut, a private road, ostensibly off-limits to through traffic—it was still better than the 405 freeway, which was backed up for miles, even this late at night. "September 30, 1955."

Alison blew a stream of smoke at him. "You're probably one of those guys who sits on his couch yelling out the answers to *Jeopardy*, yelling at the contestants when they miss."

Nick smiled. "Could you put that in the form of a question, please?"

Alison laughed. She offered Nick the joint but he ignored her, pushing back his glasses instead. "Come on, Clark," she growled, "it's reefer, not Kryptonite." She shrugged, took another hit, and rested her head on the back of the seat. Her white-blond hair was cut in a sleek pageboy, parted on one side, wispy bangs hanging into her eyes. She tucked an errant strand behind one of her small ears. Long, dangling rhinestone earrings bounced against her slender neck as the Porsche fishtailed through a turn. She looked like she was enjoying the rough ride more than he was. "You and

Perry are real good friends, huh?" she said, eyes lowered, smoke curling slowly from her nostrils.

"We go back a long way."

"Well, now," she purred, "that's not really the same thing, is it?"

Nick glanced over. Her silky lashes were crimson in the red light of the dashboard instruments.

She was in her mid-twenties, tall and athletic, an aspiring actress from a small Texas town, with great bone structure and a nasty mouth: "I can play sophisticated, I can play dumb, but my agent is pushing smart 'n' sassy. The girl-next-door-to-Melrose-Place type that *both* Dad and Junior want to fuck."

Tonight she was wearing a short, clingy dress that looked like it was made out of silver foil. A trickle of mascara ran down one cheek from when they had been caught by the storm after leaving the party. On her it looked deliberate and stylish. She caught him staring, smiled that wild cowgirl grin, and he looked back at the road, kept his eyes where they belonged.

Water dripped from the frayed weatherstripping of the Porsche's sunroof, splashing onto his bare knee. He wore baggy madras shorts, a black tank top, black combat boots, and a wrestling-team letterman's jacket from Huntington Beach High School with the elbows worn through. He was wiry and compact, just a few pounds more than his competition weight, with serious eyes and an aggressive chin. Barely five ten, he still shopped for clothes in the young men's department, but he kept his hair cropped these days—that way it didn't show the gray so much.

Alison had looked at him when he came downstairs in his shorts tonight, and said that he looked like the world's oldest teenager. Sharon had told Alison that the last time she had seen Nick in long pants was at their wedding five years ago.

The two of them were on their way back to Nick's house after attending a record-release party at The Reef, an industry hangout in downtown L.A. The Reef was a smoky dive with an incredible THX laser sound system and a cheesy, fifties shipwrecks-and-buccaneers decor. It reminded Nick of the Pirates of the Caribbean ride at Disneyland, only with four-dollar draft beers and unisex toilets.

The party was all business for Nick; he had produced the album, spent two solid weeks in the studio with the band—O.J.'s Knife—your basic, young-loud-and-pierced thrashband. The final product wasn't bad. The lead guitarist had a three-chord range, but the singer had a strong voice and there were some decent lyrics that could actually be heard now that he had cleaned up the tracks. A major-label exec who had dropped in seemed interested. Not that Nick would get anything out of such interest. In the last year he had produced albums for eight different bands. Two of them had gotten recording contracts, but the labels had their own producers. Sorry, dude, and thanks.

Nick was a big boy. He knew how the game was played. Seventeen years ago he and Perry had been up on a stage too, fronting a young-loud-and-postpunk band, Plague Dogs. Perry had been the lead singer, Nick played guitar and wrote the songs. Perry sported safety pins through his cheeks and a purple Mohawk. Nick's ensemble was black leather with lots of zippers. The drummer, Baby Steve, wore a diaper. Just a diaper. Nick smiled at the memory. Their first single, self-produced and independently released, went gold and they got the fat contract every other band in L.A. was hustling for. Nick bought the Porsche with his share. Perry and Baby Steve invested theirs in cocaine.

The silence must have been too much for Alison. "Perry told me that you guys were on *American Bandstand*," she said suddenly. "Does Dick Clark really still have pimples?"

"We never made it on *Bandstand*," said Nick. "We were

scheduled to appear, but . . ." He shook his head. "The label set up a sixty-three-city national tour. Total disaster. We were playing to half-filled houses, getting sloppy, fighting with each other. Our Detroit concert was described by the local paper as 'a new low in popular entertainment, a degrading spectacle to all concerned.' "

"Sounds like fun," giggled Alison. She must be feeling the pot. Nick could hear a trace of a Texas drawl now.

"It was fun, all right," Nick said. "Baby Steve puked all over his drum kit during the first set and kept on playing. Perry was so fucked up he couldn't remember any of the lyrics, so he decided that urinating into the audience would have to serve as his artistic statement. There was a riot. A small riot." Nick smiled. "Today this kind of publicity would have gotten us a fan club, but back then, early Reagan-era, it was considered . . . unprofessional. The label cut off the tour, and used some fine-print clause to cancel the contract. We all took separate planes back to L.A. and never played together again."

"Perry didn't tell me that," said Alison. "He said that the band could have been the next Ramones, but your temper kept getting in the way."

"How long have you known Perry?"

"About four months."

"He'll get around to the truth sooner or later," said Nick, straightening the wheel as the car drifted toward the shoulder of the dark road. "Perry likes to try out all his options first."

Alison flicked ashes onto the floor, took another hit off the joint. She stretched out her long legs, looking bored, posing for some unseen camera.

The moon came out from behind the clouds, highlighting the low hills surrounding them in gradations of purple. It was so beautiful Nick just settled back in the torn seat, driving with his fingertips, sensing every vibration in the car, every bump in the road. He listened to the wipers flop back and forth across the windshield, heard the whoosh of air as they passed through the night. The damp interior was sweet with the smell of wet leather and Alison's perfume.

The Capistrano Ranch had been the largest unbuilt section of coastal Orange County, a rolling expanse of avocado trees and mountain-bike trails. Prime real estate, too valuable to waste on guacamole. The hills had been stripped bare over the last six months, the avocado trees bulldozed into piles of sticks. Nick could see a flash flood of topsoil and pebbles pouring down the slopes, overflowing the gullies on each side of the road with muddy water. The engine whined as he accelerated, tires slipping for a moment on the wet road before biting in.

Alison yawned, reached into her mesh handbag and pulled out a flip phone. She punched in some numbers, listened, then tried again. "Perry?" She tried the numbers one more time, mouth pursed in frustration. "Perry? Hello? Damn it." She snapped the phone shut. "This whole area has lousy reception," she said. "All this static . . . It's not just the storm either, Perry says you need another microwave transmission tower. He's been complaining ever since we showed up at your house yesterday."

"Don't worry, we'll be there in about ten minutes."

"I'm not worried," she said. "I just wanted to have him order a pizza. We used to feed our hogs better than the slop y'all had laid out at the party. *Musicians.*"

Nick bristled. "You seemed to be having a pretty good time with that weasel from Virgin, the one reeking of CK one."

"He told me they're shooting a Janet Jackson video in a few weeks," said Alison. "He thinks I'd be perfect for one of the principal parts—"

"Uh-huh."

"Don't use that tone with me," she said. "I gave him my agent's number. If he's legit . . ." She smacked the dash with her hand. "I know what you're thinking. Do I look like I can't take care of myself?"

"You kidding me?" Nick glanced at the dash. "I think the weasel is the one who's in trouble."

Alison appeared pleased. "I had to talk to *somebody*," she said. "You hardly said a word all night. I know you weren't expecting there would be just the two of us going to the party like some hot date . . ."

"I'm allowed out without my wife—"

"That's not how you acted," said Alison. "Every time you introduced me to someone, you seemed compelled to mention that Sharon had a lot of legal work to finish and that I was Perry's girlfriend and Perry got sick—"

"Sharon *did* have work to do, and Perry—"

"Don't be dense." Her dress crackled as she moved. "You know what I mean. We were *supposed* to have a good time. You didn't even dance with me."

"Yes I did."

"Once. Big deal."

"You weren't suffering. There were guys lined up—"

"Yeah, and you didn't take your eyes off me the whole time. Probably counted my drinks too."

Nick pushed back his glasses. Rain spattered against the windshield so hard the wipers could barely keep up.

"I thought tonight would be different," said Alison. "I thought I'd get a chance to get to know you better. Perry has all these . . . stories about you. I was curious. You know how weird it is—*couples*—you can be friendly but not too friendly, wild but not too wild." She stuck her tongue out. "I get so tired of being on my best behavior . . ." She cracked her window and the damp breeze whipped her blond hair across her face. "I figured we could go out, just the two of us, get a little drunk, a little stoned, a little sweaty . . . What's the harm in that?"

He swallowed. "No harm at all." He meant it. "You're right, I was a little . . . defensive at the party, but things have happened so fast—you and Perry show up, no warning, and suddenly it's you and me hitting the clubs solo." Rain dripped onto his knee and he shifted in his seat. "Maybe I'm getting old, but I don't like sudden changes anymore."

"You act like sudden changes are something you have control over," said Alison, her voice barely audible over the engine's hum. She sighed. "I thought maybe the reason you were so quiet was because you were embarrassed about listening in on my phone call last night. Maybe feeling a little guilty."

Nick watched the windshield wipers move back and forth. He tried not to breathe too loudly. Tried to pretend he hadn't heard her.

"Some guys . . . they overhear a thing like that they get weird afterwards. They get ideas. You're not like that, are you, Nicky?"

"Not me. I avoid ideas. No telling when one might take root."

"Hey, I wish we had known that you and Sharon were listening," said Alison. "You know Perry—he likes to have an audience. He might have kinked things up, given you a *real* earful."

Nick forced himself to relax his grip on the wheel. "You two seemed to be doing just fine," he said lightly. He waited a couple of beats. "How . . . how did you know—"

"What do you think Sharon and I were talking about sitting around the pool this afternoon?" Alison teased, enjoying his discomfort. "That's the way we girls are, no secrets. I'm surprised your ears weren't burning." She wagged a finger at him. "Sharon wouldn't tell me, but I bet you two were tearing up the sheets afterwards. I bet you were a total Eveready battery bunny."

Nick didn't respond to that.

She peered at him through long lashes. "Sharon said you've been married five years. That's a long time . . . maybe you should thank me and Perry for recharging your love machine."

"My love machine doesn't need recharging."

She threw back her head. "You're really cute when you blush, Nicky."

"It's *Nick.*"

"You're *still* blushing," said Alison. "I can feel the heat from here." She fanned herself with her hand. "Are you trying to tell me you *weren't* turned on last night? We're adults here. Fess up, Nicky, if listening in last night didn't get you stiff, then I'm losing my touch."

Nick didn't answer.

"If I had known about that letterman's jacket of yours, I could have changed my lines, said I was going out with the captain of the *wrestling* team. Would you have liked that better?"

"Would *you* have liked it better, Alison?"

Alison bit her lower lip. "Careful now, I might tell you the truth."

"I doubt it." The Porsche hit a pothole and Nick felt the car shudder. "This is what you do on the phone, isn't it?" he said, nodding with a sudden recognition. He saw her rake a hand through her hair, let the strands drift through her fingers. "You start the conversation rolling, sweet and friendly at first, but you're always probing for the tender places . . ."

"Lighten up, Nicky. Can't you take a joke?"

"You're blushing, Alison. I can feel the heat." The inside of the car suddenly felt too small, too intimate. "Truce?"

"Don't be a baby. This is just starting to get interesting."

Moisture ran down the inside of the windows. "You said you wanted to get to know me better," said Nick, his eyes on the road. "Maybe I was wondering about you too."

She watched him. "That's better. See what happens when you let yourself have some fun, Nicky? You end up saying what you really mean." She grinned. *"Then* you're in trouble."

He shook his head in total surrender. "Tonight . . . tonight, I saw you walk into a club full of pretty women and all the serious players turned to stare. I saw you work the room with that smile of yours, and the way you held your glass, loose and playful in your fingers . . . perfect. You didn't give anything away but everyone thought you were handing out free samples. Yeah, you're something special, Alison, even the suits can tell that." He glanced at her. "So what are you doing wasting your time making prank phone calls with Perry? You can do better."

Her eyes shone. "Are you talking about me wasting my time with Perry or with the phone calls?"

Nick didn't answer. He wiped condensation off the windshield with his hand, wishing they were home.

Alison nodded like she had decided something. "You're very loyal, Nicky," she said seriously. "Most guys wouldn't miss the opportunity to put Perry down."

"Maybe it's just none of my—" Nick slammed on the brakes, the mother raccoon staring from the center line—caught in the glare of the headlights, her four babies clinging to her. The car hydroplaned across the flooded road, moving sideways, out of control. He struggled to pull them out of the skid and almost made it, but one wheel hit the soft, muddy shoulder. Alison screamed as the car started to roll.

Nick saw the red Porsche as a playing card tossed carelessly into the air, the jack of hearts flipping slowly through the darkness.

3

NICK AWOKE UNDERWATER. He could feel himself hanging upside down, dizzy, ears ringing. He fumbled at his seat belt, slipped it off, still disoriented. His face broke the surface of the water, and he banged his head. Darkness. Water poured from his nose as he gasped for breath. He reached out, felt the clutch and brake pedals in front of his nose. The Porsche was upside down in the culvert, with about six inches of air space between the water level and the floorboard. The driver's-side door was sprung, the window underwater. He could hear rain beating gently on the undercarriage of the car. Alison!

He called out her name, fumbled under the water and felt her hair billow through his fingers. He took a breath, scooted under the water. She struggled frantically against him now, clawing at her seat belt. He couldn't find the release. He stood up, took another breath and went back down, found her face and pressed his mouth against her lips.

She gasped bubbles, tickling his cheeks with her fear as he breathed fresh air into her. He surfaced, got another breath and returned to her—she grabbed his head, held him close, banging his front teeth as she filled her lungs. He stayed under, working his way down the twisted seat belt until he found the release buckle. Jammed. Red spots danced as he tore at the buckle, felt a sharp pain as one of his fingernails broke off. The buckle popped open and Alison slid free, rose with him up to the narrow air space. The water was rising, rushing around their chins. There was hardly any room left now.

Nick kicked at the door, bracing himself against the steering wheel to force it open, then squeezed out, pulling her along. The two of them were carried downstream for a few yards before they were able to reach the side of the culvert, water rushing around their legs as they slowly dragged themselves up the embankment. Nick slipped backward at the top and would have fallen, but Alison grabbed his collar, held him until he regained his footing.

They were exhausted by the time they reached the shoulder of the road, collapsing beside each other, the two of them covered with clumps of grass, hair caked with gray mud. Rain dripped off their noses. They looked like a *National Geographic* cover on primitive tribes of New Guinea.

Alison coughed and kept coughing, finally wiped her mouth with the back of her hand, smearing dirt across her cheek. She nodded, trying to catch her breath.

"I'm sorry," said Nick. "I tried to steer . . ."

"You saved my life, Nicky." Alison's eyes were huge and unblinking, dark blue eyes, the color of the ocean when you swam out over your head. "You could have pulled a Ted Kennedy, but you didn't. I'm just sorry about your car."

"Me too." Nick stared at the overturned Porsche. Only the tires were visible now, turning slowly in the current. He felt sick. He loved that car. The body was dinged, the paint faded, but it was mechanically perfect, fine-tuned and tight. "I don't even *like* raccoons."

"You're bleeding," Alison said. She gingerly touched his forehead and he winced. Blood trickled down her fingers.

"I'm okay." He tried to stand but the world was swaying, out of control. Better to sit.

She bent beside him, wiping away the mud from his face, trying to see him clearly in the moonlight.

"I just want to stay here for a minute," he said.

"You do that," she commanded, starting down the embankment, her bare feet slipping for an instant before she caught herself, skating down toward the car.

Nick was going to tell her not to go. Tell her it was dangerous. Tell her that whatever she wanted back in the car, he would get for her. Just as soon as his head stopped throbbing. He pushed his index finger against the bridge of his nose. His glasses were gone. That was a relief. It explained why things looked so blurry. He lay back on the ground, turned his face to the rain and closed his eyes.

Alison bent over him, shaking him. She looked scared.

"What is it?" His head still hurt but he didn't feel like throwing up anymore.

She smiled. "I was afraid you had croaked on me." She sat beside him, handed him his glasses.

Nick put them on. "You went back for *these?*"

"Don't flatter yourself." She held up her shoes and handbag.

She put on those hot-pepper-red Hush Puppies, rummaged in her purse, brought out the cellular phone. Water leaked out the sides. She tried a couple of numbers, tossed it aside in disgust.

They helped each other up. Her dress was torn, the thin fabric barely holding together. He took off his jacket. "Take it," he insisted. She did. The wind was picking up. "Let's go," he said. "It's only a few miles. There won't be anyone out here until the work crews come in the morning."

They slogged through the warm rain for about ten minutes without speaking. Nick's combat boots squished with every step, keeping perfect time. He could see a helicopter circling in the distance, white searchlight stabbing down. The police helicopters were out almost every night, swooping through the dark, messing up people's TV reception.

"You're a pleasant surprise," said Alison, her hands in the pockets of the jacket. "When we first drove up to your house, I was expecting you to be some major burnout with a living room full of crappy music memorabilia like the home version of the Hard Rock Cafe. I'm so sick of Perry's rock 'n' roll dinosaurs— whoops. Hey, sorry. No offense."

"Don't worry. I've got a brain the size of a fava bean. Me and the other sauropods won't be smart enough to take offense for fifty million years."

She squeezed his arm so hard it hurt. "I love that wry sense of humor. Most guys I know, strictly Beavis and Butthead."

There was a small lake on one side of the road, filled with clean runoff from the irrigation lines the developers had run in, part of a championship golf course slated to open next year. Alison walked off the road and stepped onto the new grass surrounding the lake.

"What are you doing?" called Nick.

Alison peeled off his jacket, dropped it on the ground. "I'm going to wash." She kicked off her shoes. "Otherwise, by the time we get to your house, I'm going to be raw in places I don't want to hurt." She reached behind to unzip her dress.

Nick saw the fine bumps of her spinal column as the zipper slid down, averting his eyes as the dress fell away, but not before he got a glimpse of Alison stepping out of her white thong. Nick remembered Perry yesterday, proudly identifying her tight butt in a magazine ad for a brand of French blue jeans Nick had never heard of.

Alison dove underwater, came up squealing happily, her breasts bobbing in the moonlight. He had to keep reminding himself to turn away. She dunked herself again and again, scrubbing at her hair, her legs, rinsed out her dress.

Nick stood on the road, looking at the stars, listening to her sing. She had a country-and-western voice, a little twangy, a little flat. Not too bad. He could sweeten it up in the studio . . .

"Come on in, Nicky!"

Nick's tank top was plastered to his skin, his madras shorts caked with mud. He itched all over. "I'm fine."

"Come on in, I won't look!" Alison was treading water, only her head visible, her hair white in the moonlight. "Your modesty is safe with me." She clucked like a chicken, daring him, then turned away, backstroking across the surface of the lake.

Nick unlaced his boots, not looking at her, then quickly took off his tank top and shorts, mud slaking away. He waded in up to his waist, rinsing his clothes, then took off his underwear. Alison was still swimming away from him. He left his clothes on the grass and dove in, swimming out about twenty yards. He floated on his back for a long time, the rain misting on his face, feeling the knot in his stomach smooth out. Too soon, he headed back.

Alison stood on the shore, her back to him. She had her

clothes back on now, the wet silvery dress clinging to every curve. She must have given up on the thong.

As he splashed onto the cool grass, Alison turned around, watching him with a smile, not making any attempt to hide her gaze from his nakedness, enjoying his discomfort.

"What about my modesty?" accused Nick.

Alison smiled.

The walk home went quickly after that, the two of them walking close, brushing shoulders. Nick wasn't sure if it was the accident or the swim, but it felt like they had known each other for years. He wondered how Perry had managed to get somebody like her. Same old story, probably. Perry was lazy. He was arrogant and selfish and always broke. He was also great-looking and had a pair of green eyes that could melt a glacier. Women had always been crazy for him. Why should Alison be any different?

"You're awfully quiet all of a sudden, Nicky."

Nick pushed back his glasses. "This thing last night . . . that game with the phone. Do you and Perry . . . Is that part of your regular routine?"

"This is the nineties, Nicky—the phone is just another love toy." She looked at him, her tongue peeking out of the corner of her mouth. "You really got off on listening in last night, didn't you?"

"I'm just curious. It's a juicy little hobby, that's all."

Alison's laugh cracked the night. "Oh, it's more than a hobby, and you're more than just curious, Nicky. You got off on it. It's okay. So do I. So does Perry. Mind games . . . better than the real thing."

"No way," said Nick.

"You're such a straight guy, Nicky." Alison smiled to herself. "That's nice." She reached out and grabbed his pinky, held it in her hand, swinging it as they walked. It felt like high school. It felt good.

They walked for a few more yards, separating to circle a huge puddle. "What did you mean before?" said Nick. "You said the phone calls were more than a hobby?"

"Ask Perry," said Alison.

"I'm asking *you*. What's the matter? I thought you were the one who said whatever she felt like."

Alison stopped to watch the clouds sliding across the moon, wisps of gray turning to rust. "Perry makes tapes of the calls. It's all about contacts, Nicky. There's a whole circuit of people who are into tape games. Important people. Producers, actors, casting directors, it's like an underground club. Perry says it's just a matter of time until the right person hears one of my tapes and gives me my big break." She shrugged. "Posing for *Playboy* is passé." She looked at him. "That's what Perry says, anyway. You probably think that's bullshit."

"What do I know?" said Nick, wanting to smooth the edge off her voice. "The only break I'm going to get will probably be my neck." He smiled at her. "I hope the phone calls and the tapes work for you, Alison. I really do."

She watched him. Kissed him on the cheek, her lips lingering, brushing his mouth as she pulled away.

They walked on. The rain had started up again. Nick wished they had more time. Wished they could just keep walking.

As they entered the outskirts of Rancho Verdes, Nick could hear the sound of traffic from the nearby freeways, a steady hum, day and night. It made him realize how rare was the relative silence he and Alison had been walking through for the last hour. Just rain and crickets and the sound of their own voices. So quiet it was almost illegal.

The last time the freeways had been wide open was right after the most recent earthquake, when the overpasses collapsed and the mayor and governor asked everyone to stay home. Nick had taken the Porsche out, punched it up to 130 miles an hour on the deserted Long Beach freeway.

Rancho Verdes was a rugged enclave of California dreamers—ex-hippies, New Age capitalists, surf bums, software engineers, and organic gardeners—a small town notable for its large, secluded lots, high taxes, and lack of a master plan. Live and let live. Spanish-style pink stucco mansions were sited next to wood-frame ramblers and solar-powered geodesic domes.

They were just a few blocks from Nick's house now, their wet clothes flapping as they hurried down the street.

Nick stopped as they turned the corner onto his cul-de-sac. There were red and blue lights flashing in front of his house, blurry lights flickering in the rain. He heard Alison call his name as he started to run. His wet shoes fell heavily on the sidewalk, the breath pounding through his chest.

Yellow police tape ringed his property like ribbon on a birthday present. Nick could hear a police radio crackling from the black-and-white unit parked in front. A strange car was in the driveway, a big, green Pontiac. Don and Donny, the next-door neighbors, were standing around outside in their matching bathrobes. They turned away when they saw him. Nick could see flashes of light from the rear of his house.

Nick jumped over the tape. A young cop yelled at him from the front door, but Nick just ran faster, ducking through the bamboo grove alongside the house, leaves scratching his face as he headed for the back. He emerged onto the patio, blinking in the bright lights. He slowed, hesitant now but still moving forward, unable to stop himself.

A police photographer stood on a stepladder beside the hot tub, snapping away, strobe flaring with every shot. Nick barely noticed. His attention was on the large black man bending over a woman sprawled facedown a few yards from the hot tub. A woman lying nude on the edge of the patio, almost to the grass. A woman with dark curly hair and the whitest skin . . . stark white skin in the popping of the strobe. Water dripped off his glasses and ran down his cheeks. Sharon. Nick felt his knees buckle.

Nick must have cried out, because the black man looked up. He wore a gray suit and an elegant, pearl-gray homburg streaked with rain, the surgical gloves and booties incongruous with that dapper outfit. He held a small tape recorder, his lips still moving as he watched Nick.

Nick was grabbed from behind and spun around. He saw the cop from the front porch standing there, face flushed, shaking with anger. "This is a crime scene, asshole!" he shouted, grabbing Nick's wrist. "You're under arrest!"

Nick stepped in close, twisted the cop's thumb backward, forcing him to his knees. It was instinctive. Nick was somewhere outside himself, watching the pain on the cop's face. Disinterested.

A huge hand drifted onto Nick's shoulder. Nick looked up at the enormous black man who towered over him. "This *is* a crime scene, sir. You don't belong here." He had kind eyes.

Nick shrugged him off. "I *live* here." He bent down beside Sharon's body. Her wet hair was in ringlets across her shoulders, covering one side of her face. Her hands were curled up beside her, one leg drawn up. There was a hole under her left shoulder blade. A tiny hole with a red center. Such a tiny hole. Nothing really. He took her hand. It was cool and spongy. "This is my wife."

"I'll take care of this, Harris," the black man said to the cop. He turned to Nick. *"You're* Nicholas Carbonne?"

Nick didn't answer. He lifted Sharon's hair from her face. Closed her eyes. She looked like she was sleeping now. He watched her, wanting to remember the softness of her hair, the curve of her lips. He stayed there, not speaking, kneeling in the lake of pale pink water that seeped across the flagstones.

The black man helped him to his feet, lifted him up and away from Sharon. "I'm Sergeant Calvin Thorpe, Mr. Carbonne," he said, his voice deep and resonant, the words tolling through the night. "I'm a detective with the Rancho Verdes P.D. I'm sorry that my officer tried to stop you. We were told that you and Mrs. Carbonne lived alone, and we just assumed that . . . well, that you were the individual in the hot tub."

Nick looked over. Perry floated in the hot tub, his nude body bobbing up and down in the foam. Most of his face was blown away, his teeth shattered. Nick felt the warm rain dripping off his glasses. "No," he said softly, "that's not me."

"Someone must have surprised your wife and . . . this gentleman while they were soaking in the—"

"No."

"I beg your pardon?" said Calvin Thorpe.

"My wife wouldn't have shared a hot tub with Perry," said Nick. "She didn't even like him in the house with her."

"Oooooooh!" Alison stood on the edge of the patio. She covered her mouth as the young cop patted her arm.

Nick walked over to Alison, took his jacket off her, then covered Sharon with it. The detective tried to stop him, said something about "protecting evidence," but Nick was too fast, bending low, sweeping the jacket across her body. Sharon wasn't evidence. She was his wife and he needed to protect her, to shield her from the photographer and the cops staring, but the jacket wasn't big enough to do the job. Her arms and legs stuck out, and there was all that blood . . . Someone was crying.

"That's all right, buddy," said Calvin Thorpe, wrapping a huge arm around Nick, folding him in his embrace. "You let it all out. I'd do the same thing if I were you."

Nick's tears were lost in the drifting rain.

IN A DREAM of fire, Nick heard bacon sizzling. A sound like a lit fuse. He shifted, trying to stay asleep, but the aroma pulled at him now, dragging him up into consciousness. Sharon didn't believe in cholesterol. She liked bacon and eggs for breakfast, butter on her toast, cream in her coffee. She'd be standing over the stove now, poking the bubbling strips with a fork, humming to herself. A memory jabbed at him, sharper than a fork . . .

He opened his eyes. Blinked through crooked glasses jammed across his nose, sunlight filtering through the rattan shades into the living room. He lay on the sofa, holding Sharon's favorite pillow, breathing in her perfume. He let the pillow go, watched it tumble onto the rug.

There was dried blood on the pillow. He touched the side of his head, felt his hair crusted where he had hit the steering wheel last night. Last night . . . the sound of screaming lost in the storm.

Nick got up slowly, hearing voices in the kitchen. One of them sounded like Alison but he couldn't be sure, his ears were ringing. He was barefoot, wearing white shorts and a baggy white T-shirt. He remembered changing out of his wet clothes last night—this morning actually—after walking through the house with Detective Thorpe, trying to determine if anything had been stolen. He glanced down at the pillow. Anything else. His cheeks burned.

He had sat on the couch afterwards waiting for dawn, listening to the police radios crackle, unable to bring himself to watch what was going on outside. He remembered the glare of arc lights from the patio, throwing grotesque shadows on the living room wall as he slumped into sleep.

Nick shuffled toward the kitchen, groaning with each step. Everything hurt.

"Morning, buddy," Thorpe called cheerfully. Bacon crackled and popped on the stove, while he stood over the butcher's block, his shirtsleeves rolled up, rapidly chopping onions. His big hands cradled the chef's knife like a Cordon Bleu graduate, keeping the point in place with his fingertips, letting the blade do the work.

Nick hung on to the counter, trying to make sense of this bizarre domestic tableau: the Galloping Gourmet with a .38 clipped to his belt. Laughter tumbled from Nick's lips, surprising him—he didn't feel amused, he felt helpless, overflowing with conflicting emotions.

"Nicky?" Alison rose from the bench in the breakfast nook where she had been curled up, her eyes puffy, rimmed with red.

"Are you okay?" She wore faded jeans and a man's white dress shirt, her blond hair pulled back. She embraced him, and he could feel her trembling against his chest. It wasn't just her, either. They were both shaking, hanging on to each other like a couple of shipwreck survivors.

The only sound in the room was Thorpe steadily dicing onions as he watched them, not even looking at his hands. His head almost brushed the low ceiling—he was at least six four, broad-nosed and soft-bellied, with satiny black skin and short hair parted on the side like the young Nelson Mandela. His gray suit jacket was folded over the back of a kitchen chair, his matching homburg drying brim-up on the seat. "Hope you don't mind me making myself at home," he said to Nick. "It's been a long night and I think better on a full stomach."

Alison peeled herself away from Nick, wiped her eyes with the back of her hand. "I was fine until you got here, Nicky," she said, plucking at his shirt, not wanting to separate from him. "Calvin here's been cheering me up . . . just what this country girl needed on a badass morning." She picked up her coffee cup from the table, sloshed a little over the brim. "He makes good coffee too." There was a slight quaver in her voice, but she fought it.

"Thank you kindly." Thorpe beamed.

Nick could see the patio through the kitchen window—there were small puddles of rain around the swimming pool, and blood staining the concrete. Someone had put the cover back on the hot tub, but they hadn't put it on right. One corner stuck out, streaked with fingerprint powder. Leaves drifted in the swimming pool, turned lazy circles in the breeze. He was going to have to skim the pool; Sharon liked to swim when she came home from— He bit his lip.

Thorpe followed his gaze. "The medical examiner took your

wife to the coroner's office about an hour ago. Just before sunrise. I am sorry." His voice was a warm, slow rumble.

"You should have awakened me."

"He tried," said Alison. "We both did, Nicky, but it was like you were in a coma."

"You took a real whack to the head last night," said Thorpe. "Alison told me how you pulled her out of the wreck. That was really something."

Nick shivered as though he were underwater again, struggling to free her. "I was just reacting."

"That's what counts," said Thorpe. "Heck, we're all cowards when we've got time to think."

"You boys play nice," yawned Alison, stretching, "I'm going to go wash my face and try to get beautiful."

They watched her leave. She walked like she knew there would always be a man watching.

"She's not going to have to try too hard," said Thorpe, separating a head of garlic, crushing the unpeeled cloves with the flat of his knife blade. "The uniforms were falling all over themselves last night trying to get her attention—'buffing the badge,' that's what we call it." He deftly freed the fractured cloves from their papery sheaths with his thick fingers. "She said she was in a TV commercial for suntan oil once."

Yellow police tape marked off the patio, loose ends fluttering in the breeze. Sharon's tomato plants were in the sunniest part of the yard, carefully staked, drooping with ripe red tomatoes. Sharon hated store-bought.

"Nick?" said Thorpe. "I said the ME suggested you get a CAT scan. You may have a concussion or—" The knife was poised over the garlic. "You don't look so good, buddy. Why don't you sit down?"

Nick stayed where he was. Beyond the pool the backyard became increasingly overgrown, the ground rising to a line of eucalyptus trees that sheltered the yard from view of the neighboring houses. The young cop from last night walked slowly across the damp grass, his eyes on the ground.

"What's *he* looking for, Detective?"

"Call me Calvin." Thorpe flashed his pearly incisors. "Not Cal," he cautioned. " 'Cal' is some skinny white guy with red hair, a goiter, and bib overalls." His grin widened. "Now 'Nick,' *Nick* is a feisty little monkey, whereas Nicholas—"

"My wife has been murdered. You going to tell me what you found or play the fucking name game?" There wasn't enough air in the room.

Thorpe stared at Nick, unable to make up his mind about him. "We haven't found anything yet," he said finally, starting in on a pile of mushrooms, slicing them thin as paper, barely moving the knife. "I doubt if we will either. Not back *there*. The shooter most likely came through the house or around the side the way you did . . ." He saw the question in Nick's eyes. "Your wife was running away from the house when she was shot," he explained. "I think she and Perry were surprised in the hot tub and she took off for the darkness of the backyard—"

"That's bullshit. I told you that last night."

"Lots of people take a friendly soak without it meaning—"

"Sharon couldn't stand Perry."

"The two of them were naked, buddy," Thorpe said, his hands absently aligning the mushroom slices on the cutting board so that the mushroom appeared whole again. "I could smell chlorine from the tub on her skin."

"If Sharon was in the hot tub with Perry, she didn't go willingly," insisted Nick. "Maybe the killer forced them into the tub, so he could isolate them while he checked the house, to contain them while he searched—"

"Their clothes were folded and protected from the rain," Thorpe said patiently. "They had towels ready." The mushroom fell apart. "Nothing was stolen. All your fancy audio equipment, VCRs . . ."

"Maybe the killer wasn't interested in stereos and VCRs." Nick glanced away. His face darkened. "Hey!" He stalked to the sliding glass door, shoved it aside so hard the glass cracked. "Hey, you!"

The young cop looked up, startled, one of Sharon's perfect tomatoes in his hand. He had a skimpy mustache that twitched like a bunny.

"That's not yours!" Nick stepped out onto the patio, his head pounding so loudly he had to shout to hear himself. "Put it down!"

The cop laid the tomato on the ground, backed away, his hand on his holster.

Nick barely noticed. He stood staring at the chalk outline of Sharon's body on the flagstones. The last of the rain had eroded the edges, cutting through her outline. Ever since he woke up, there had been a part of him that kept expecting Sharon to walk downstairs, fresh from her shower, her hair still wet . . . A hand drifted onto his shoulder.

"Quit scaring my uniforms," Thorpe teased, "you're going to break their spirit." He squeezed Nick's shoulder. "That's some temper you have there. Used to have one of those myself but had to give it up. Kept getting me in trouble."

Thorpe tried to ease Nick around, steer him into the house, but Nick was rooted, his knees slightly flexed, his center of gravity located at the center of the earth. It was an aikido exercise, part of his wrestling training, part of him now. Thorpe grunted, straining, then straightened up and left him alone.

Nick was aware of Thorpe's struggle but his attention was

on the faint yellow chalk outline. That was all he had left of Sharon. Her body was at the morgue, but that wasn't her. That was a discarded shell. A seashell. Hold it up to your ear and hear . . . nothing.

"Nick?" Thorpe said. Polite, not touching him. "Why don't you come inside. Have some coffee."

Nick walked back into the kitchen, took a bottle of beer out of the refrigerator. He shook four aspirin tablets from the bottle on the counter, chewed them slowly, enjoying the sharp taste, then washed them down with a long swallow of beer. He looked toward the patio, his attention drawn there in spite of himself. The breeze blew orange fingerprint powder off the lawn chairs.

"I like a beer in the morning myself sometimes," Thorpe said, "particularly after a rough night—"

"Did you get any fingerprints from the patio? Or inside?"

Thorpe looked perplexed, his forehead bunching into knots trying to keep up with the sudden shifts in Nick's behavior, maybe still working out his inability to strong-arm the much smaller man. "We got plenty of hits on prints," he said, refilling his coffee cup, "but they all belong to your wife or Perry or Alison. Or you." He eyed Nick. "Killer must have worn gloves."

"I saw muddy footprints everywhere . . ."

Thorpe tried to hide his smile behind the rim of his cup. "Yeah, I've seen those TV shows too. Columbo looks at a footprint and announces that the murderer was a New Yorker, six feet one inch tall, wearing Italian lace-ups—"

"So what *have* you got?"

"We're a small department," Thorpe said good-naturedly. "Even if we had all the fancy tools, we still have a fouled crime scene. When we got the 911—"

"Sharon called 911?" Nick moved toward Thorpe. He didn't care how big the detective was. "How long did it take for you and your band of merry men to respond? They running a special at the doughnut shop?"

"I gave you more credit than that," said Thorpe. "Next you're going to tell me that you pay my salary."

"How long did she wait?"

"Sharon didn't call in the 911." Thorpe picked the crisp bacon strips from the skillet with his fingertips, laid them on a paper towel and patted off the grease. "We don't know *who* it was. The call came from this Circle K mini-mart at eleven-oh-three P.M. A man told the operator to send a car to your address. No mention of homicide. A 'situation,' that's what he called it. 'A situation that requires police attention, so beam your ass over there.' Then he hung—"

" 'Beam your ass over there'? Who placed the call, Captain Kirk?"

"We're still trying to find out who he was." Thorpe licked his fingertips. "The uniforms arrived here at eleven thirty-two. Not a bad response time. We get lots of false alarms from these mini-marts. High school kids pick up a six-pack, drop a dime on their friends. Ha-ha." He swabbed the pan clean with another paper towel, drizzled on some olive oil, and put it back on the gas burner. "These two uniforms showed up expecting a party in progress, maybe catch a few kids smoking pot." He sighed. "They were rookies. Instead of securing the scene, they chased around, weapons drawn. Those muddy footprints you saw were theirs. The crime scene was compromised. Forensics just rolled their eyes."

"Was Sharon still alive when the call came in?" Nick was amazed at how steady his voice sounded.

"No." Thorpe tilted the pan, spreading out the oil, which was just beginning to smoke. "The ME is having a hard time pinning down a time of death, but we're sure about that. I don't know how much you want to know—"

"*All* of it."

"Okay." Thorpe averted his eyes. "Time of death is always an approximation. The ME places a thermometer under the rib cage, inserts it into the liver to get a body temp . . ." He dropped the crushed garlic into the pan, keeping it moving. "Anyway, the ME says the hot tub and the rainstorm throw off his calculations, but he estimates that your wife and Perry were murdered sometime between seven and ten last night." He adjusted the flame. "Alison said the two of you left about seven-thirty for this record party. That right?"

"I guess. I don't know."

"So the killing must have happened sometime after seven-thirty. You have any balsamic vinegar?" Thorpe opened cabinets. "I found it. Wow. Villa Modena Reserve. What is this, forty bucks a bottle?" He tossed a handful of onions into the pan, stirred them with a wooden spoon. "I have a problem, though." He added a splash of vinegar to the onions. "Your wife was killed by a single shot, but Perry . . . somebody got up close and personal with him. Five shots. Right in the face." He slid the pan back and forth, flipping the onions with a steady rolling motion. "Alison didn't come right out and say it, but I got the idea that Perry was a real hustler. Fast and loose." He added the mushrooms. "That kind of guy can piss people off."

"So what's your problem?" Nick said, irritated by Thorpe's rambling discourse.

Thorpe broke brown eggs into a bowl, using only one hand, tossing the shells into the sink. "I've been working on the premise that Perry was the intended target and your wife was simply a bystander. That may not be what happened." He tugged at the waistband of his trousers. "I know you don't like the idea, but if your wife and Perry were caught in the hot tub, maybe somebody thought it was *you* in there with her, getting all steamy and romantic. You're about the same size, and it was dark and rainy . . . Even at close range, mistakes could have been made." He whisked the eggs into a froth, adding a splash of Tabasco. Then another. He looked at Nick. "Maybe you pissed somebody off too?"

Nick waited a couple of heartbeats. "Plenty of people. None that would want to kill me, though."

Thorpe poured the eggs into the skillet and they exploded in the hot pan. He smiled at Nick through the fragrant mist. "Hey buddy, don't sell yourself short."

5

NICK LISTENED TO Detective Thorpe's fork cut into the frittata, the metal clicking onto Sharon's good china. There was something offensive about the sound.

"We're not so different, you and me," said Thorpe.

"Oh, yes we are," said Nick. They sat across from each other in the breakfast nook, plates of food steaming in front of them, Nick's bare knees brushing against the detective's gray suit pants.

"Don't be so sure of that," said Thorpe, talking with his mouth full. "You ever do any preaching?"

Nick took another swallow of beer. He was working on his third bottle, still sober. He looked around, wondering what was taking Alison so long.

"I know you're a musician, used to be anyway," said Thorpe. "I'm a lay minister myself," he said, lifting another forkful of omelette to his lips, "still do a bit of testifying when the Holy Ghost moves me. Musicians and preachers, we're more alike than you think . . . we each hear the call of the spirit."

"You should listen to some of the bands I've worked with," Nick said sourly. "You wouldn't say that."

"Man can follow the spirit to heaven or to hell," ruminated Thorpe. "The path we choose . . . that's up to us, isn't it?" The detective chewed slowly, savoring the taste, his broad face shiny with pleasure. He had garnished each of their plates with thin slices of orange and three raspberries. "Alison showed me your gold record after you went to sleep. Said it wasn't real gold, though. Not solid gold anyway."

Nick could hear Thorpe, but his attention was drawn to the detective's wide mouth, the sheen of sweat on his upper lip. Thorpe's emotions floated across his smooth face like the main feature on a drive-in movie screen, displayed without excuse or equivocation. He either had nothing to hide, or wasn't afraid of being found out.

"You haven't touched your food," said Thorpe. "Are you trying to hurt my feelings?" He speared one of Nick's raspberries, gobbled it down. "This band of yours, Plague Dogs . . ." He delicately extracted a raspberry seed from his large, white teeth with a fingernail. "I never heard of you. No offense. Alison said it was about fifteen years ago. That's a long time in the record business, isn't it?"

"Fifteen *minutes* in the record business is a long time."

"You must miss being onstage," said Thorpe, placing the raspberry seed on the edge of his plate. "All those girls screaming, riding around in limos . . ."

Nick let his gaze wander. The cop with the skimpy mustache

was still walking off the yard, his shoes soaked from the wet grass, keeping well away from Sharon's tomatoes. Nick wanted to go outside, give the kid one of the tomatoes, tell him to take all he liked, tell him he was sorry for yelling at him. He stayed put. He watched the yellow butterflies hovering over the swimming pool, saw them dart off in tandem, their flight erratic, struggling in lust. Oblivious. Easy pickings. He turned back to the kitchen. Still no sign of Alison.

Thorpe must have seen his disappointment. He had good eyes.

"Alison will be here soon," said Thorpe, "don't worry. Sometimes I think we spend half our lives waiting for a woman. Ah well, a woman like her is worth waiting for." He patted his belly, a jaunty black Buddha with all the answers. "She sure thinks a lot of you. It's Nick this and Nick that, and when she talks about you she gets a little smile around the corners of her mouth. She didn't say much about Perry without me asking, but *you*, she just goes off." His eyes twinkled. "You must have a magnetic personality."

"Yeah, can't you feel my aura?"

Thorpe laughed with his mouth open wide, head thrown back, drinking up the morning. It wasn't that funny. He finally stopped, wiped his eyes and picked up a piece of toast slathered with orange marmalade. "Oh, I almost forgot . . ." He took a bite and chewed slowly, waiting until he swallowed before finishing his sentence. "When you said you and Alison left the house around seven-thirty last night, you meant the *first* time you left, right?"

"The first time?"

"Alison said after you had been driving for a while, you suddenly turned around and went back home."

"I forgot my business cards. Left them on my dresser," said

Nick. "The party . . . I was hoping to get producing gigs from some of the bands that were there." He hesitated. "I need the work." He couldn't stop his legs from bouncing, keeping time to the song that ran through his head. It was cramped in the booth—every time he moved he banged against Thorpe. Sitting still was worse, feeling the heat that poured from the big man, enveloping them in a warm cocoon.

"Your wife must have been surprised to see you walk in the door."

Nick didn't answer. He already knew where this was going.

"Alison said she waited in the car listening to music while you went inside. She likes it loud I bet." Thorpe heaped more marmalade onto the last of the toast. "She told me she couldn't remember how long you were gone. She doesn't wear a watch. Doesn't believe in time. Must be nice, huh?"

"I was only inside for a few minutes."

"She said she sat there in the car, feet up, music cranked up, smoking a doobie." Thorpe shook his head, chuckling. "She dropped that little misdemeanor into the conversation like she was talking about a new pair of shoes." He swirled his knife in the marmalade. "Were you and the wife having troubles? You said you were married five years. Sometimes—"

"When did I say that?"

"Last night. Right before you went to sleep." The knife dripped with marmalade, thin slivers of sour orange peel lacing the sweetness. "Don't you remember?" Thorpe leaned forward, concerned. "Maybe you *should* check with a doctor?"

There was a rap on the sliding glass door to the patio. A uniformed officer stood there, waiting, then opened the door in response to Thorpe's beckoning wave. He bent down, whispered in Thorpe's ear.

"What was that about?" asked Nick after Thorpe had dismissed the man.

Thorpe stifled a yawn. "Nothing much." He tugged at his earlobe. "So were you and the wife having troubles? You have to admit it looks . . . funny. You and Alison go off joyriding while she and Perry—"

"Joyriding?" Nick felt his jaw tighten. "Yeah, we went off in my hot rod to meet Betty and Veronica at the malt shop."

"You know what I mean," said Thorpe.

"Yeah, you want to know if I surprised Sharon and Perry in the hot tub and went homicidal," said Nick.

Thorpe ran a fingertip across the knife, licked marmalade off his manicure. He saw Nick staring and put the knife down, embarrassed. "I got a sweet tooth. My wife used to get on me about it. I told her I had a metabolism problem, but I don't think she believed—"

"Are we almost through here?"

Thorpe smiled. "You're quite a character, Nick. I've seen a lot of next of kin. Most of them are in a state of shock, stupefied, weepy, and eager to please. I've never seen anybody like you. Ah well." He blotted his lips with his napkin. "Don't worry. I've got a feeling about this case."

"That's a comfort," said Nick, enraged by Thorpe's bonhomie. "Your rookies show up late for a 911 call and screw up the physical evidence, but you've got a feeling."

"Mistakes were made," said Thorpe, prickly now, his fingers drumming the table, "but mistakes are part of any investigation—anybody who tells you different never ran a case." He smoothed his tie, adjusted the knot. "Nick?" His eyes were bright. "Do you believe in God?"

Nick didn't know if Thorpe was serious.

"I've had my faith tested too," said Thorpe. "Some of the things I've seen . . . You wouldn't believe what people do to each other, do to people they *love* . . . It's like they're trying to prove something." He ran a hand over his scalp, the bench creaking as he fidgeted. "I believe in God, but I've seen things that gave me doubts."

Nick looked away toward the hot tub.

"What choice do we have?" said Thorpe. "We *got* to believe in God. A man would go crazy on his own, he'd fly right off into outer space. Never get back home without God. Never." He was rolling now, a deep bass rumbling from his chest. "That's what you want, Nick. That's what we all want." His head bobbed in affirmation. "We want to get back home."

"I have a whole shelf of gospel albums," said Nick, "the real stuff: Bells of Joy, Swan Silvertones, Mahalia Jackson. I love the purity of the music and the way it makes me feel inside. I believe in the music, but do I believe in God, Calvin . . ." Nick leaned over the table, the two of them so close that it looked like they were about to kiss. "I haven't got a clue."

Thorpe studied him with those dark eyes. "If you want to talk to me about anything, Nick, *anything*—"

"My wife is dead," Nick said softly. "Talk can't change that and neither can God."

"You always refer to your wife being killed," said Thorpe, slowly buttering a piece of toast. "Never Perry. Like he doesn't count. Why do you think that is?"

Nick flushed, a hot tide boiling up from his heart.

The knife scraped across the bread. "I like you," Thorpe said, "but I'm troubled by your coming back to the house last night. You've got a temper, we both know that. I keep wondering"—the knife stopped—"just what did you walk in on last night?"

"Nothing. Perry was watching TV downstairs, Sharon was working. I was only there a few minutes."

"Personally, I believe you. Professionally . . . well, we'll have to see." Thorpe squared his shoulders. "It's been a long night. We're not going to settle anything now."

"There's nothing to settle," growled Nick.

"You are something," Thorpe said, impressed. "Last night you're crying in the rain, this morning you're ready to tear a chunk out of anyone who gets in your way. I respect that." He sat back and spread his hands across the back of the booth, like a man on a park bench surrounded by pigeons.

Nick stared back at him. The two of them smiled at the exact same instant. Nick didn't know why either of them was smiling. The house was so silent that he could almost hear the dust falling. Silent snow, secret snow. Ashes to ashes. That was a prayer for the dead before it was a David Bowie song.

He heard the front door open, heard Alison walking toward them. She trod lightly for such a tall girl. He wanted to close his eyes to appreciate the sound. The morning after she and Perry had shown up, Nick had lain in bed listening to her moving around the house at dawn, imagining her slim, strong ankles while Sharon slept beside him. Thorpe hadn't reacted to the front door. He sat there, stirring his coffee, the spoon tinkling in the quiet kitchen. Nick was pleased that he was the only one to hear her approach.

"Hello, boys . . ." Alison's voice was soft, a little out of breath, a tired drawl. Her blond hair hung loose at her shoulders now, cheeks flushed. She looked like Daisy Mae with a wild glint in her eyes. "Hey, Calvin," she said, then scooted down beside Nick, laid her head on his shoulder, settling into him like she never wanted to leave. She smelled of sunshine and soap.

"How you doing there, pretty thing?" asked Thorpe.

"I'm tired." She clung to Nick's arm.

"Where were you?" asked Nick.

"You're sweet, Nicky." Alison's eyes were half closed. "I went for a walk. I wanted to be by myself for a while."

"You shouldn't have gone off alone," said Nick.

"He's right," said Thorpe.

"I *had* to," said Alison. "I needed to walk past houses where it was just another Sunday morning, a morning where people were getting ready for church or reading the paper with the TV on." She ran her hand along the edge of the pine table, eyes downcast. "A couple blocks over I saw these two little kids in bathing suits washing their old man's car in the driveway, getting each other soaked with the hose, laughing, and it was like . . . it was like last night never happened." She looked up at Nick. Her eyes shimmered. "It did happen though."

Nick slowly nodded.

6

NICK STEPPED OVER the yellow plastic police ribbon that drooped listlessly across his porch. Behind him, he heard Alison thank the cop who had given them a ride back to the house. As he unlocked the front door a white business card fluttered onto the welcome mat: "Donald Fisk, *Orange County News*." A note on the back asked Nick to please call the reporter ASAP. Nick crumpled the card, tossed it away.

Their neighbor Krinol came out of his house across the street, got into his Cadillac. He avoided looking at them as he backed out of the driveway and drove away.

Nick went inside first, standing in the entryway listening for a full minute while Alison waited outside, shaking her head at his caution. He heard water in the pipes from the leaky toilet. He heard birds cooing in the roof beams and the ticking of Sharon's antique pendulum clock at the top of the stairs. Safe noises. He slowly unballed his fists.

"Nicky?"

He beckoned to Alison, closed the door after her and threw the dead bolt. When he turned she was right beside him. "It's going to be all right," he said.

"You don't sound convinced."

They had spent the last three hours at the police station while Thorpe took their statements separately. Nick had watched the ancient reel-to-reel recorder as he answered Thorpe's questions. The plastic reels were slightly bent, wobbling round and round. Lot of wow and hiss. Cheap microphone, too. Thorpe had noticed his expression and apologized for the city's outdated equipment and bad coffee, complaining about budget cuts since the county went bankrupt in 1995. Then he had a forensics tech take Nick for a paraffin test, to see if there was gunpowder residue on Nick's hands or face. Thorpe hadn't apologized for that.

Nick left her and went through the house checking doors and windows. When he returned, Alison was in the kitchen, standing in front of the sliding glass door, looking out at the patio. The crack in the glass door had spread, thin fingers reaching across the frame toward her.

"I'll go if you want to be alone," Alison said, not turning, seeing him reflected in the sliding door. She had already fired up a joint, her hand shaking as she brought it to her lips. "I've got friends . . ."

"I think we should stay together."

Alison smiled at his reflection, turned around and faced him. Her jeans were tight, the tails of her baggy white shirt loosely knotted around her waist, framing her belly button. A tiny gold ring pierced her navel, gleamed in the afternoon light. If he were to touch it, it would be warm as his wedding ring. She held out the joint to him.

"No, thanks." Nick looked away, out at the still-soggy back-yard—the sun slanted through the trees, throwing shadows across the grass. The surface of the swimming pool was a dull mirror reflecting a cloudless sky. He had lived in the house for ten years, long before he and Sharon were married, but at this moment he stared through the cracked glass and didn't recognize anything.

Alison laid her hand on his arm. "I still can't believe it," she said, trembling, the tremor running through the both of them, a strange intimacy. "Yesterday . . . *yesterday,* the four of us were splashing around in the pool, Sharon riding on your shoulders, all of us getting loose . . ." She wiped tears from her eyes. "I didn't know Sharon very well, but I liked her. I think she liked me too. I make a lot of girls nervous, but Sharon was a confident person." She shook her head. "I promised myself I wouldn't cry anymore."

"Why don't you go lie down," said Nick. "Get some rest. I think we're okay for now."

Alison took another drag on the joint. "What do y'all mean 'for now'?" Smoke trickled from her nostrils.

Nick watched the smoke twisting in the air.

"You trying to scare me, Nicky? 'Cause I never liked the fun house at the carnival, things jumping out of the dark at me, some pimply guy grabbing at my tits like that's going to protect me from the bogeyman. Made me mad."

"Why don't you ease off on the pot?" Nick said gently. "It's not helping."

"You're not my daddy." Alison defiantly took a deep drag, started coughing. She stubbed out the joint. "I was done anyway, so don't look so happy with yourself."

"Was Perry in some kind of trouble?"

"Depends on what you mean by trouble."

"Don't play games," said Nick. "Perry said he needed a place to stay until you two could find a new apartment—"

"I wasn't going to move back in with Perry," said Alison. "It was all over between us. Four months was plenty."

"I didn't know . . . Perry never said anything." Nick lowered his eyes, feeling like he had intruded. "Did Perry need to move because he was afraid of somebody coming around? Somebody who tracked him here? Was Perry dealing? Maybe cutting the product—"

"Like I told Calvin, Perry was no dealer, he was strictly recreational." The joint had burned down almost to her fingertips. "We moved because his old apartment was small and hot and Perry owed a couple months' rent. The only person he was afraid of coming around was the manager."

"Then what kind of trouble was he in?"

The phone in the kitchen rang and they both jumped. On the sixth ring the answering machine switched on and a reedy voice said, "This is, ah, Donald Fisk at the *Orange County News*. I'd like to talk to you about your, ah, tragic loss. Please call me back at 827-3766."

Nick glared at the phone. "I thought I had an unlisted number."

"Yeah, right." Alison yawned. "I'm going to take a shower."

Nick waited until she went into the guest room before starting up the stairs.

The sun warmed the master bedroom, the scent from the red and yellow blossoms in the window box sweetening the air. They were just flowers to him—Sharon was the one who knew their botanical names and what kind of soil they needed. The flowers weren't going to make it. For a while he'd remember to water them, but eventually he'd forget and they would wither and die. Nick felt like tearing them out by the roots right now to save the waiting.

He heard Alison moving around downstairs. Opening drawers. Closing them harder than she needed to. The shower came on.

Sharon's desk was in one corner of the bedroom, a plain, bird's-eye maple. Her pens and legal pads were lined up, the dust cover on the computer. She kept just one photograph on the desk, a snapshot of the two of them on vacation—Nick giving Sharon a boost so she could peer over the fence of a nudist colony, Nick looking up her skirt. Peekaboo. He smiled. After all the arguments and silences, only the good times remained. In photographs, at least.

He sat in her chair, placed his hands on the desk, *her* desk, hoping to get a sense of Sharon, some lingering part of her that continued to exist in her things. Nothing. The ache in his heart was all he had left and it was fading too. He felt a surge of guilt, but even the guilt was momentary. Sharon didn't care if he grieved for an instant or forever. She was dead.

He avoided the bed as long as he could, circling the room, walking past the professional stereo system before lying down, head on the pillow. He reached for the remote control on the nightstand, flipped on the CD, but it was stacked with Tony Bennett and he was in no mood. He bounced the infrared remote off the ceiling and turned on the cassette deck. He had expected to hear the Moby ambient tape he had been listening to yesterday but there was something else on.

There were two electronic beeps, then a phone ringing three

times before a man picked up. Nick heard Alison's voice on the tape and sat up on one elbow, listening.

It's me, said Alison. Nick glanced at the bedroom door.

I was hoping it was you, the man gushed. *How's my girl?*

Turn out the lights, Doc, said Alison.

Way ahead of you, dahling, said Doc, a hint of prep school in his speech pattern. Nick could hear classical music playing softly in the background.

There was a silky rustling. *My panties are cutting into me,* said Alison. *My skin is so tender. If you breathed on me, I'd bruise.* She sighed, somewhere between pleasure and pain, and Nick heard her panties rustle again, imagined them sliding down her long legs. *Ohhh, that's better.*

Nick swallowed. Alison said she and Perry made tapes of their phone calls . . . but what was this tape doing *here?* Alison sighed again. He should shut the door but he was tired and didn't want to move. He hit the remote, lowered the volume, and closed his eyes.

Just the two of us, said Alison, *alone in the dark. No secrets, no shame, no regrets. You trust me, don't you?*

You know I do, said Doc.

You trust me, don't you? repeated Alison.

Nick nodded involuntarily.

Trust is all we have, all we need. Her voice rose and fell, shifting smoothly from a husky erotic pout to coy invitation . . .

Nick lay with his eyes closed, carried forward by the rhythm of her words, unaware of the meaning, the sound purely tactile, music more ancient than speech, a warm tide lapping at his consciousness, pulling him toward her. He tried to concentrate on Sharon, tried to remember the last time they had made love . . . It was so long ago. Alison's voice filled the room, resonant and compelling as the sea.

Just the two of us, whispered Alison.

Nick laid his arm across his face. The sun must have been pouring through the windows, because his skin was hot, but he couldn't see a thing. They were alone in the dark.

Open your mouth, said Alison. *Go on. Open it. Yeah, just like that. Shhh, don't say a word, just open wide.*

Nick heard the man groaning. He heard someone else groan too—the sound coming from his own throat.

Yeah, like that, said Alison. *Ummm, I'm so . . . tight and slippery down there, I can't put more than the tip of my—*

"Nicky?" said Alison, her voice the same smoky murmur as on the tape. "Are you all right?"

Nick blinked in the sunlight, saw her standing in the doorway, fresh from her shower. She wore an oversize white embroidered Mexican wedding shirt; her legs were bare, her hair wrapped in a towel. He hadn't heard her climbing the stairs. He was almost as startled by that fact as by her presence in his bedroom.

You like that, don't you? Alison said on the tape.

Nick fumbled for the remote but it was lost in the sheets. "What . . . what is this we're listening to, anyway?" he said. It was too late to pretend but he had to try.

"Perry must have left the tape there," said Alison. She saw his surprise. "He was using your bedroom system to make copies," she explained. "I thought you knew. Perry said the stereo equipment in your living room wasn't as good—"

"Perry never asked me—"

What the fuck are you doing here? demanded Doc, no trace of prep school in him now.

Nick sat up, his anger at Perry evaporating.

Hey, bro, Doc said, louder now, *you surprised me, man. Caught me with my pants down, heh-heh.* There was a thump and the phone hit the floor. Doc groaned. It was different than before. It wasn't passion now. *What are you* doing, *bro?* said Doc, this time from somewhere in the room, his voice hollow.

Nick found the remote, turned up the sound. His heart was beating fast. He heard a metallic click. Then another. *This is so fucking . . . inappropriate, bro,* wheezed Doc.

Alison unpeeled the towel from her head, tossed it aside and combed her fingers through her wet hair. There were tiny red and yellow birds embroidered on her shirt—they seemed to float in the air as she moved.

Glass shattered on the tape, and Doc was moaning, the words indistinct. Nick leaned forward, listening. *Careful, man,* gasped Doc, *you don't watch out . . . you're gonna kill me.* Doc laughed weakly. Nick strained to hear, jerked upright as Doc's laughter was cut off by a loud blow. Then silence. In that terrible silence, Nick could still hear the sound echoing in his mind, the sudden, overpowering impact of something hard against something soft and yielding, a slaughterhouse symphony.

Nick glanced at Alison but she was still combing out her damp hair. He felt a drop of warm water hit his wrist.

On the tape Nick heard the phone being picked up from the floor. Someone breathed into the receiver. *Doc?* said Alison. She sounded worried. There was only the breathing for an answer. *Perry?* Alison said, more concerned now.

Keep going, said Perry. *Tape is still rolling.*

Silence again. No breathing now. Just silence.

What . . . what's the matter, Doc? Alison asked. *Don't you wanna play anymore?*

The phone was very carefully put back onto the cradle.

Nick looked at Alison in her bright wedding shirt. "He heard what Perry said. He knew you were taping him."

"That's part of the fun, silly."

"No," said Nick. "Not . . . Doc. The one who was *killing* him."

"That was just playacting, Nicky," said Alison, motioning toward the tape deck. "Don't feel bad, Doc almost had me fooled too. Really freaked me out at first." She sat beside him on the bed, bouncing as though testing it out. "That was *Doc* doing the heavy breathing. He was joking."

Another phone call came on the tape, Alison using her sexy cowgirl drawl. Nick clicked it off. "I don't think that was a joke." He looked at her. "I want to hear it again."

"I bet you do," smiled Alison, their faces just inches apart. "Judging from what I saw when I walked in, that tape sure worked on you."

Her smile held him. It took an effort for Nick to break away and walk over to the stereo. He slid out an armor-aluminum case from under the cabinet, removed the small Mackie 1604 console mixer—and a multitrack cassette deck—and hooked it up to the receiver. Then he patched a parametric equalizer into the Mackie, plugged in a set of headphones.

"What are you doing?" Alison stood behind him.

He didn't answer, just plugged in another pair of headphones and handed it to her. She squatted beside him on the floor, waited for him to say something.

Nick took the cassette out of the deck, slipped it into the Mackie, and rewound it to where Doc was interrupted. His finger stabbed PLAY. He isolated certain frequency groups with the equalizer, not Doc's voice but the background noise, jagged points on the digital screen of the equalizer. He boosted the background. REPLAY. Nick heard a floorboard creak on the tape. Doc's surprised voice muted now, then the first impact.

Nick found the exact point of the last blow, the killing blow, and boosted the signal. He was listening so intently he could feel tiny beads of sweat gather along his hairline. He heard the impact even more clearly this time, immediately followed by the exhalation of breath, an explosion of air from Doc. Hard to fake that.

Alison put her hand on his arm.

Nick rewound the tape to before the final blow, boosting the vocal range now. *What are you* doing, *bro?* said Doc. *This is me, man. This is* me. Nick could hear the fear in him, barely contained, trembling at the edges. He could see it on the screen, a quavering hieroglyph of pain.

Alison pressed the headphones against her ears as he let the tape run.

Careful, man. You don't watch out . . . you're gonna kill me. Doc laughed and Nick tried to prepare himself for what was coming. *Wham!* Nick rested his head in his hands, suddenly looked up. What was that? A faint clatter in the silence . . . Nick rewound the tape, keyed the spot. "You hear that?" he said to Alison.

"What was it?"

He played it for her again, filtering out as much of the extraneous noise as possible. There. Wood against wood. Not wood striking wood. Hardwood dropping on a wood floor, discarded now. The distinctive ring of a baseball bat tossed aside, a Louisville Slugger, its job done. Nick felt the sweat run down his jawline as he heard the phone being picked up, and the sound of ragged breathing as the batter listened. Nick turned off the tape. "Now do you believe me?" he said to Alison.

Alison took off her headphones.

"Doc was beaten to death," said Nick. "Didn't you *hear* it?"

Alison shook out her hair. "Maybe that's what it sounded like. That doesn't mean that's what happened." She looked like she felt sorry for him. "Nicky . . . when I'm playing phone games and I'm cooking, I mean when I'm really hot, I can make you believe I'm all alone or in the middle of a slumber party. I can make you believe I'm in church waiting to get married or broken down on the freeway and scared of the dark. I can make you believe *anything,* Nicky."

THE BLUE ANGEL kept his hands in his pockets as he strolled down the sidewalk on Pacific Avenue, a narrow street in Sunset Beach, sand crunching underfoot. He wore soft, powder-blue penny loafers and no socks. The cool wind off the ocean whipped his blue suit, rippling the light fabric and lifting his fine blond hair. The Angel. The Blue Angel. Always blue. Peacock blue. Royal blue. Midnight blue. Blue—the color of the sky.

The tiny houses across the street were right on the beach, wood-frame shacks with lousy plumbing and mildewed walls that rented for two thousand dollars a month. A dozen surfers would move in, sleep all over the floor, then leave when the waves were right in Mexico or the garbage piled up too high in the kitchen.

It was late afternoon, the sun pink and mottled through the pollution, the ocean an ugly gray. The Angel scanned the street as he walked, watching from behind his sunglasses, not moving his head. It was a quiet Sunday, rusting VW vans parked on the brown lawns. No waves today—the surfers were staying in, probably watching *Ren and Stimpy* reruns and drinking tap water instant coffee.

The beach was almost deserted—a solitary, thick-waisted jogger trudged along the tide line, headphones on, mouth open. The jogger stumbled and fell to one knee, got up slowly, brushing seaweed off his leg. The Angel smiled, but it never reached his mouth. He walked past the cottage he was looking for, noted the two chopped-out Harleys on the sagging porch, chrome gleaming in the sunlight. A white Lincoln Town Car was backed up to the porch steps. He memorized the license plate with a glance, kept walking.

The Angel glimpsed his reflection in the cracked window of a Nissan pickup truck, noted the powerful shoulders and graceful bearing. His face was smooth and oddly sensuous, the features elongated, blue eyes cool and haughty behind his sunglasses—the wide-set eyes of a predator. He preferred to see his image in dusty surfaces and broken glass, to gaze upon himself from afar, but not directly. A glimpse was all he needed to take in his own radiance.

A woman had told him once that he was so beautiful it hurt to look at him, like staring at the sun. He was thirty-two years old now, still beautiful, untouched by time. Tiger, tiger, burning bright . . .

He crossed the street and cut between the houses to the beach, moving easily across the soft sand toward the house with the Harleys on the porch. Effortlessly. Weightless as a thought, a premonition of pain. The Angel's eyes were bright with pleasure.

He heard a sound like distant thunder, turned and looked out to sea, shading his eyes with his hands. Far out over the Pacific he could see a pair of thin white jet trails moving parallel across the sky. A couple of FA-18 Skyhawks out of Mira Mar probably, streaking toward Catalina Island at Mach 2, the pilots strapped in tight, controls at their fingertips, the fighter an extension of their nervous systems. Instantly reactive. Pure destruction. The Angel watched the jet trails until they disappeared. He had no idea how long he had been standing there, head high, heart pounding like a drumroll.

The windows of the cottage were open wide to the sea, curtains billowing in the salt breeze, flapping wildly, the ends frayed. The Angel stepped onto the bleached wood of the back deck, moving quietly, unhurried. Empty beer cans lay scattered across the deck, an overturned metal picnic table chained to the railing. He could hear voices inside the house and an intermittent clicking sound. They were shooting pool inside the room. He smelled cigarette smoke and something else, too. His nostrils flared at the stink.

Windblown sand stung his face, but he didn't flinch. He wondered what the Skyhawk pilots were doing at this exact moment, what they were seeing, what they were feeling . . . Even a gradual banking turn upped the gravity, doubling, then tripling your body weight. The Skyhawk could pull 9 G's and it was like the hand of God squeezing the sweat out of you, the sweat cold as ice water soaking your flight suit. You learned not to shiver. The best pilots loved the cold.

Someone cleared his throat inside the house, spitting. The voices were louder. Three different voices. The Angel drifted closer, standing right beside the window now, so close that the flapping curtains brushed his arm. The beach was deserted now, gulls swooping low over the waves, their cries harsh against the foam.

The Angel picked up a conch shell ashtray from the deck, weighed it in his hand, then lobbed it over the cottage. It shattered on the front porch and he heard yelps and footsteps inside. The Angel slipped through the billowing curtains, right through them, not touching the sill, stepped inside the house, moving silently as smoke.

The three of them stood in front of the open front door, their backs to him, looking out. A slate pool table was at the center of the small room—a hastily discarded cigarette burning on the ratty green felt, right next to the 11 ball. The two bikers wore filthy jeans and studded leather vests, bare-chested. The other was older, a stocky, balding man in a red nylon jogging suit and neon-yellow running shoes. That would be Ben Telaris.

Anyone else would have looked ridiculous in that bright red outfit, but Telaris had a flair for the dramatic. Ten years ago he had ridden with the Evil Dead, a Bakersfield outlaw biker club that specialized in contract arson, rape, and extortion. Telaris had deposed the former warlord of the club, beat him unconscious, then pulled out his teeth with a pair of needle-nose pliers. He had strung the teeth on a necklace and worn it on an all-night ride celebrating his own coronation.

Telaris had quickly expanded the Evil Dead into methamphetamine production and distribution, always learning, increasing his operation, setting up legitimate businesses as fronts. Telaris was no longer warlord of the Evil Dead, not officially. He didn't even ride a Harley anymore—he had kidney problems, and was more likely to attend a Kiwanis breakfast at the International House of Pancakes than a sorority girl train-pull. He still kept a pair of pliers under the front seat of his Lincoln.

A fly buzzed past the Angel. His hand darted out, grabbed the fly, shook it in his fist like dice and bounced it off Telaris's bald spot.

Telaris jerked around, startled. His eyes widened when he saw the Angel but he stayed steady.

The two bikers turned and immediately separated, flanking him. One biker carried a stumpy sawed-off shotgun—a stupid, wasted felony—the other didn't need anything. The one with the shotgun was tall and gnarly, with pocked skin and a scraggly goatee. The other was shorter but twice as broad, his face flat as an anvil, huge arms covered with tattoos. The Angel waited. They were so slow. Earthworms struggling through darkness. Ignorant of the light.

"It's okay, boys," barked Telaris, back in command, not even looking at them. He was a beefy man with hard eyes, bloodshot now, like he hadn't been getting enough sleep and it was starting to tell on him. "You're the Angel?"

With those fighter-jock eyes of his, the Angel could count the pores in Telaris's cheeks, the individual hairs in his wild eyebrows, yet his peripheral vision was so sharp that he was aware of the rest of the room, from the sagging sofa to the motorcycle posters peeling off the walls. A pile of empty black trash bags was stacked beside the sofa, rippling in the breeze.

"You didn't need to play games coming through the window," Telaris said. "You could get yourself hurt that way." The gold Rolex on his thick wrist was lost in the curly hair that rolled up from the back of his hands. His chest and back were probably matted with fur. An alpha ape leading other apes, but an ape just the same, gibbering in the mud.

"Shit, Ben," said the one with the goatee. "This the dude you were worried about? Mr. Prom King?"

"Shut up, Maynard," said Telaris, still watching the Angel.

"Maynard's right," said the anvil-headed biker. "Dude looks like a commercial telling you to drink milk."

"Yeah," rasped Maynard, "like healthy bodies and shit."

The Angel smiled.

"Shut *up*, Maynard," said Telaris. "You too, Rollo."

"Were you worried, Ben?" the Angel asked. "Tough guy like you? I'm shocked."

"Let me show you what I called about," Telaris said, ignoring the sarcasm, as he walked toward the rear of the cottage. "It's not pretty, but I'm sure you've seen worse."

The buzzing sound grew louder, a cloud of flies rising as Telaris and the Angel walked into the bedroom, then settling back down onto the three bodies sprawled across the room like the remains of a slumber party. The air was thick with the smell of bad meat.

A long-haired biker wearing leather chaps over his jeans was splayed in one corner, a bullet through his right eye. Blood had leaked out the eye socket and dried down his cheek like a dirty tear. One of the couriers, a man in a black suit, lay on the bed, one side of his head blown away, flakes of unburned gunpowder tattooing the raw flesh. Someone had shot him point-blank as he turned away. The other courier was crumpled on the floor in a corona of dried blood. It looked like he had been reaching for the pistol in his shoulder holster.

"Your man Lomax did all this? Doc? That's what you call him?" The Angel paced around the bed in his powder-blue penny loafers, trying to reconstruct the scene—where the shooter stood, how he must have moved in that crowded room, the killing arcs . . . The geometry of death. "Doc was a busy fellow. Greed will do that. Nine million dollars can turn a good man into a runner."

Lomax must have started with his partner, the biker with the chaps. He was the only one shot direct, too surprised to flinch. Curious choice. The Angel usually took out the most suspicious person first, the one most likely to already have his finger on the trigger. Lomax must have been making a statement to himself by starting with his partner—there was no going back after that shot. The Angel was pleased. Lomax was weak. He didn't trust himself to kill his partner when the man could see it coming.

Telaris bent down beside the body of the biker. The room buzzed louder, like the static between radio stations. "J.B. here was with me from the beginning," he said, touching the man's tangled blond hair with the back of his hand. "J.B. and those damn chaps, like some candyass Hollywood cowboy. He got a lot of pussy with those chaps. More than me, anyway. Yeah, we shared us some wild times . . ." He punched him lightly on the jaw. "Evil Dead forever, bro."

"What a tender moment," said the Angel. "Why don't you toss a couple of *Easy Rider* centerfolds into the trash bag with him? Give J.B. something to beat off to in hell."

Telaris stood up, perplexed, not certain he had heard the Angel clearly. "Are you *trying* to make me mad? Just find Doc. That's your job."

"I don't work for you, Ben," the Angel said, positioning himself so that he could see into the living room. "You know that."

"I didn't mean—"

"You borrowed four million dollars from my associates," said the Angel, enjoying the sight of Telaris chewing on his lower lip. "Payback time. Three days ago you were supposed to deliver nine million dollars to our couriers. Cash. Nonsequential hundreds." He glanced at the bodies. "What we have here, Ben, is a loan in default. All that money . . . you really should have been more careful."

"I had a backup on the beach with an Uzi—"

"Ahhh," said the Angel, drawing out the exclamation. He loved the drama of these moments, the erotic tension, tightening, tightening . . . "A *backup*. Where is this backup?"

Telaris ground his teeth. "We found him on the sand when we got here that night. One shot to the brainpan. Uzi was still in his hand. He was an ex-marine, real handy with a weapon, and he never even flipped the safety off."

"Three dead in the house. One outside. This Lomax is very . . . capable. Once he sets his mind to it."

"I trusted him," Telaris said bitterly. "Lomax set up our first big meth lab practically by himself. Motherfucker turned out some great crank . . ." He shook his head. "Damn college boy. I should have known he'd fuck me over."

"That's right," the Angel said. "You should have known."

"What's that supposed to mean?"

"You were being squeezed pretty bad, from what I understand," said the Angel. A car with a bad muffler drove slowly past the cottage. He waited until it faded in the distance. "A D.E.A. agent I know told me the Mexican Mafia and Vietnamese gangs are cutting into your crystal meth franchise." He clucked. "That's some serious competition."

"I ain't worried." Telaris blotted his forehead with the back of his hairy mitt.

"You've lost the whole Riverside market," said the Angel, fingering the lapels of his suit jacket. "Mexicans torched your labs, hired away your best cooker and killed the rest."

"Just part of the cost of doing business," said Telaris, looking away. "Diversification, that's the secret to survival. That's why I borrowed the money. We got the corner on this new designer drug, Lovetron. It's somewhere between pharmaceutical coke and Ecstasy. You fuck for *days* on this shit. Kids are going crazy for it."

"Is that so?" The Angel puckered his lips. "I hear things that make me wonder. Your ranch in Santa Barbara—you had it on the market for two point five million. Somebody told me you dumped it last month. Didn't even clear a million. That's an act of a desperate man."

"Real estate is in the toilet. You know that."

"Were you worried about repaying your loan, Ben?" the Angel asked solicitously, his voice soft as cotton.

"A temporary cash flow problem," said Telaris. "We're not fully operational on the Lovetron. The chemistry is pretty complicated . . ." He shook his head, as though waking up. "Look, you got your money. It was a stretch, but I paid it back."

"That's just the point," said the Angel. "You *didn't* pay it back." He watched the flies dance in the warm air, a hypnotic ballet, dipping and soaring through ʻhe stink. "Your old friend Doc ran off with the money, remember? At least, that's what you said."

"You calling me a liar?"

The Angel gave a slow, exaggerated shrug. "You know how people always brag how they can spot a lie and a liar?" He took a last look around the room. "Truth and lies, Ben—I'll be honest with you, I can never tell the difference." He started down the hall.

"You think I ripped myself off?" Telaris hurried after him. "If I had done that, you think I'd stick around to try and explain it to you? You think I'm that *fucking* stupid?"

Maynard and Rollo looked up from their game of pool as the Angel entered the living room and stood beside the window.

"You borrowed money." The Angel stared at the sky through the flapping curtains. "Now you have to pay it back."

"This ain't right."

The Angel could feel Telaris behind him, but he didn't bother turning around. "Plus late charges, of course—"

"I'm tapped out," snarled Telaris. "You know that."

The Angel watched the curtains float in the breeze. He could see Maynard reflected in the windowpane, saw him move away from the pool table, quietly lay down his cue stick. The Angel focused on the sky, the endless blue . . . "Tapped out? My goodness, Ben," he said, his voice flat as glass, "I wouldn't want to be in your shoes."

8

NICK KNOCKED OVER a stack of Perry's cassette tapes in his haste, scrambling around on his hands and knees beside the bed in the cluttered downstairs guest room, clothes and audio equipment everywhere.

Hello, said a man.

I found your number in Janet's pocket, you needle-dicked son of a bitch, said Alison.

What . . .? said the man. *Who is this?*

I'm Janet's girlfriend, said Alison. *She's a slut but she's my slut, understand?*

I don't know no Janet, lady—

*Don't you lady me, mac, I'm no lady and I'll prove it if you
stick that bone where it doesn't belong one more—*

Nick popped the tape out, tossed it onto the heap, and went
back to rummaging through the mess on the floor. A police scanner was overturned, cord trailing. Three of Perry's hot cell phones
lay on top of some crumpled blue jeans, another peeked out
from under a pile of Alison's underwear, lost among the silky
wisps—panties and fishnets and lacy brassieres. She probably
didn't own a pair of panty hose. He averted his eyes, picked
among the tapes.

Alison watched him from the bed. "When I'm on the phone
I pretend I'm in acting class, working out a role," she said.
"Sometimes I'm a West Texas cowgirl, sometimes I'm Malibu
Barbie getting a bikini wax, sometimes I'm their raging bitch of
a boss leading them around by their pecker. I enjoy it, won't deny
that, but it's not just idleness, Nicky. Actors have to keep in practice. Otherwise . . . well, we get stale, don't we?"

Most of the tapes were unlabeled, some marked with Perry's
scrawl: "Head job," "Car fone talk," "Confessions." Nick
slapped "Confessions" in, adjusted the volume as the tape hissed.

"I told you, they're just party tapes," Alison said. She was
still wearing the white embroidered wedding shirt, but had
slipped on a pair of unraveling cut-offs, sitting cross-legged on
the rumpled sheets. Through the window behind her, Nick could
see the trees in the backyard stirring in the wind.

*It . . . it's been six weeks, no seven, since my last confession.
I have had impure thoughts—*

Be more specific, my son, said Perry.

Pardon me, Father?

What exactly do you mean by impure? said Perry.

Alison leaned off the bed, stopped the tape. "I don't like that
one. Perry sneaked into a church with a recorder under his priest

outfit, real proud of himself. Not me. I don't mess with people's religion—I'm strictly fun and games."

"Fun and games. Party tapes. You make it sound so innocent. Just a little mind-fucking between strangers, an acting class assignment." Nick held up the cassette he had brought downstairs. "This tape got Sharon and Perry killed. Some fun, huh?"

"You don't know that, Nicky, so don't you blame me."

Nick shook his head.

"Guys are always pulling stuff like that. They pretend to have heart attacks, pretend that the cops are busting in—"

"This tape that Perry left upstairs is a copy," said Nick. "Where's the original? You couldn't find it." He indicated the scattered cassettes. "I can't find it. Where did it go?"

"I don't keep track of Perry's tapes," said Alison. "*Perry* couldn't either." Her voice softened. "Maybe Perry taped over the original. Erased it. He did that with the junk. I thought Doc's murder trick was pretty good—I mean, I still get chills when Doc says, 'You're not careful, you're gonna kill me.' Yeah, he fooled me, at first anyway, but he didn't fool Perry. 'Junk.' That's what he called the tape."

Nick heard a car door slam out front. A familiar thunk. That would be Krinol from across the street, home from his regular half-price Sunday matinee. They were going to bury him in that old Coupe de Ville.

"This call to Doc was local?" said Nick. "You're *sure?*"

Alison nodded. "Perry bitched about it—said it wasn't even long-distance and he still couldn't get through with one of his cell phones."

Nick cleaned his glasses on his T-shirt. No way to trace a local call. Alison didn't know Doc's number—she said Perry always dialed. He put his glasses back on. The world was in focus again. Right. He bent down, started going through the tapes.

"Why don't you have any other calls to Doc in here? You said he was one of Perry's regulars."

"He was, but I don't know if he brought any of them here. Perry had boxes of tapes stashed—"

"Let's go get them," said Nick.

"I don't know where Perry kept his stuff," Alison said. "We were splitting up, remember? My things are in a storage locker until I find a new apartment. I didn't even want to come here, but Perry begged and pleaded and said it would be a good time. I think he hoped I'd change my mind." She grimaced. "It had worked before." She looked at him. "What's the big deal with these other tapes, anyway?"

Nick hesitated. His instinct was always to keep his own confidences. Sharon told him once that he was willing to share everything but himself.

"Nicky?"

"I need them to figure out Doc's phone number—I've got the last two digits, an eight and a four."

"What are you, 1-800-PSYCHIC?"

"Perry left two dialing tones on when he made the recording," said Nick, "an A-flat and a C-sharp. A-flat is the number eight, C-sharp is a four. I thought maybe Perry left more tones on the other Doc tapes."

"You can really do that? That is so cool."

Nick spotted some tapes under the bed, reached under and scooped them toward him. "Did anyone know you two were staying here?" he said, stretching for the last of the tapes, his head under the box spring.

"I didn't tell anybody," she said, her voice muffled by the mattress.

"This guy Doc," said Nick, sitting up, wiping dust balls off his forehead, "what was his real name?"

"Who knows?" Alison shrugged. "He's *strange* . . . always talking about how tuned in we are together, asking me if I feel it too." She snorted. "Yeah, for sure. Doc keeps trying to impress me with how smart he is. He *is* smart, but he works too hard at it—like having that Beethoven music in the background."

"Mahler."

"Ma-who?"

"Mahler," said Nick, sifting through the tapes, finding nothing with Doc on the label. "It was Mahler in the background. Ninth Symphony."

"Why do you have to correct me all the time? Who *cares* who it was?" Alison blinked away tears. "Geez, Nicky, you act like you're the only one who lost somebody last night. You don't think I wonder about that call to Doc too?" She pulled at the tiny buttons of her shirt. "Maybe if I hadn't called Doc, they'd still be alive."

Nick watched her lower lip quiver. "Exactly."

She bit her lips shut, eyes flaring. "Well, *fuck* you."

Nick let her response linger. He wanted to tell her he was sorry . . . tell her it wasn't her fault, but he wasn't sure that she would believe him. He turned one of the tapes over and over in his hand, thinking.

"Just about the time I start liking you, Nicky, you turn into a real prick. I shouldn't be surprised but I am." One of her shirt buttons had come off with her twisting.

"Alison," he said, still thinking it through, "these tapes you and Perry made . . . was he blackmailing people with them?"

"Not with my tapes," said Alison. "Nobody cares about dirty talk anymore. It's a brave new world, Nicky."

"Not with *your* tapes maybe," said Nick, "but you're not on a lot of these."

"No," said Alison. "Perry had been making tapes long before he met me—"

"This one from the church confessional and the power trip tapes . . . Perry might have turned a buck with them. Perry had to have a reason for making them."

"I told you, it turned him on," said Alison. "The idea of intruding into strangers' lives . . . he got off on that whole forbidden-zone thing. At the beginning it was just fun, but then he figured out we could use the tapes to get jobs. I got a Frosty Cola commercial from this one tape, ran nationally too, and Perry got some voice-overs, you know, commercials—"

"I know what voice-overs are," Nick said, distracted, for the first time wondering if the Doc tape he had listened to upstairs was faked.

"That's how Perry and I met," said Alison. "There was this audition for a Cherry Crisp spot—it's this cereal that tastes like cherry pop. I got the part of the college girl who eats 'C.C.' straight from the box while she studies. I don't remember what part Perry was going after, but he got cut right away. Then, out of the blue, he launches into an a cappella version of the C.C. jingle. The actors were all like, 'Wow, the cat has balls.' The producer still didn't hire him. Perry mostly landed cartoon voices, Saturday morning stuff. *Local* market. Grampa Droid, Mrs. Wiggily-Jiggily . . . God, that one was pathetic." She tossed her head. "I talk too much, I know it." Her fingers worried at another shirt button. "So, okay, Perry liked voice-overs; the money was good—"

"And he was back in the studio." Nick finished the thought. "Almost as good as being onstage. I tried it myself. I wasn't very successful."

Alison nodded. "Neither was Perry. At first. There was too much competition. Like *thousands* of people are going after those jobs, people with connections: TV actors with their own series even, and movie actors with too many wrinkles . . . Old rock stars are a dime a dozen, and Perry could sing but his speaking voice wasn't all that good. This casting director told him he didn't have texture." She moved closer to Nick. "Perry was afraid of ending up behind the counter at Tower Records bragging about his gold album to kids who never heard of him. He needed a hook. That's where the tapes came in. Lots of people in the industry swap tapes. Not just party tapes, there's all kinds of twisto stuff passed around. Yuck." She winced. "I kept waiting for one of my tapes to pay off big-time—you know, a real movie or maybe a mini-series . . . Perry said we should just hang on. He said he had a feeling we were going to hit it soon." She sniffed. "We hit it all right."

"Maybe one of Perry's other tapes came back at him," said Nick, talking to himself as much as to her. "Some people would kill to keep their secrets."

"So *now* you don't think it was my call to Doc that—"

"I don't know."

"Upstairs you knew," she said angrily. "It was all my fault that Perry and Sharon got killed. Now you're not sure. Now maybe it's one of Perry's other tapes. Make up your mind!"

"I said I didn't know."

"Why are we even arguing?" said Alison, hugging a pillow to herself. "Give the tape with Doc to Calvin. Let *him* decide. It's not our job to figure this all out. This is what he's paid to do."

"Who were Perry's customers?" persisted Nick. "Who did he trade the 'twisto stuff' to?"

"I don't know. Perry only took me around when he was peddling our party tapes. I guess I was good for business."

"I bet you were."

"Shut up, Nicky. You think I'm just some bimbo does the heavy breathing number and gets guys all sticky?"

"I didn't say that."

"I thought you understood," said Alison. Her lower lip quivered. "All that stuff that happened on the walk back last night . . . You talked to me like I was a person." Her eyes flashed. "I thought you were different, Nicky. I thought you understood me better than that."

"I'm sorry," said Nick. He was, too. "I didn't mean—"

"You think a sexy voice is all you need to make tapes? No way. There's plenty of guys would be scared off by sexy. Maybe sexy makes them hostile. Everybody is different, Nicky, and there's no road map. It takes instinct and brains and knowing when to back off and when to move in close." She smacked the pillow in her lap so hard that a feather floated in the air.

"I said—"

"Lots of times they can't even give me a made-up name for themselves," snapped Alison, "so *I* make up names for them, a nickname, a pet name, maybe a name they always hoped somebody would call them." She beat her chest with her hand. "It takes *heart* to connect with strangers, to know what they want to hear, to know what they want to say. It takes heart to get them to open wide. Perry was making tapes before he met me. I'm not the first girl he worked with. I'm just the best."

"I'm sorry," whispered Nick.

She turned away from him. "Someday . . . someday, Nicky, you're going to see me on the big screen and neither you or anybody else in the audience is going to be able to take your eyes off of me."

Nick watched her profile. He could see three holes in her earlobe—no earrings this afternoon. He sat there and he wanted to lean over and kiss the three tiny slits in that pink cartilage, which made no sense. No sense at all.

Nicky. Even when he asked her not to, she called him that. It was a little boy's name, mischievous, a reminder of a carefree childhood. Nicky was a name for a playmate. Or a lover. She was good. Maybe she *was* the best. He stared out the window, watched the yellow police ribbon billowing across the backyard. It looked like a going-out-of-business sale.

9

"I DON'T WANT trouble with you," grumbled Telaris. He was an aging bully, not used to being challenged, barely keeping his anger in check. "You find Doc, you'll find your money. Then we're all happy."

"I'm happy now," the Angel said brightly.

Rollo twirled the cue stick in his huge hands, watching the Angel, trying to make sense of the conversation.

"Don't push me," said Telaris, the hairy tips of his ears tinged with red. "Do you know who you're talking to?"

"I know all about you," said the Angel. "I know about your house in Corona del Mar, the one with the ugly yellow carpeting in the master bedroom." He saw Telaris's eyes widen. "Lousy water pressure in the Jacuzzi, Ben. I think you were taken." He was aware of Rollo and Maynard sliding into position, flanking him, but he stayed right where he was, holding the center.

Telaris didn't react. He was digesting the implications of what the Angel had said, evaluating the sudden knowledge that the Angel had been inside his house. His bedroom. The Angel smiled to himself seeing Telaris's calm—nice to see a proud man who didn't let his pride trip him up. No wonder he had lasted so long in a dangerous game.

Rollo approached the Angel, rolling from side to side as he walked, his dull eyes narrowed into slits.

The Angel waited for him, radiating a cool contempt, poised on the balls of his feet. The room tingled with energy, the flies buzzing louder, moving around the room like mad molecules, bouncing off the walls.

"Look, we're all in this together, right?" Telaris said to the Angel, trying to defuse the situation.

"Where did you get that idea?" laughed the Angel.

"Then what are you doing here?" demanded Telaris.

"Relax, Ben. You're not a young man anymore. Probably eat too much red meat and don't get enough exercise. You could have a stroke right here. You'd be on the floor, unable to speak, unable to move. You might still have bladder control, but you'd need someone to carry you into the bathroom. You'd need someone to hold your penis. To shake it off when you were done." The Angel looked from Rollo to Maynard, considering. "Which one of these two cretins would get the honor? I bet Rollo would be first in line—"

Rollo snarled, swung the heavy end of the cue stick like a home run hitter, charging forward full speed. He might as well have been moving in slow motion for all the good it did him. The Angel wasn't bound by the same laws as the rest of them. He wasn't a prisoner of gravity, plodding through the mire with his burden of flesh. Oh, he was a different creature entirely.

The Angel swiveled, felt the whoosh of air as the cue stick narrowly missed his head. Instead of retreating, he moved in closer, close enough to smell the sweat and rage on Rollo, close enough to deftly take the cue stick from him. His timing was perfect—not jerking the stick away, not trying to win a tug-of-war with the behemoth, but simply plucking it from his startled grasp as though it were a bouquet of flowers offered by a suitor.

The Angel whipped the end of the cue stick against Rollo's face, shattering his nose in an explosion of blood. He saw Maynard dive for the sawed-off as Rollo fell to his knees. The Angel punted Rollo's head, drove his face into the side of the pool table, then pivoted toward the couch, moving faster now, gliding across the room as Maynard reached the shotgun and turned, smiling his rotten teeth as he pulled back the two hammers with his grease-stained thumb.

Maynard's eyes went wide as the Angel drove the cue stick into him, shoving it through his belly in a single smooth movement, pinning him to the back of the couch. The sawed-off fell from Maynard's grasp, his fingers twitching as he stared at the Angel. He looked like a beetle in a science display, arms and legs jerking.

The Angel watched Maynard struggle, utterly at peace with himself—he felt a warmth in his fingers and toes, as though some vast electrical circuit had been completed. He leaned closer to Maynard, right in front of his face, hoping to hear what he was saying, but the words were caught somewhere in Maynard's throat as he jerked spasmodically, teeth chattering.

"Jesus," whispered Telaris, just standing there, unsure of what to do. He had a .32 tucked into an ankle holster on his left leg, but it was a long way down and the Angel moved quicker than anyone he had ever seen. He looked from Maynard to where Rollo was splayed under the pool table, motionless, blood leaking out of his head.

The Angel sat down on the couch, right next to Maynard, the slight movement of the seat cushions causing the biker to cry out. "Come on, Ben," the Angel called, patting the cushion on the other side of him. "Sit down, take a load off. We still have matters to discuss."

Telaris watched Maynard claw at the end of the cue stick protruding from his abdomen, his dirty nails scratching against the wood. Telaris half closed his eyes, as though that would drown out the sound. He had grown up in a house infested with rats, had gone to sleep every night hearing them scurry in the walls, making that same scratching noise.

"Get over here," commanded the Angel.

Telaris walked slowly toward the couch and sat down, keeping as far from the Angel as possible.

"You have the information I asked for?" said the Angel. "A recent photo of Lomax? List of friends, associates, relatives . . . all the bits and pieces of his life."

Telaris reached into his jumpsuit, pulled out a manila envelope and passed it over. His hand trembled, the gold Rolex bouncing against his wrist, but he fought down the fear, taking pride in his self-control. He indicated Maynard with a nod, taking care not to really look at him, not at his face, not at his eyes. "Was this for my benefit?" he blustered. "Because you didn't have to—"

"For *your* benefit?" The Angel threw back his head in delight. "What a lovely thought, Ben. No, I must confess, I didn't do this for you."

Telaris wiped his forehead. The room was stifling. "Yeah, I should have known that. I seen your work."

"The videotape?" The Angel lit up. "You recognized my voice, did you? It took me less than two weeks to find that particular runner. He had fled the country, gotten himself a new identity, dyed his hair, grew a beard . . ." The Angel shrugged. "The world is but a speck, and there's not really that many places where someone with a great amount of money would want to live. Why steal millions if you have to sleep in a grass hut and slap mosquitoes all night? Most people don't appreciate that fact until it's too late."

"I thought I'd seen it all," said Telaris, "but that video . . ." He swallowed. "That was some sick shit."

"We send a copy of that video to all of our clients." The Angel inclined his head toward Telaris as though sharing a confidence. "We had a runner almost every month before we made the video. Afterwards . . . well, this little problem of yours is the first incident in over a year." He smiled. "If I'm not careful, I'm going to put myself out of business."

"You could always get a job at a fucking slaughterhouse," Telaris grunted, wanting to beat that smile off the Angel's face with a tire iron.

"You misjudge me," the Angel sighed. "I'm not a sadist, I'm a moralist." He saw Telaris's lack of comprehension. "Trust is the basis of all things," he explained, "and the basis of all trust is fear."

"You made your point," said Telaris.

"I don't think so," said the Angel. "The money you owe is incidental to the grand scheme. If a client thought he could default on his responsibilities with impunity, that would introduce doubt into every transaction, large and small. What kind of world would that be? A world out of balance. Beyond good and evil. A world adrift, loosed of its moorings. I could *never* allow that, Ben."

Telaris didn't answer. In the silence they heard Maynard gasping, the cue stick rising and falling with every breath. "Why don't you put him out of his misery?" rasped Telaris. "If you won't, I will."

"No, you won't," the Angel said, not raising his voice. He turned his head, whispered in Maynard's ear: "No one is going to put Maynard out of his misery. That wouldn't be any fun at all." He looked back at Telaris. "First, I'm going to find Lomax. Then I'll find out what *really* happened in this little house by the sea."

"What really happened?" said Telaris, confused. "You *seen* what happened—"

"Look at that." The Angel pointed to Maynard, whose arm was inching along the cushions toward the sawed-off. "Bravo."

Maynard wheezed as he reached slowly for the sawed-off, his arm acting independently, the rest of him still stuck to the couch. Blood ringed the cue stick where it penetrated his abdomen, trickling onto his Harley belt buckle as his hand strained toward the shotgun.

"Come on, Maynard," the Angel urged. "You're almost there."

Maynard hooked the trigger guard with his index finger, dragging the sawed-off toward him. He groaned, eyes fluttering as he weakly lifted the shotgun into his lap.

The Angel spread his arms wide. "Take your shot, Maynard. I won't move. Come on, don't keep me waiting."

"*Do* it, bro," hissed Telaris, getting off the couch, away from the Angel.

The Angel basked in the moment.

"Do it!" shouted Telaris.

Maynard tried to lift the shotgun, but his hands were shaking and it slid off his knees and onto the floor. He started crying, then jerked convulsively. His head flopped forward and he was still. The room was quiet.

The Angel looked disappointed.

"Maynard had an old lady and four kids," Telaris spat, angry at the Angel, even angrier at himself for not doing something to stop him.

"You're sweating, Ben. Maybe you should change brands of antiperspirants. That was a generic I saw in your medicine chest. You get what you pay for."

"You think you know everything," said Telaris, pinpoints of color erupting across his cheeks. "Well, I heard some things about you too."

The Angel looked down his nose. "Really."

Telaris licked his lips.

"What did you hear, Ben?"

"I heard you went to the Naval Academy," Telaris said. "You were going to be some fancy jet jockey but washed out when something showed up on your psychologicals." He puffed up. "Right at the last minute too. Just before you got your little gold wings. Must have broke your fucking heart."

"What a strange tale," mused the Angel. "Who would have told you something like that?"

"The Navy dumped your ass quick," Telaris crowed, eyes wide under those bushy eyebrows. "They marched you to the front gate with an armed guard and everything. Sayonara, swabbie, and don't come back." He licked his lips. "What did the Navy psychs see when they looked inside you, Angel? It must have been something *really* special to scare them like that."

"Who told you a story like that, Ben? I'd like to know . . ."

"I bet it was a real shock getting caught like that, especially for a punk like you," sneered Telaris. "You probably figured you had everybody fooled with that choirboy face of yours."

"It is a beautiful face, isn't it?" The Angel gave him a profile, then a close-up. "You'll see me in your dreams, night after night. If you're lucky."

"What does that mean?"

The Angel watched him with those cool blue eyes.

"I . . . I'm not afraid of you," said Telaris.

The Angel smiled.

"I mean it," said Telaris. "You . . . you just find Doc. Get your money back. Then we got no hard feelings, you and me. Just find him."

The Angel pulled the handkerchief out of the breast pocket of his suit jacket, leaned over and wiped down the handle of the cue stick. He stood up and walked toward the open window.

"I'm not scared of you!" called Telaris.

The Angel stepped through the curtains and out into the afternoon.

10

"ARE YOU *STILL* out here, Nicky? It's after three A.M." Alison stepped out onto the patio. She wore a lacy white slip, shivering in the damp night air, her legs bare, her hair loosely braided. The night sky was overcast, the stars streaked with clouds—twenty yards beyond the swimming pool shadows ruled. She glanced toward the hot tub, quickly turned away. Nick had done the same thing earlier, unable to look at the stains around it. She looked around, rubbing her arms for warmth. "Why don't you come back in the house? At least turn on the outside light. I can't hardly see a thing."

"That's the idea," said Nick. His voice sounded to him like it was coming from the bottom of a deep well.

She laid her hands on the back of his neck, massaged the tight muscles, kneading his shoulders. He resisted for a moment but his heart wasn't in it, feeling himself drawn out of his restless thoughts by the immediacy of her, giving in to her touch. Grateful.

The wind lifted the yellow police ribbon strung along the backyard and Nick ground his teeth. "I keep going over how it must have happened," he said, moving away from her. "The killer would have come this way from the street"—he pointed—"*through* the bamboo, because the garbage cans are on the other side and he'd have made too much noise—"

"It doesn't matter how it happened."

"Perry was probably in the hot tub," said Nick. "He was feeling sick and a soak might have made him feel better. That's where the killer found him. Sharon . . . she was in the house. She had work to do, but the killer must have made Perry call her out to the patio—"

"You can replay it any old way you want, but it's not goin' to change what happened last night," said Alison. Her white slip shimmered in the darkness. "I'm a realist, Nicky. I have to be. Girl starts giving in to wishes, she ends up like my little sister, with a passel of babies in dirty diapers and a man that goes out on her."

Nick was too tired to argue. He stepped forward, crunched a snail underfoot and jumped like the patio was booby-trapped. Alison laughed and so did he. "For a minute I thought you were going to have to perform CPR on me," he said.

"I'm ready," said Alison.

Nick didn't mess with that one. A small cardboard film carton floated in the pool, making lazy circles. More police debris. "Couple of hours ago I spotted headlights in the alley that runs along the back of the property line. A car stops. Engine turns off." He felt Alison tense. "Then I hear a beer can open. *Swush—*"

"You heard that? It's got to be fifty yards away."

"Sixty," said Nick, "but the neighborhood was quiet and I know that sound. I heard a can open. Then another." He shook his head. "It's probably a couple of kids sneaking out to get drunk—'Check out the house where those two people got smoked, dude.' "

"When I was in high school we used to park next to the graveyard and make out," said Alison.

"How romantic."

"Oh, with the right boy it's better than Disneyland." Alison grinned wickedly and he was envious of a boy he had never met. She must have seen the look on his face, because she straightened, glanced at the dense foliage surrounding the property. "This is a nice place," she said, changing the subject. "I bet you and Sharon had some good times here."

Nick felt the breeze on his face. Crickets sawed away in the night, the sound resonant with memory. "One night . . ." He smiled in spite of himself. "One night, Sharon and I were in the hot tub, bubbles everywhere, and suddenly we spot this coyote, big gray one looks like a skinny wolf, padding across the yard carrying the neighbor's Siamese in his mouth. Sharon actually wanted me to chase him down, get the cat back." He shook his head.

"I bet you did too, city boy."

"You should have seen me," chuckled Nick. "Here I am, bare-assed in the moonlight, one hand over my crotch, running after this coyote, yelling, 'Drop that kitty!' "

"I bet that coyote was scared," teased Alison.

"He looked at me like I was top sirloin."

"You're lucky all he did was look," said Alison. "Coyotes don't take any shit."

"It seems like a long time ago," he said softly.

They stood there, the two of them, watching the darkness. "I was surprised to see you wearing glasses," she said. "I like them, don't get me wrong, but the only pictures Perry had of you were these old photos of the band—you guys were *so* young and trying so hard to look tough. Don't get that hurt look. Men, you're all so vain."

"Tell me about it. You probably put makeup on before you came out here."

"Wake up, Nicky, you're having a wet dream."

Nick laughed in spite of himself.

"I'm getting to you, aren't I?" She punched him lightly. "You can't help yourself." She scratched her hip, the sound of her nails against the slip electric. "This is nice . . . just being out here. All Perry ever talked about was the old days and the band. He'd get stoned and talk about that one perfect summer, when no matter when you turned on the radio, you heard a song from the Plague Dogs album. Best dope in the world, he said, and the groupies . . . Perry sure loved his groupies."

"Yeah."

"It's all right, Nicky, I don't care. I didn't care about his girls when he was alive . . ." Alison cleared her throat. "I sure as hell don't care now. Yup, boys will be boys." She straightened. "You ever see that other guy in the band?"

Nick shook his head. Baby Steve had OD'd . . . must have been ten years ago. No. Twelve, last month.

"What's wrong?"

"Nothing."

The breeze stirred the hem of her slip. "Perry told me that

you didn't go in for that groupie action," she said lightly, her face in profile, full lips slightly parted. "They used to tease you about it."

"I had a girlfriend."

"They all had girlfriends, Nicky," she said, trying to laugh it off.

The two of them fell silent. No words. Just the wind in the trees and the faint hum of traffic in the distance. No matter the time of day or night, there was always the sound of traffic, a constant rhythm, pervasive as a pulse. She shivered and Nick put his arm around her. He told himself he wanted to keep her warm.

"Perry talked about you all the time," said Alison, "but I look at you now and think he was talking about someone else."

"He tell you I had sold out?" said Nick. "Did he tell you I had lost my edge, gotten boring?" She didn't answer and Nick liked her even more for her silence, her unwillingness to speak ill of the dead. "Don't worry about it, Alison—that's what he told me, too."

She hung on to him. The darkness was soothing now. He had felt attracted to Alison the first time they met—was it only five days ago? Perry had walked in the front door, not bothering to ring the bell, walked in, shouting his name. Nick had hugged him, smelled bourbon on his breath at ten A.M., and over Perry's shoulder he had seen her in the doorway, hands on her hips, framed by sunlight.

"I hardly ever think about the old days," Nick said. "We were such friends in the beginning—Perry and I had these cheesy, swap meet guitars, Baby Steve didn't even have a complete drum set." He smiled. "We survived a whole year eating out of a McDonald's Dumpster. One of the girls who worked there was crazy for Perry, used to leave bags of hamburgers right on top."

"He still charmed every damned waitress he ever met."

Nick pushed back his glasses. He heard the flapping of wings. An owl on the hunt. "I remember the exact moment I knew we were going to make it. The moment I knew we weren't going to be eating out of trash cans anymore. We were playing at the V.F.W. in Long Beach. Five other bands on the bill, cover bands, 'haircut bands' we called them because that's all they had going for them. We were last up, three A.M., crowd already streaming for the exits, and we came on like fucking D-Day. I was playing so fast my fingers were numb, and Perry, he was beautiful, screaming this song I had written only the night before. The crowd went nuts, jamming the stage . . . I looked at Perry, and he looked at me, and we both knew. We *knew*."

"Perry told me about that concert," said Alison. "He wasn't nearly so . . . poetic, though. He told me that the promoter tried to rip you off, talking about overhead and expenses, but you stared him down. He said the promoter had this big ol' bouncer beside him and you still got the money. Your 'psycho-killer stare,' Perry called it."

"I forgot about that," laughed Nick. "Yeah, we had some good times in the beginning," he said, feeling his smile sag. "We should have quit after Long Beach. We believed in what we were doing then. By the end we were just going through the motions. I'm glad it's over."

"Give me a break," said Alison.

"What?"

" 'I'm glad it's over,' " mimicked Alison.

"Why don't *you* go back inside?"

"You think I'm stupid, Nicky? You'd *love* to be on top again, fancy hotels and press conferences, selling out the arena. Who wouldn't?"

"It was fun," Nick admitted. "For a while."

"I'd settle for 'a while,' Nicky. I'd settle for five minutes of being a star. I'm so tired of being nobody. Tired of being 'the one in the bikini,' or 'the one with the lips,' or 'the one with the hair.' " She tossed her head, blond hair flashing in the night. "When you're a star you get a name. I'm going to make it too. You wait."

"I believe you," said Nick.

Alison took his hand, delicately touching his callused fingers like he had broken something. "It must be terrible to get to the top and lose your spot. I don't know how you handled it. Perry didn't handle it worth shit."

"Yeah," Nick said seriously, "and the worst part is I think my spot went to Hootie and the Blowfish."

Alison burst out laughing, then stopped. "What's that?"

"What?"

"What's that in your pocket?"

"Maybe I'm just happy to see you."

"Old joke, Nicky."

He slowly pulled the pistol out of the front pocket of his shorts, holding it awkwardly. "It's a gun. Okay?"

"It's not a gun," Alison said, taking it from him. "It's a nine-millimeter Glock semiautomatic." She popped the magazine and racked the slide. "Nice action. Doesn't look like it's ever been fired." She frowned at him. "You told Calvin you didn't own a firearm."

"The nine-millimeter is Sharon's. When I was out late, it made her feel better to have it around. I don't like guns, but now—"

"You lied to him, Nicky. Why would you do that?"

"I don't know. Maybe because he acted like he had all the answers, and I wanted to know something that he didn't."

"You shouldn't lie to a lawman. Calvin is just doing his job."

"If you say so."

She slapped the magazine back in with the palm of her hand, gave it to him, butt first. "There's no safety on a Glock, so be careful." Her eyes sparkled. "You don't want to blow off anything you might need someday."

Nick stared at her, slowly tucked the pistol back into his pocket, feeling like he should let Alison keep the gun . . . the Glock. Whatever.

"My daddy was deputy sheriff of Waxahachie, Texas," she said proudly. "He said it was a badass world, and a woman needed to be able to take care of herself. So watch your step, buster." She dragged him by the hand to the edge of the patio and onto the grass, giggling at the dampness on her bare feet. "Loosen up, Nicky, I'm not going to bite."

"I don't know, you kind of remind me of that coyote."

Alison growled at him.

"It's funny," said Nick. "Sharon used to complain . . . well, not really complain, but she used to say that I never talked to her anymore. Now, here we are, going at it . . ."

"I like playing with you," said Alison. "It makes me feel like we're in this together, that I'm not just Perry's girlfriend you got stuck with." She dragged a toe through the moist earth and the smell of wet grass rolled around them. "You want to go back inside?" she asked. "We could smoke a joint. It'll help you sleep."

"I'm fine."

"You sure are," Alison said softly. She caught herself. "Geez, I didn't mean to say that. I'm embarrassed."

"No you're not."

"No, I'm not." She listened to the sound of a helicopter in the distance. "Perry told me that you loaned him money when we got here. Why'd you do that? You knew he was never going to pay you back."

"Old habit," said Nick. "I've been loaning Perry money for as long as I can remember."

Alison had a good, strong laugh, but the darkness swallowed the sound. "Why is it the really cool guys never have any money? Just once I'd like to go out to dinner with a guy worth fucking and not have them seizure up when I order the lobster." She shook her head. "Perry was always near broke, but he was a good time, and he was a *great* kisser." She sighed and Nick was jealous of her memory. "A lot of guys are pile drivers in bed, but a man who can kiss . . ."

Nick stared at the hot tub. There was a balloon inside his chest, slowly inflating, getting bigger and bigger.

Alison must have noticed. "Did . . . uh . . . Calvin ever call you back?" she said.

"No," said Nick. "I left three or four messages, but no response. There must be a special at the Pancake House."

"Calvin's a good man," said Alison. "He won't let us down."

"You weren't there when he was questioning me this morning," grumbled Nick, turning away from the hot tub. "You didn't help either, telling him I was in the house for ten or fifteen minutes last night—"

"You *were*, Nicky."

"I was in and out," Nick insisted.

Alison shook her head. "No way. I smoked a whole joint waiting for you. If I hadn't had that Pearl Jam tape to listen to—"

Nick put his hand on her arm, silencing her as a match flared in the darkness at the far edge of the backyard. The match went out and they watched the red glow of a cigarette, the tip bobbing slightly as the smoker breathed.

"It's probably more kids," said Alison.

Nick eased her into the shadows. He saw the cigarette tip move up, imagined it poked high from the smoker's mouth. Someone was standing out there watching the house through the trees. Just watching.

"Nicky? Come on."

"It's a little late for kids to be out," whispered Nick, "and sightseers would get a better look in daylight."

"It's more fun in the dark," said Alison. "Everybody likes a good scare."

"Would you lower your voice?" whispered Nick.

The two of them stayed on the edge of the grass, watching the red ember glow bright with every drag, then dim, bright, then dim, but never moving from the smoker's mouth. Nick stared at that hot red dot and he saw again the hole in Sharon's back, her face hidden by her wet hair, as though she were embarrassed to be found like that.

"Maybe we should go back inside," said Alison.

"Maybe you should."

Alison stayed. Nick kept hoping the smoker would move toward the house, but he remained where he was. Out of reach. Clouds drifted overhead, making the night even murkier. The cigarette suddenly arced through the air in a flicker of sparks, hit the wet ground, and died. Nick leaned forward, listening, trying to see, but there was only the darkness and the faint rustling of the trees. Alison finally went inside but he waited. It was only at the first streaks of dawn that he was sure there was no one out there. Not anymore.

11

DETECTIVE THORPE SLOWLY took off the headphones, stopped the portable tape player. He hadn't said a word since he started listening to the tapes Nick had brought for him.

"Well?" Nick said, raising his voice to be heard over the crash of bowling pins. Thorpe had finally answered Nick's phone messages this morning, had given him the address of the Hillside Bowlerama and said he had to make another call. "Thorpe? What do you think?"

Thorpe wagged a finger at Alison, grinning. "I think my mama would have washed your mouth out with Lifebuoy, young lady—"

"Well, aw shucks and sha*zam*, Andy," said Nick, irritated

from lack of sleep. "Could we cut out the bumpkin routine, Calvin? You heard the tape—"

"I *liked* the Andy Griffith show," Thorpe said, standing beside the ball return in his dress shirt and necktie, his suit jacket across the back of his chair. "I always wondered why there weren't any black folks in Mayberry, but still . . ."

"What are we doing here, Thorpe?" said Nick. "Why couldn't we meet someplace . . . private. Someplace quiet, at least?"

"I like it here, buddy."

The electronic pin setter at the opposite end of the building swept aside the remaining pins in lane one, clanking and hissing as it worked. It was midmorning and the bowling alley was nearly empty, the only other bowlers a matronly foursome wearing orange shirts with *Kegler Kuties* embroidered across the back in green script. A pall of cigarette smoke drifted over the manager's cage, the wizened coot inside watching the Kuties through his squint.

Nick took a deep breath. "Look, Perry may have been blackmailing people—that might have been what got him killed, him and Sharon. Or it might have been the tape you just heard—I think maybe that man, Doc, was really being murdered at the end of the call."

"May have? Might have? Maybe?"

"Yes," Nick said. "Have *you* got anything better?"

Thorpe didn't respond. "That last tape *did* sound like a man being killed, but that doesn't mean anything." He dried his right hand over the air blower, raising his voice to be heard. "I've seen *Forrest Gump*. People who know what they're doing can make you believe you heard and saw anything they want you to." He shook his head. "I'd still like to know how they made it look like Forrest was meeting President Kennedy." He picked up his bowling ball, balanced it in the palm of his hand, sighting down the alley. He glided across the polished hardwood, releasing the ball so smoothly there was only a whisper of contact. Thorpe's red-and-black-streaked ball started out on the far right side, almost in the gutter, then veered straight into the pocket. Strike! He looked at Nick. "You keep your tapes, buddy."

"Don't be like that, Calvin." Alison was wearing a denim blouse and a short cowgirl skirt with fringe that bounced as she moved. "Nicky thinks one of those tapes got Sharon and Perry killed. Maybe he's right."

Thorpe bent over his score sheet, the paper covered with X's. He took in Nick's baggy Australian-print shorts. "Don't you own any long pants, buddy? Between you and her, no one dresses like a grown-up anymore."

"I'll go over the tapes with you," Nick offered. "I'll—"

"Why bother?" said Thorpe. He turned to Alison. "This last tape, you're talking dirty with Doc when he suddenly acts like he's being killed. You laughed at him. You didn't call the police. Why? Because you didn't *really* believe he was in danger. Isn't that true?"

Alison hesitated.

"You thought it was a game he was playing," Thorpe said gently. "Just like you were playing a game with him."

"That's what I thought, but now . . . I don't know." Alison took the scoring pencil from him, laid it down. "Take the tapes, Calvin. Please? Nicky was up half the night making copies for you. Take them. What can it hurt?"

"That's quite an endorsement." Thorpe picked up the tapes, tossed them onto the bench. "I can always turn them over to vice. You sure you two don't want to roll a few lines? Nothing like bowling to relax a person." He surveyed the vast space of the Bowlerama, hands on his hips. "I love it here. I love the way the light hits the wood and the sound of the pins being tumbled, the clean smell of wax and—"

"Yesterday it's Calvin Thorpe, short-order cook, today it's the Zen bowler," said Nick. "When do I get to see you actually do some work?"

"Oh, I've been busy," said Thorpe, his voice hardening. "You think I just go home after my shift, put my feet up on the couch and watch TV? The job never ends, buddy. I make calls. I ask questions. I keep at it. Maybe I'm not the smartest guy in the world, but then I just have to know how to add things up. Police work isn't trigonometry, it's just simple addition."

It felt like somebody had turned up the air-conditioning in the Bowlerama.

"Are those really all your trophies in the case by the front door, Calvin?" asked Alison, trying to defuse the situation. "Did you see them, Nicky? All these perfect-game plaques and Bowler of the Year awards."

"Your paraffin test was inconclusive, by the way," Thorpe said to Nick. "According to forensics, that mud bath you stopped off for on the way home took care of that."

"Tough," said Nick. "Where's my car? I called a tow truck and they couldn't find it."

"I had it taken to the impound lot," said Thorpe. "We need to run some tests. Another waste of time, probably." His expression dropped. "The coroner is finished with his exams on your wife and Perry—he moved them to the head of the line as a personal favor to me. I thought you'd want to start making funeral arrangements."

"Thanks," said Nick. "I'll take care of it as soon as—"

"What was the murder weapon, Calvin?" Alison asked quietly. She didn't look at Nick.

"Ballistics says it was a thirty-eight," said Thorpe. "I don't really want to release any more information—"

The manager shuffled over to their lane, ashes from the cigarette in his mouth drifting onto the tray he was carrying. He was a skinny old man, bent as a pipe cleaner, eyes bright and birdlike as he set the tray down next to Thorpe.

"Morning, Lorenzo."

"You got lucky on that last strike, copper," said Lorenzo. "You dropped your shoulder on the release." He glanced disdainfully at Nick and Alison. "Too many distractions. You should practice by yourself."

Thorpe sipped the coffee Lorenzo had brought him. Picked up one of the doughnuts. "Where's my chocolate-sprinkled?"

"That's what you get for showing up late," said Lorenzo, cigarette bobbing. "I hold my *best* lane for you every morning. Least you could do was be on time."

Alison took in the virtually empty Bowlerama.

Thorpe cleaned powdered sugar off the corners of his mouth with a fingertip, the whiteness stark against his skin. "I apologize." He licked the finger.

"You got a tournament coming up and you ain't near ready," said Lorenzo, scuffling back to the manager's cage. "Apologize to yourself."

Calvin positioned himself behind the foul line, holding the ball just above his waist as he sighted down the alley.

"If you're too overworked to run down all the tapes, at least listen to the one with Doc again," said Nick. "I think it's genuine. Thorpe?" he said to his back. "If you won't follow up on the tapes, then I'll do it."

"Buddy," Thorpe said, still facing the pins, "why don't you take care of the funeral and let me handle the investigation?" He made his approach, but dropped his shoulder again. The ball hit wide, left a 7-10 split. Lorenzo's cackle bounced off the walls.

Thorpe glared at Lorenzo as he retrieved his ball. He stayed on the line for what seemed like five minutes before laying down the second ball, but he actually picked up the spare, the ten pin sliding over into the seven. Thorpe whooped it up, but Lorenzo pretended not to have seen. Alison applauded like Thorpe had levitated.

Thorpe finished out the game with five strikes, then sat and added up his score: 255. "Why don't you go find a ball and I'll give you some pointers?" he said to Alison. "Just take off those cowboy boots before Lorenzo calls in a SWAT team." He watched her pull off her boots and walk over to the rack of balls. "Not too heavy, now. *Control* is the name of the game." He glanced at Nick. "Not muscle."

Alison stepped onto the alley in her socks, holding the ball with two hands, intent on the pins.

"You know, Nick, you're so insistent about this Doc tape . . ." Thorpe waited as Alison rolled a gutter ball. "Have you asked yourself how this killer found Perry? Did Doc know where Perry was staying?" Alison shook her head. "Well, finding someone isn't all that hard if you know who you're looking for," said Thorpe. "The real question is why do it? Why would someone kill two people who are no threat to him? This man who supposedly murdered Doc, he never speaks on the tape. Doc never calls him by name. So why does the killer bother tracking Perry down? It makes no sense."

It *didn't* make sense, but Nick wasn't going to let that stop him. He couldn't. When you have nothing else to hang on to, you grasp at straws. "Then why were Sharon and Perry killed?" Nick asked. "Why, Thorpe?" he demanded, his voice shrill now, moving closer, close enough to smell the detective's peppery cologne.

"You said it wasn't robbery. Two people alone in a house, nothing taken . . . What did they do wrong?"

Thorpe didn't move. "You tell me, buddy."

Nick flinched at the crash of pins from the far lane. He could feel Alison beside him. "Did you find out who made the 911 call?" he said to Thorpe. "Maybe he saw the killer. Maybe he *is* the killer. That happens, doesn't it? Like firebugs report the fire they just set."

Thorpe watched him, his large eyes black as silence.

Nick stood under the detective's unblinking stare. If it was supposed to unnerve him, Thorpe had picked the wrong guy. Maybe it worked with doubt-ridden gangbangers and low-life cockroaches who hit up old ladies at ATMs, but Nick was comfortable in the spotlight. Perry used to throw up before every concert, but Nick was steady. Let Thorpe stare. Nick could wait him out.

Thorpe looked irritated. It was the first time Nick had seen his confidence slip. "Go ahead and roll, Alison," he said, "this is between me and Nick. If you want a little advice, start off on your right foot and follow through."

Alison looked at Thorpe, then put the ball back on the rack and went over and sat beside Nick.

Thorpe's face gleamed under the fluorescent lights. "You're a lucky man, Nick. That can make a fella think he's smarter than the rest of the world. That's when he starts making foolish mistakes." Nick didn't respond and it only made Thorpe more irritated. "You lied to me, buddy. I should be used to it by now, but I liked you. It's my own fault."

"What are you talking about?" said Nick.

"I asked you if you and the missus were having problems," said Thorpe, "asked you every way I knew, and you looked me in the eye and told me, 'No problems. Nothing more than the usual.' I believed you, buddy, but I still checked. I checked because it's my job, and I take my job seriously."

"Sharon and I *weren't* having problems—"

"I went through her bank statements," said Thorpe. "That in itself got my attention. Separate bank accounts? That's like separate beds—you know there's trouble."

"It's a new day, Thorpe. Women can vote, drive—"

"The missus had all these payments to the Saddleback Clinic," Thorpe said. "Every week. I thought maybe she had a medical problem, so I checked. Turns out Saddleback's a counseling center. Marriage counseling."

"I don't know about any—" Nick was aware of Alison watching him, her eyes guarded. "What?" he said.

"Nothing," said Alison.

"What is it?" Nick said to her. Thorpe was interested now.

"Sharon told *me* that y'all were having trouble that day we sat around the pool, girl-talking with our strawberry daiquiris," Alison said lightly. "I gave her the word about me and Perry splitting, told her she should count her blessings." She looked at Thorpe. "Lots of times girls tell each other things they wouldn't think of letting on to their man." She smiled, trying hard. "Got to keep you boys in the dark much as we can."

Thorpe was unfazed. "I went through your wife's Daytimer," he said to Nick. He let that announcement settle for a few moments. "This Thursday she had an appointment with Rita Alvarez. Ms. Alvarez is a divorce attorney, a very good one, from what I understand. I guess you didn't know about that, either."

"I don't believe you," said Nick, the words like lead.

"I'll be happy to show you," Thorpe said. "It's all there in black and white."

Nick slowly sat down, steadying himself like he expected the bench to be pulled out from under him. "Sharon and I . . . we had some rough spots, but I thought we were working it out."

"One of your neighbors said he used to hear you and your wife arguing," said Thorpe. "We didn't even have to ask him, he volunteered the information. A concerned citizen."

"So we argued," Nick said numbly. "You never argue with your wife?"

Thorpe didn't answer.

Nick looked at Alison. "Why didn't Sharon tell *me* she was leaving?"

"Maybe she was worried about how you'd react," said Thorpe.

"I wasn't talking to you, Thorpe," said Nick. He turned back to Alison. "She should have told me," he said. "She should have given me a chance."

Alison watched him. "I would have," she said quietly.

12

Nick sat in the passenger seat looking straight ahead while Alison drove, barely registering the traffic around him. He thought he knew Sharon. Maybe they weren't happy anymore, but they were working things out. Yeah, that's why it took a homicide detective to inform him that she was planning to divorce him. He thought he knew her. If he was wrong about that . . .

"You're mumbling to yourself," said Alison. She pumped the brakes of the Range Rover as the cars ahead slowed, all four lanes of the northbound 405 freeway stacking up. She could feel a vibration in the steering wheel—bearings in the front wheels were shot. "Are you okay?"

Nick didn't even bother answering. He didn't know what he

was talking about anyway. Thorpe had proved that. Nick could say he felt fine and have a brain tumor.

Alison downshifted, hearing a rattle in the transmission. Getting worse. Most of the time she needed to double-clutch to get it into gear. Four months ago she had starred in a low-budget horror movie—the producer had run out of money in postproduction, offered to pay her off with his old car. Take it or leave it. She took it all right.

Nick watched a couple in the orange VW bug ahead of them making out, the young woman pressed against the guy driving, snuggling close.

She was playing with the guy's hair now, running her hands through his dirty-blond curls. "Why don't you get into the right lane?" said Nick. "You're following too close."

"Why don't you sit back and relax?" Alison said. "I've seen the way you drive and I've still got mud in my hair." She gave him a sly glance. "You want to buy this car? Face it, Nicky, the Porsche's totaled."

"I *hate* this car. I don't even like riding in it."

"It's a great car, runs good—"

"I feel like I should be wearing a safari jacket and a pith helmet," said Nick, "like we're heading off for Kilimanjaro or something. And it runs like shit, by the way. It sounds like a coffee grinder."

"It's supposed to sound like that," said Alison, the wind whipping her hair, lifting the fringe on her cowgirl skirt. Yeehaw.

"Keep your status-mobile," said Nick. They drove for a few minutes in silence, enjoying the light mood. Nick tried to stop himself from ruining it, but he couldn't. "So . . . what else did Sharon tell you during your cocktail party around the pool? She tell you that I wanted to have kids and she didn't? Did she tell you why, Alison? She never gave *me* a straight answer, I thought maybe—"

"Nicky, *don't*."

"Did she tell you why she was leaving me?" said Nick, holding his voice perfectly steady.

Alison kept her eyes on the road. "She said you brooded when you couldn't find work, and when you got a job you were angry because you never got the chance to do the job right. She said she tried to help you, but you wouldn't go to the meetings she set up—"

"Okay, I get it."

"She said you didn't pay attention to her for weeks at a time. She said she woke up in the middle of the night a few months ago, looked at you sleeping next to her . . ." Alison swallowed. "She looked at you and couldn't remember why you two ever fell in love with each other. She said she didn't even cry, just laid her head back down on the pillow . . ." Alison glanced over at him. Sad-eyed girl. "I'm so sorry, Nicky."

"I asked, you told me. I'm grateful."

"Did you want me to lie?"

"No."

"I could—"

"No lies," Nick said sharply. "I don't want there to be any lies between us. Let's just try the truth for a while."

"The truth?" Alison thought it over. "Gosh, you *really* are a perv, Nicky."

Nick smiled. The wind rushing past smelled of exhaust fumes and flowers. "Thanks, Alison."

"For what?"

"For talking to me." Nick felt warm. Maybe it was the sun. "I get . . . lost sometimes in my own head. Talking with you helps me find my way back."

"You get lost? Tough guy like you?"

"Well . . . it's dark in there."

She laughed with him. "You're welcome, Nicky." She looked pleased, stretching out her legs, one hand on the wheel, sunshine splashed around her like gold.

"Alison? What about you?" Nick put his hand on her leg, needing to make the connection. "How are *you* doing with all this? You act so . . . steady."

Her nails drummed against the wheel. She stopped herself with an effort, mouth tightening, eyes on the road. "Well . . . that's what an actor does, Nicky—she acts."

"Is there anything I can do?"

She shook her head. "Just keep your hand on my leg." She laughed as he jerked away, then tentatively put his hand back. "That's better." The radiator was running hot, edging into the red zone. "We can't get in touch with Perry's agent until after five," she reminded him, watching the gauges. "He walks on the beach near Huntington. He got Perry started with the tapes."

"Doesn't he have an office?"

Alison shook her head. "He's got an answering service. Dirk's not much of an agent, but then Perry wasn't much—"

"Dirk?"

"I know, I know. In Texas, he'd get his ass kicked every day with a name like that, but out here . . ."

"You heard about Perry?" said Alison.

"This morning," huffed Dirk Malone as he power-walked along the tide line of Huntington Beach, pumping ridiculous one-pound pink dumbbells. "Don't you worry about me, though, Dirk 'gets you work' Malone has a client list longer than a donkey's dick."

"Why would I be worried about you?" said Alison.

"Don't be so self-centered," said Dirk, stumbling on the sand. "You were Perry's girlfriend, but *I* was his agent."

"Yeah," said Nick. "Dirk was Perry's agent. He's got the donkey dick."

"You're right," said Alison. "I was just his girlfriend."

"Lift your knees higher," said Dirk's trainer, Ingrid, a young, pigtailed Valkyrie with the deep voice and thickened jawbone of a chronic steroid user. "Work your arms, too. That's better. Tough and buff, that's it, that's it."

Dirk beamed in the setting sun, momentarily increased his pace, puffing merrily. A cellular phone dangled from the waistband of his paisley stirrup tights. His doughy arms flopped out of the oversize Gold's Gym tank top.

The ocean was flat in the carcinogenic light, the hard-packed sand at the water's edge dotted with dirty plastic and small, dead fish that even the seagulls avoided. The beach was still crowded, sunbathers stretched out on their towels, tape decks blaring. The four of them walked through Doppler zones of salsa, heavy metal, acid-house, tejano, and rap. Nick moved differently as they passed through the differing musical tastes, unconsciously taking on the rhythms of whatever he heard.

"Are you still represented by Barb Shapiro?" Dirk asked Alison, slowing down so he could talk without panting. "Barb's a good girl, but she really can't offer her—"

"I'm very happy with her," said Alison.

"You ask Ingrid here what a first-class agent can do," persisted Dirk. "I may have landed her a regular spot on *American Gladiators*. Isn't that right, babe?"

"I'm waiting for my callback," said Ingrid. She wore a striped crop top over her flat chest, and shorts that showed the corded muscles in her ass. "Pump, pump, pump."

Dirk looked at Nick, eyes narrowing. "You've got yourself

an opportunity here too, Nick. If I leak the story that you and Perry were planning on re-forming the band . . . whatever the fuck your band was, and in spite of this senseless tragedy et cetera, et cetera, et cetera, you're going to continue—"

"I don't think so."

"I see a Golden Age of Punk tour," Dirk said expansively. "I've already been in contact with Sid Vicious—"

"Must have been a séance," said Nick. "Sid is dead."

"Well, it was one of the Sex Pistols—I never liked them anyway, fucking noise . . . I'm not talking about you, of course. Give it some thought, Nick, you might not get a chance like this again. Take these, Ingrid," he said, handing her the pink dumbbells, "I'm afraid I'm going to pull something."

"We're trying to find out if Perry gave you any tapes with someone called Doc on them," said Nick. "Alison said you were the middleman for a lot of his recordings and—"

"I resent the term 'middleman,' " sniffed Dirk, kicking through clots of brown seaweed. "I consider myself a collaborator in the creative process." He smiled his porcelain caps at Alison. "A good agent is always finding ways to utilize his clients' talents, and Perry had a flair for phone sex. I was able to use his ability to secure him work." He held out his right arm and Ingrid pressed her fingers against his wrist, checking his pulse rate. "I haven't given up on you, my dear," he said to Alison. "You're underutilized. I've had inquiries about the woman behind the voice on Perry's most recent tapes."

"We can talk about representation another time," said Alison. "Right now, Nicky and I need to know if any of Perry's tapes might have gotten him into trouble."

"Trouble?" Dirk brushed aside Ingrid. "Am *I* in any danger?"

"Dude! Nick! Over here, dude!"

Nick looked around, saw somebody waving to him from one of the concrete fire rings on the dunes overlooking the beach.

"Alison? Am I in danger?"

"You know him?" asked Alison, ignoring Dirk.

Nick stared at the wildly jumping figure, a bare-chested young man wearing a tartan kilt. He smiled. "It's Rebar. He's a musician I worked with a few months ago. Good guy."

"Dude!"

"Why don't you go talk with him?" said Alison. "I may have better luck with Dirk if you're not around."

"You're sure?" said Nick.

"Shoo!"

Nick turned around to check on her when he was halfway up the dunes, saw her talking with Dirk, reassuring him, squeezing his puny biceps.

Rebar walked down to meet him, hugged him. "Jesus, *shit*, man, sorry about your old lady getting smoked," he said, shaking his head sadly. "I liked her, man, she was like the only real adult who dug my music. Except for you, but you're not an adult. You're just like . . . old."

"Thanks," said Nick. "Nice skirt."

"It's a *kilt*, dude."

"Whatever you say."

"I want you to meet somebody," said Rebar. He was a wiry teenager with a bleached buzz cut, his arms scrimmed from wrist to shoulder with elaborate tattoos—dragons and wizards, gnomes and elves, knights and princesses. He was a storybook of skin and when he played guitar the story came alive.

There was a small group of runaways standing around the fire ring, tossing cardboard boxes onto the feeble blaze, wet driftwood, and balled-up fast-food wrappers. Most of them were dressed in Salvation Army castoffs, scrawny urchins with dirty hair and defiant eyes. They watched Nick with suspicion, ready to run.

Rebar squirted lighter fluid onto the fire, not flinching as it flared up. He kicked at a paper bag. "I got hot dogs here, come and get 'em." He watched the runaways tear into the bag, ripping open the plastic packages. Hot dogs tumbled out onto the sand, were quickly brushed off, impaled on splintered sticks, and held over the oily flames. Rebar turned away from the feeding frenzy. "Nick, this is Gwyneth." He said it like he was presenting royalty.

Maybe he was. Gwyneth was slender and strong-featured, an exotic creature with the haughty bearing of a ballerina. She wore a short black skirt and a lacy black brassiere, her hair a stubbly orange buzz. She watched Nick with cool cat eyes, timeless and ravening. A tattoo of entwined flowers and skulls circled her left wrist.

"Hello," said Nick. Neither of them had moved but it appeared that they were closer. Nick could almost hear the scratching of her lace bra against her skin as she breathed.

"Gwyneth says 'Hello,' too, said Rebar.

Nick looked quizzically at Rebar.

"She doesn't like to talk out loud," said Rebar. He scratched his bare belly. "I can usually hear her in my head . . . so I do it for her."

"What does she do when you're not around?" Nick said, watching Gwyneth. She returned his gaze.

Rebar hesitated. "She finds somebody else."

"Sorry to hear it," said Nick. "How are *you* doing? You got any gigs happening?"

Rebar shook his head. "Band broke up. Those guys were just too indier than thou. I'm no sellout, man, I just want to make enough for gas money. What's wrong with that?"

"Don't give up," said Nick. "You've got talent."

"Thanks." Rebar looked at Gwyneth. "She wants to know if you're a musician."

"Why?"

Rebar licked his lips, uncomfortable. "She only fucks musicians and cops. She *knows* you're not a cop."

"Musicians and cops?" Nick was amused. "One end of the rainbow or the other, nothing in between?"

"What are you talking about?" Rebar checked the sky. "There's no rainbow." The fire was going good now, but he emptied the lighter fluid onto it, tossed in the empty can, the flames whooshing up. He looked at Gwyneth. "Oh, okay. She says you're wrong. Cops and musicians, they play the same song. I don't understand it either," said Rebar. "I'm just glad I got a guitar, you know, be part of the club."

Nick felt Gwyneth's eyes on him, expectant. "I *used* to be a musician," he said to her. "I don't perform anymore."

Rebar nodded. "She says too bad."

Nick bowed to her. "My bad luck."

"She says you have no idea. She's right, dude."

Nick patted Rebar on the back. "I have to go. Good seeing you again. You have a place to stay?"

"I'm set," said Rebar. He pointed toward a small abandoned house up the beach. "My parents sold it, but they're letting me stay there till escrow closes."

"Well, you let me know if you want to go back into the studio," said Nick. "I'll help you—" He stopped, turned to Gwyneth. "Do you know any cops in the Rancho Verdes P.D.?"

She watched him with those cool gray eyes.

"She says yes."

"Do any of them . . . Does one of them owe you a big favor?"

"She says why?"

"My wife was murdered Saturday night," he said to Gwyneth. "Can you get me a copy of the 911 call? It was made around nine o'clock. I know it won't be easy—"

"I hear you," said Rebar, bobbing his head at Gwyneth, "but that CD of mine you liked, Nick worked the board. Didn't charge me nothing either." He stared at Gwyneth for a long moment, then looked at Nick. "She says there's a cop at Rancho Verdes who's very grateful and should be."

"You can really get that for me?" Nick asked Gwyneth.

"She says yes," said Rebar.

"Okay . . ." Nick said to Gwyneth, not really convinced. "I'm going to go catch up with my . . . friend. Umm . . . thanks." He looked at Rebar. "You have my number. The sooner the better. Thanks again." He trotted down the beach toward Alison, running faster now. He glanced behind him once, saw Gwyneth and Rebar watching, lit by the flames of the fire ring.

13

THE VIDEO CAMERA panned across trees swaying in the breeze, worked its way across the overgrown yard, and settled on the swimming pool. Zoom in to Sharon and Alison in bright bikinis, the two of them lying side by side on chaise longues, drinks in their hands. The camera was too far away for the microphone to pick up what they were saying, there was just a happy buzzing between them, and the sound of Alison's laughter ringing out.

Sharon slathered oil onto her perfectly tanned shoulders and down her arms. Too far away to know if it was coconut-scented. The camera jiggled slightly. She reached for her drink but her hand must have been slippery because it shot out of her grasp. She caught the glass between her knees, sloshed whatever she was drinking onto the chaise, staining the concrete beneath. An ice cube skidded toward the pool.

The two of them were silently laughing now, Alison handing her a towel, refilling the glass. Alison ran her fingers through her blond hair, stretching. The sun was warm and buttery on their bodies, arms and legs akimbo, dizzy with the heat.

Sharon got up, a little unsteady, dove into the pool, her body scribing a perfect arc through the air, diving below camera range, surfacing in a spray of water, shouting, happy. The sun made rainbows across her skin. She beckoned to Alison, waving her in. A shadow rolled across the yard, darkened the scene as a cloud edged over the sun.

Jump cut to darkness. Sheets of rain spatter the lens. The angle is low, almost ground level, high grass brushing across the frame as the camera scuttles closer, the image bouncing. The sound track is thunder and constant rain. A faint tinkling sound can be heard near the camera.

In the near dark a couple can be seen nestled in a hot tub. Cowering actually. Maybe cowering. It's hard to tell. They are lit only by the faint lights from the kitchen of the house. Rain streaks the lens as the camera continues moving closer. Stops suddenly. Someone else is standing there. Next to the hot tub, obscured by a tree.

Lightning flash. For the first time we see the gun, held at arm's length, jabbing at the two shadow people in the tub. Sudden darkness and the thunder crashes a moment later. The camera focuses on the man with the gun, but he is hidden, the gun visible only because it is constantly moving, poking out at the people in the tub. The camera is shaking slightly, the sound track overshadowed by heavy breathing.

The camera bounces forward, crawling through the tall, wet

grass. There is the tinkling sound again, louder, then receding, a counterpoint to the steady, drenching rain.

The man in the tub seems to be talking, hands up. The gun jabs in from the edge of the frame, backlit by the house lights, and the man in the tub stumbles backward, falls with a splash. The woman tries to move away from him, one hand on the tub.

The sound of breathing is harsher now, louder even than the rain and the howling wind. The man in the tub has regained his feet, starts to climb out when the gun zooms in, a close-up, an inch from his face. The muzzle flash is more startling than the lightning—gunshot, gunshot, gunshot, gunshot, gunshot—the man is thrown back by the force, pieces of his head flying through the rain.

The image is shaking so hard it's impossible to see. The camera steadies, catches the woman vaulting from the tub, heading toward the camera, a running nude framed by a corona of house lights. Lightning flash and she's caught in the sudden glare. It's Sharon, mouth open, glancing behind her as she runs, legs pumping, heading toward the house like she's about to cross the finish line.

Gunshot.

Sharon acts like she doesn't hear it, or thinks it's just more thunder, running a couple more steps before slowing down, putting her hand out, searching for something to hold her up, but there's only the rain between her fingers. She crumbles onto the patio, just short of the grass, her head hitting the wet flagstones with a tiny splash.

The video image trembles, jerking in time to the deep, gasping breaths on the sound track. The image tilts and we see darkness and weeds, as though the camera is trying to burrow into the earth. Rain splatters the lens.

Lightning crackles and the camera lifts, the image off center, prismed by the rain, but for an instant the screen shows a man in a bright red jacket, his back to the camera as he bends over Sharon, the gun pointed at her head.

Shadows and storm. Darkness and the steady sound of rain. Then the sudden snow of blank tape.

Silence in the room for a long moment. Then . . .

"Let's see it again."

14

THE ANGEL CLOSED the front door of Remlinger Cycle Design behind him, relocked it. *By Appointment Only,* the door had said, a discreet business in an upscale Irvine industrial park, home to start-up computer software companies and engineering consultants. No lunch wagon pulled in at noon. Earlier today the parking spaces had been filled with Lexuses and Infinities. Most of them were gone now.

The security alarm was on the opposite wall, red light blinking. Thirty seconds. He removed the plastic housing of the alarm, took the small pulse generator out of his jacket and attached its three alligator clips to the alarm leads. He aligned the polarity between the alarm and the generator. Eighteen seconds. There were six numbers in the alarm's electronic code, and the Angel calmly watched as the diodes on the generator flashed through the possibilities. The alarm was disengaged with three seconds to spare.

The Angel moved through the empty office and stood in the doorway. In contrast to the tiny office, the workshop was large, high-ceilinged, and immaculate, every tool in place, not a spot of oil on the concrete. A motorcycle was on a padded rack at the center of the room, a rugged beast with deep red tank and forks, chrome pipes gleaming in the overhead lights. Another motorcycle was in pieces on a large sheepskin rug nearby.

Remlinger bent beside the bare frame of the disassembled motorcycle, welding goggles on, torch cascading sparks as he fused a joint in the metal. His coveralls were pressed, smudged around the knees where he kneeled on the concrete floor. Busy, busy—the endless spinning of the mortal coil.

The Angel watched him for several minutes, enjoying the precision of the man's movements. The walls were covered with color blowups of customized motorcycles and schematics of futuristic motorcycle designs that would never see a racetrack or a freeway.

"Hey!" Remlinger snapped off the torch, flipped his goggles onto his forehead. "What are you doing in here? I thought I locked that front door. Listen, mister, I don't like drop-ins. Call tomorrow and make an appointment." He took in the Angel's blue three-piece suit and loafers. "I'll tell you now, though, I don't mess with any aftermarket shit. No ready-mades, no bolt-ons, no Christmas trees. Strictly custom or pure restoration. You get my drift?"

"I understand you exactly, Douglas," the Angel said, making no move to leave. "My, that is lovely." He pointed to one of the blown-up schematics, a low-slung motorcycle shaped like a teardrop, clean and powerful, with not a hint of excess. He stepped into the room. *"Flawlessly* aerodynamic."

Remlinger laid down the torch and stood up. He was tall and rangy, with large, red-knuckled hands and a spray of brown hair.

The Angel strolled around the shop, admiring the work on the walls as though he were on holiday at the Louvre.

"I'm real busy, mister," Remlinger said. "You're going to have to take off and let me get back to work."

"Does this motorcycle belong to Doc?" said the Angel, indicating the red bike at the center of the room. "I thought I saw a photograph of it at his home."

"I don't talk about my clients," said Remlinger.

The Angel went to the clipboard on a nearby bench, ignoring Remlinger's shout, read the name on the work order before it was snatched so rudely out of his hand.

"Get your ass out of here," said Remlinger, holding the clipboard to his chest. "You want me to call the cops?"

The Angel kicked the bottom of the clipboard, drove the edge of the metal clip under Remlinger's chin, sent him reeling, falling back onto his seat, blood streaming down his neck.

"My, that looks nasty," said the Angel. "An inch either side and you'd have opened your carotid artery."

Remlinger held a hand over the wound in his throat, his eyes big with fear, staring at the Angel.

"I mean you no harm," said the Angel. "Do you understand that, Douglas?"

Remlinger nodded. Blood leaked through his fingers.

"Good," said the Angel. "It's important that we understand each other." He pointed to the red motorcycle on the rack. "This belongs to Doc. I respect your desire to maintain your clients' privacy, but I'd like for us not to have any secrets."

"Can I get up?" said Remlinger.

"I think not," said the Angel, hands in his pockets.

"I've . . . I've got a first-aid kit on the wall."

"That's very wise of you," the Angel said gently. "You have so many dangerous tools here. Hammers, saws, metal presses . . ."

Remlinger didn't move.

"This motorcycle of Doc's, I don't think I've ever seen one quite like it."

"No shit. That's a 1951 Indian. Twelve hundred cubic centimeters of power. Perfectly restored. There's not more than five or six of that model in the world, not in that condition, and the only one not in a museum. Every bolt, every bulb is straight stock. Even the paint job is original mix. Took me two years to locate that exact shade of cherry red he wanted. Mr. Lomax is a perfectionist. Just like I am."

"A very admirable trait, Douglas." The Angel smiled. "Doc called you at the workshop last Friday. Nine twenty-eight in the morning. It was the last call he made from his home. He seems to have gotten lost and I'm trying to find him."

"Yeah? Okay, he called me Friday." Blood trickled down his fingers. "Can I get up now?"

"Not just yet." The Angel walked over to the acetylene torch, brought it back to where Remlinger sat, the hose trailing behind him.

Remlinger jumped up, but the Angel tripped him, sent him sprawling onto the floor.

The Angel stepped on the man's anklebone with one foot, holding him in place—rocking lightly on that tender fulcrum.

"You're hurting me, mister!"

The Angel popped on the torch, adjusted the flame until it was a perfect white-hot cone.

"Look, *please,* I don't know what you want—"

"What was the nature of your conversation with Doc last Friday?" said the Angel, holding the torch lightly in his hand as it hissed away like some slender serpent. "You're a perfectionist—you should be able to recall your conversation exactly."

"He asked if his bike was ready," hurried Remlinger, staring at the flame of the torch. "I told him it was ready. I said if he was going to be home for the next hour I'd crate it up and deliver it myself." He swallowed. "Could you put my torch down, mister?"

The torch continued to hiss a few feet from Remlinger—the Angel could see his cheeks redden from the heat. "Why didn't you deliver the motorcycle to him?"

"He didn't want me to," said Remlinger, trying to pull away, his ankle still trapped under the Angel's foot. "He asked me if I had put ten coats of paint on and I told him yes, hand-rubbed after each one just like he wanted." Remlinger looked up at the Angel. "He said he decided he wanted sixteen coats. I said fine, you're the boss. That's how he was. When it came to his bike, it was only the best."

"I see." The Angel nodded. "Doc could have had his motorcycle on Friday morning but he told you to keep working on it."

"Y-yes."

"Douglas, I'm going to ask you a great favor. I'm looking for Doc. It's very important. If he contacts you, I want you to inform me. *Immediately.* He may not call you himself. He may send a letter. A fax. He may send someone else to pick up his motorcycle for him. No matter what, I want you to do nothing without first contacting me. You can call me anytime, day or night. I'll give you my beeper number so you'll have no excuse for failure."

"I'll call you, mister."

The Angel released Remlinger's ankle, reached down and grabbed him by the front of his overalls with one hand, and effortlessly lifted him to his feet, drawing him closer to the hissing torch, watching the blue gas-flame reflected in the man's terrified eyes.

"That's good," said the Angel, "because I wish you no harm. I consider you an artist and I value artistry more than you will ever know, but if you violate my wishes, I will find out. When I do find out," he said, speaking slowly, "I am going to burn off your fingers with this welding torch. I will burn them off one by one. Do you like barbecued pork, Douglas? Skin crackly and the meat inside juicy and sweet? Yes? Well, you won't when I am through. Do you understand?"

Remlinger jerked his assent, blood streaming from his chin.

The Angel released him. Turned off the gas. There was a pop as the flame went out, then a sudden silence, broken only by the sound of Remlinger's teeth chattering.

15

"You looked like you were having a fine ol' time," said Alison, whipping the Range Rover into the Circle K parking lot, taking the parking space in front of the two phone booths, slamming on the brakes at the last minute. "That's all I said."

Nick's arm and legs were sore from bracing himself against the frame, but he waited until she turned off the ignition before relaxing. "I told you, Gwyneth may be able to help us. She knows a lot of cops—"

"I bet she does."

Nick didn't answer. He wasn't sure this Circle K mini-mart was where the 911 call had been made, but it was the closest one to his house, just five or six miles away. He got out of the car, walked over to the two phone booths. You couldn't see the cashier from either of them. A religious tract was on the floor of one of the booths, a small comic featuring a rock 'n' roll Satan luring impressionable teenagers to hell with his electric guitar.

An alarm buzzed as Nick and Alison walked through the double doors of the Circle K, but the clerk didn't look up. Neither did the two young skateboarders lounging across the magazine rack reading *Thrasher* through their hair. A security camera perched in the far corner, red light blinking. The door had a sign that said, *NO DOGS ALLOWED EXCEPT SEEING EYE DOGS,* but a small wirehaired mutt was curled up next to the clerk, gnawing on a microwave burrito.

An older man in paint-spattered overalls signed a credit card receipt for a case of generic beer.

The clerk checked the signature against the one on the card, then tossed it back so that it slid off the counter and onto the floor. "Good catch, Stumbo," he said.

The older man grunted as he bent to pick up his card, then lugged the beer past Nick, so busy eyeballing Alison that he bumped the side of the door.

The clerk put his hands on the counter as Nick approached. He was a scraggly, long-haired twerp in his early twenties, wearing a *LOSER* T-shirt, baggy jeans, and a cultivated aura of boredom. An intellectual in exile among the Vienna sausage. "Let me guess," he sneered at Nick, "you ran out of KY Jelly."

Nick heard the skateboarders snicker. He looked at them and they turned back to their magazines. "Are you talking to me?" he said to the clerk.

"Great, now we're playing *Taxi Driver.*" The clerk preened for Alison. "Me and Travis Bickle here."

"I just want to ask you a couple of questions," said Nick.

"Just a couple, Travis?" the clerk said, leaning forward on

his hands, still watching Alison. "Why limit your opportunities for enlightenment?"

Nick covered the clerk's soft hands with his own, held him down as he struggled.

"Let me go," said the clerk, jerking helplessly against Nick. "You're on camera, mister," he threatened, watery brown eyes wide and frightened. "My boss can see everything. You're in big trouble."

Nick smiled in his face. The clerk had acne scars embossed on his cheeks; his breath smelled of Altoids.

The clerk slammed his forehead into Nick's head. Nick didn't budge but the clerk's eyes rolled backward and his knees buckled. Nick wasn't just holding him down now, he was holding him up, too.

"Nicky, don't," warned Alison.

"I didn't do anything." Nick slowly released the clerk's hands once he was sure the young man could stand.

"I saw that move a hundred times on TV," the clerk said, still groggy, "I was supposed to knock *you* out . . ." He suddenly pulled away from Nick, blinking. "I'm going to sue you, man. I hope you're a lot richer than you look."

"You're in for a big disappointment," said Nick.

"Do it again, mister!" chimed in one of the skateboarders.

"Yeah, *good* move, Bradley!" said the other skateboarder. "Kung fu fighting—"

"Dy-no-miting," harmonized the other skateboarder. The two of them wrestling across the magazines, laughing, karate-chopping the air.

"Hey!" the clerk called to the skateboarders. "Get off the magazines! Get out of here!"

Alison handed the clerk a tissue, watched as he wiped his eyes, then blew his nose. She bent down to where the dog was licking the now empty burrito wrapper, scratched him behind the ears. He lifted his snout toward her, his collar and tag jingling.

The skateboarders got up slowly, walked out the door, and rolled off into the night. One of them flipped the clerk the finger, not even bothering to turn around.

"He is *so* cute," said Alison, looking at the clerk, still petting the dog. He looked like he was mostly terrier, but he had a beagle's long snout and ears. She kissed the dog's nose. "Is he yours?"

"I'm not into ownership of other species," sniffed the clerk.

"Me neither." Alison smiled as the dog rolled over on his back for her attention. "He's your animal companion."

"Exactly," said the clerk.

"Like Tonto," said Nick.

The clerk gave Nick a grim look but kept out of his reach.

Alison stood up, brushing dog hair off her cowgirl skirt. "We just wanted to ask you a couple questions . . . Bradley. Were you working here Saturday night?"

"I already talked to the cops," said the clerk.

"So this *is* where the 911 call was made from?" said Nick.

"You reporters?" asked the clerk. "I don't want my picture in the paper."

"We're not reporters," Alison assured him.

"Why don't you want your picture in the paper?" asked Nick.

"I like my privacy, if it's any of your business, which it *isn't*," said the clerk. "You ever heard of the Fourth Amendment, or did you flunk out of high school before they covered that?"

Nick restrained himself.

"I'm sure the police already asked you plenty of questions," said Alison, "but we were hoping—"

"There was this black cop calling all of the shots," said the clerk. He smiled at her. "Big dude, looked like the guy on the Cream of Wheat box. He was okay, not particularly bright, but I never met a cop who was. He brought me chocolate chip cookies though. You believe that? Good cookies too. Homemade. Loaded with macadamia nuts."

"You didn't see the person who made the 911 call?" said Alison. "It was raining so hard that night, I wouldn't think you had many customers around . . . when was it, Nicky, eleven o'clock?"

"Eleven-oh-three."

"I'll tell you what I told the cop," the clerk said to Nick. "Nobody came in around eleven. Nobody came in asking for a cherry Freezeroo or tube socks or any of the other junk you and the rest of Dickhead America can't live without. It was a perfect shift— no leaky milk containers, no morons telling me we're out of relish and they can't eat their ratburger without relish, hardly any customers at all. I sat here reading until I closed up at three. I wish it stormed like that every night."

"Did Thorpe . . . Did the cop take the security videotape from Saturday night?" asked Nick.

The clerk glanced at the camera in the corner, snorted. "That's just a dummy unit. A security placebo. Fooled you, didn't it?"

"You must have heard a car pull up in front of the phone booths Saturday night," said Nick. "You must have heard a car door slam. Maybe somebody came in asking for change?"

"I don't make change," said the clerk. "Why do you care about all this, anyway?"

"We knew the two people who were murdered," said Nick.

"Oh . . ." The clerk swallowed. "Well, boo-hoo."

Alison watched the clerk with a look of intense calculation. She reminded Nick of a card counter at a Vegas blackjack table.

"You said that *hardly* anybody came in all night," Nick said to the clerk. "So you did have some customers."

"Good for you, Travis," the clerk said, "that cerebral cortex of yours is really smoking." He looked at Alison. "You want to go out with me? There's an Eric Stoltz festival at the Balboa this week. You ever see *Killing Zoe?* It'll change your life."

"So would going out with you," Alison said coldly. "I'd rather eat dirt than be seen in public with you."

The clerk looked shocked.

Nick was startled too at her sudden shift in attitude toward the clerk. "Give me an idea of who came into the store Saturday night," Nick said to him. "I'll be happy to pay you for your trouble."

"I don't need your money," said the clerk.

"Nicky, don't waste your time on this flunky," said Alison, her voice sharp as a scalpel going for the soft spots. "He's too stupid to remember what happened five minutes ago, let alone Saturday night."

"What . . . what are you saying?" mumbled the clerk.

"Point proved," said Alison.

"That's not fair—" said the clerk. The dog at his feet scratched himself, his tag jingling.

"Bradley here is like one of those dancing chickens we had down South," Alison said to Nick. "You'd see 'em in filling stations, sitting in a little cage with a tin floor—put a quarter in the slot and the chicken starts tap-dancing. Impresses all the rednecks."

"You don't know me," said the clerk, voice cracking.

Alison ignored him. "The chicken *seems* smart," she said to Nick, "trained and everything, but it's just that he's standing on a hot plate that turns on when you drop in your money. He's not dancing, he's just trying to get off that burning griddle. That's

Bradley. He's got wiseass moves, but he don't have the brain-power to make it stick. Bradley's barely bright enough to work the register."

"Yeah?" the clerk said belligerently. "There was two frat boys came in for rolling papers and a jumbo bag of caramel corn around seven o'clock," the clerk recited. "A Mexican bought three Hungry Man dinners and a quart of milk a little later. A girl with braces and big tits bought a bottle of diet pop and acted like I had Ebola—wouldn't even talk to me."

Alison waited. "That's it? You're sure?"

"I have a photographic memory," the clerk said proudly.

"You have no idea who might have made that 911 call?" asked Alison. "Not even a guess?"

The clerk shook his head. "If I did, I'd tell you." He lowered his eyelids. Maybe it was supposed to look sexy. "Now that we're done playing Mr. IQ, how about you and I going out?"

"No, thanks." Alison turned and walked toward the door.

"You're making a mistake!" the clerk yelled after her. "I don't just ring up pork rinds and cigarettes. This isn't my whole life!"

16

"ANGEL!" MOUNTAIN MAMA's broad face split into a toothy grin, showing off a gold incisor with an inset rainbow. She wrapped him in a warm patchouli embrace under the porch light, all unfettered breasts and hips, rolling him against her mounds of flesh in a fertility dance ancient as the stars.

The Blue Angel went along with it. She was harmless. More than that, in her own way, she was connected to the infinite. He hugged her back, felt her coarse hair against his cheek, a thick black mane shot with gray.

Five children watched them from the floor of the living room, their expressionless eyes filling their faces. Like their mother they were barefoot, dressed head to toe in tie-dye pajamas, swirls of red and purple, blue and yellow, a whirlpool of color. Beaming down from the wall was a life-size oil painting of Jerry Garcia with the inscription "May the Four Winds Blow You Safely Home."

"Come on in," said Mountain Mama, pulling on the Angel's hand, "Rainbow's in the workshop. Have you eaten?" She beckoned to the worn purple velvet couch. "Sit down, I'll get you some blackberry wine. I know you don't drink, but it's organic." Her round cheeks flushed. "I made it myself." She pressed the intercom as she headed toward the kitchen. "Rainbow! It's Angel, honey bun!"

The children stared up at the Angel, not moving. He brushed against them as he walked past and still they didn't move, merely swiveled their heads to track his passing. It was after ten P.M.— they were up late. No rules.

The Angel sat at one end of the couch, feeling every spring in the old sofa. The coffee table was a wooden door placed on two concrete blocks, the table strewn with loose joints, finger cymbals, and half-eaten bowls of cereal. A whole apple pie lay on the table with five forks stuck in it. Spiral incense burned in a brass holder beside the pie, pungent lotus smoke drifting in the air. The Angel barely breathed. The room was overheated and there were too many smells. Perfume. Incense. Pot. Sweat.

The children still stared at the Angel. They were of indeterminate age and gender, long dirty-blond hair braided with glass beads and the bones of small animals. Their legs were skinny and scabbed, feet beating listlessly to the music on the stereo, an endless Grateful Dead boogie.

Mountain Mama drank from a green glass jug, balancing it on her forearm, Dogpatch style. She smacked her lips and offered the jug to the Angel. He shook his head. She flopped down beside him on the sofa, and for some reason the Angel thought of the scene in the beach house, he and Ben Telaris sitting on the couch as Maynard struggled to pull the cue stick out of his belly button.

Mountain Mama giggled, misinterpreting his smile. She bobbed her head to the music, her legs spread wide, covered with her voluminous skirt. She reached out, felt the Angel's blue suit between her thumb and forefinger. "I like blue," she said, taking another gulp from the jug. A trickle of wine ran down from the corner of her mouth. "Blue is the color of cosmic consciousness, but a suit . . . it doesn't allow you to breathe. It's uptight, colonialistic. You should slip into a pair of cotton drawstring pants."

"I'll take that under advisement," chuckled the Angel as she took another long drink.

"Evening, Angel." Rainbow stood in the hallway, a short, chubby man with long frizzy hair and a wispy beard, wearing tie-dye shorts and a faded *Dead at the Great Pyramid* T-shirt that didn't quite cover the half-moon arc of his stomach. "Come on back."

"Take the pie," said Mountain Mama as the Angel stood.

"Angel doesn't want no pie and I don't either," groused Rainbow.

"Take it," said Mountain Mama. "You might get hungry later."

Rainbow grabbed the pie off the table, muttering under his breath. Mountain Mama drank deep from the wine jug, smacking her lips. One of the toddlers crawled up beside her, freed one of her enormous breasts and shoved it into his mouth.

Spilled dry cereal and who-knows-what crunched underfoot as the Angel followed Rainbow down the hall and out the back door, the little man scuffling along the dirt road through the trees in his tire-tread sandals.

The house was located at the far eastern edge of Orange County, butted against the Angeles National Forest—rugged terrain, desolate and smog-free. The stars overhead were brighter than the lights from the coast. They walked in silence, the narrow, overgrown logging road twisting in the dim moonlight, until they got to the clearing where the magic bus was parked: a full-size, custom Greyhound covered with mandala murals, three satellite dishes on the roof.

Lights came on as Rainbow unlocked the bus. He locked it behind them, tossed the apple pie into a wastebasket, and wiped crumbs off his hands. He picked up a portable RF bug detector, mumbling an apology as he ran it over the Angel's body. When Rainbow bent over to check his shoes and cuffs the Angel could see a bald patch on the crown of his skull.

The bus was a streamlined bunker, air-conditioned and immaculate, the windows tinted, the walls and ceiling insulated with acoustic tile. A large air filtration unit was set into one wall, humming softly. On the ceramic-composite desk running the length of the bus were four different computers, an extended-range wireless transmitter detector, five telephones, and other, unrecognizable pieces of equipment. The Angel had no idea how Rainbow got power to the bus. Maybe one of the rooftop dishes beamed it in directly from Mars.

Rainbow straightened up with a grunt. He laid the bug detector on the desk, sat down on a swivel chair. "Before we get down," he said, his voice clipped and professional, with just a trace of a New York accent, "we need to clarify my compensation requirements." He flipped up one finger. "Payment is to be wired directly into my Cayman Islands account, but I don't want you transferring funds from a U.S. financial institution. Use Luxembourg or Hong Kong banks." Another finger went up. "Secondly, this time I want to be paid in Swiss francs. I took a fucking on the yen last year, and I'm not about to let that happen again. Strictly stable currencies. The world's been out of balance since Jerry died; the whole global axis has shifted."

"Those terms are acceptable," said the Angel.

"Groovy," said Rainbow, his eyes sharp as darts. "What can I do for you?"

The Angel let the question linger for a moment. "I need you to run down some financial data for me. Credit history. Recent transactions. Current balance. Safety deposit boxes, if any. I don't have the account numbers—"

"No problem. You got names, birth dates . . ."

The Angel handed him a piece of flash paper with the information he had on Ben Telaris and Lomax. Rainbow memorized the paper with a glance, set it afire. The Angel watched it flare. "I'd also like you to retrieve some phone numbers. Last time we talked you said you could trace *incoming* calls."

"I can do anything," Rainbow said, rocking back and forth in the swivel chair. "Time, money, and my love for the Dead, those are the only constants."

The Angel didn't want to argue with him. He handed him Lomax's home number. "I want to know who has been calling him. Long-distance and local. You really can do that?"

"Every call gets forwarded to a billing unit," explained Rainbow. "Even if there's no cost, it's still recorded." He read Lomax's number. "I'll have to hack into the A.T.T. central office that feeds this local loop . . ." He pulled at his scraggly beard. "These incoming calls . . . how long ago were they made?"

"I'm only interested in the last five or six days."

"That's okay," said Rainbow, nodding to himself. "The central-office memory buffer only holds numbers for a week before dumping them. I might still be able to retrieve them after that but—"

"The last five or six days will be fine."

Rainbow scratched his belly. "This number, is it governmental, defense-related, financial?"

"It's a residence."

"Good. It's still not going to be easy, though—central office, they got some righteous security programs. Encryption codes—"

"That's why I came to you."

Rainbow grinned. He had tiny, stained teeth, worn down from all those grains and vegetables. "Tell you what—fifteen K, and I'll yank out all the outgoing calls made from this number in the last month. Special offer, just for you."

"I've already secured that information," said the Angel. "It's the incoming calls I'm curious about."

"Yes, outgoing is easy, any moron can . . ." Rainbow rubbed his gums with his thumb. "Cost you fifteen K anyway." He looked at the Angel. "Hey, man, cracking the encryption is only half the problem; you got to cover your tracks."

"I'm not arguing with you," said the Angel.

"Come back tomorrow," said Rainbow. "I'll have everything."

Angel sat down on one of the other chairs, crossed his legs at the knee. "I'll wait. I may need you to do some follow-up on the information that you find."

"Up to you." Rainbow checked his watch. "Comsat eight comes over in twelve minutes," he said. "I'll uplink with that little satellite and do a bouncy-bounce to avoid a trace." He folded his hand across his belly, rocking away. "About six months ago, I read in the *Wall Street Journal* that the IMF okayed a three-hundred-and-fifty-million-dollar loan for Brazil to upgrade their phone system. Bastards are burning down the rain forest, but we're giving them our tax dollars. Corporate greed, man. Anyway, the Brazilians put in this great fiber-optic network, but they didn't spend shit on encryption. Maybe they don't have hackers down there." He checked his watch. "I'll skip from Comsat to Brazil to Nigeria. Lousy switching system in Africa but no international oversight. Yeah, Brazil to Nigeria, back to Brazil, then up here."

"Just do it."

"You sound like a Nike commercial," said Rainbow. He checked his watch again, suddenly hunched over the computer keyboard, waiting. His fingers tapped across the keys. "You have any kids?" he said, not taking his eyes off the screen.

The Angel smiled.

"You should," said Rainbow. "It's a biological imperative." An international dial tone hummed from the scrambler. His fingers flew across the keys, the computer beeping happily as the signal bounced around the globe. "If you have kids, though, make sure you don't send them to public school. It just fucks them up. Home-school them, man. That's what we do. Everything they need to learn they can learn on the net. None of that corporate shit."

"I'll remember that."

Rainbow typed away, sometimes waiting several minutes, fingers poised, before beginning the next level. The air conditioner hummed louder. Rainbow nodded toward a bulging, brushed-chrome machine at one end of the desk. "See that? When I finally get to the billing unit, *that's* going to help me bust in. It's a numbers sequencer for cracking codes—got a capacity of two hundred million combinations a minute. It's called a Garcia Sequencer. I bought it from a fifteen-year-old Deadhead at the last gathering of the tribe. He made it himself. Never went to school either." He rapped the desk sharply. "Here we go!" he said, typing furiously, "Down to Rio, Rio, where's the phones are free-o!" He watched the screen with delight. "You know, Angel, forget paying me in Swiss francs. Make it Malayan dollars. I feel lucky."

17

"WHAT HAVE YOU got for me?"

Nick jumped at the gruff reverb from the intercom but Alison barely registered the sudden demand.

"Let us in, Elliot, will ya?" said Alison.

"Business before pleasure, you know that, Alison." The voice came from a speaker on the ten-foot, chain-link fence, blaring out from the coils of razor wire that topped the fence. "Show and tell."

Nick felt the damp breeze against the back of his neck. It was deserted up here at the crest of Lookout Point, a high, steep promontory jutting straight up from the strip malls and fast-food joints of central Orange County. The narrow road to the house had wound up the hill, turning from asphalt to gravel, the Range Rover churning up mud from the weekend rainstorm as Alison gunned it, giving a rebel yell as they fishtailed through the slop. Some fun. Neither of them was laughing now.

Nick could see cars stacked up on the 5 freeway, creeping along on their morning commute. Alison said that Elliot's mother had left him the property—a swank restaurant previously occupied the site, but it had burned down about ten years ago. Its concrete foundation was nearby, cracked and blackened, covered with gang graffiti. Broken glass gleamed in the hazy morning light.

Elliot's house was on the far side of the fence, out at the very edge of the point: a large, irregular structure, a hodgepodge of bricks, wood siding, and corrugated aluminum. No architect in his right mind would have signed off on this house; it was as though Elliot had walked into a scrapyard and ordered a couple of truckloads of whatever was available.

"You must have *something* for me," said Elliot, his voice over the speaker making the fence vibrate. "You were the one who called. Ring-ring, ring-ring. I was having a very pleasant morning, but I took time out to see you. I'm a busy man, Alison." It sounded like he was snapping his fingers. "Don't keep me waiting."

"I'm not going to discuss business out here," said Alison. "If you're too busy to talk to us inside, then we'll go away and you can go back to jacking off to Regis and Kathie Lee."

"Tokyo girls' field hockey finals," corrected Elliot, chuckling.

The house had hardly any windows, and those few were crisscrossed with iron bars. What a waste of a view. On a clear day you could see the ocean from the top of the hill. Today, with the smoggy haze, Nick could barely make out Anaheim Stadium to the north, the giant A logo still tilted from the earthquake last year. The city was going to have to condemn the sign or turn it into a tourist attraction.

"Who's the four-eyed fuckhead with you?" said Elliot. "You didn't tell me you were bringing company. Naughty-naughty. Elliot spank."

Nick could hear a faint electrical whine, spotted a small video camera pivoting atop the fence, framing him in its sights. There were two more cameras hidden along the length of the fence facing the road. Make that three cameras. Four. He took a few steps to the side. The cameras tracked him. He stepped back.

"Make the fuckhead stop that," said Elliot.

Alison smiled at Nick and he smiled back at her. The camera perched over the intercom stayed right on her, zooming in with a whir. Going for the close-up. Alison didn't seem to mind, looking directly into the lens. "It was a long drive out here, Elliot, and it's getting hot. You going to let us in or not?"

"What have you got for me?" said Elliot. "I'm not going to ask you again."

"We need your help," said Alison.

"Show me your tits," said Elliot.

"You've got your own tits," Alison said evenly. "Go look in the mirror."

"*Nasty* girl," said Elliot. "Come on, flash 'em."

"No," said Alison.

"Why should I help you then?"

Alison stayed cool, keeping her eyes on the camera, waiting.

Nick pressed his lips against her ear. "You don't have to put up with this. Let's try one of Perry's other—"

Kissing sounds came from the speaker. "I'm shocked at you, Alison. Dry-humping the fuckhead practically on my doorstep. What would Perry say?" Crackling from the speaker. "Where *is* Perry, anyway?"

Alison hesitated. "He's not . . . here."

"Oh yeah, that's right," warbled Elliot, "silly me. Perry's on

ice, he's got a reserved parking place in the county meat locker."
The intercom squawked laughter. "I read about it in the *Times*.
They said he was shot to death. What do you think, a jealous
husband perhaps? The paper didn't come right out and say it,
but I got the feeling our little man died in the saddle. Giddy-yap!"

"Elliot . . ." Alison warned.

"Alison, I'm shocked," Elliot said. "Surely he didn't find a
better ride than you?"

"Let's get out of here," Nick said to Alison.

"It wasn't even much of a story, Alison," Elliot said, his
voice syrupy, "not even a photo. Perry was blown off the front
page by a quadruple homicide in a Santa Ana welfare office."
Ugly laughter. "No TV coverage for Perry. No radio, not even a
slobbery Casey Kasem retrospective minute." Gagging sounds.
"The *Times* described him as a 'former rock singer,' not a 'star.'
Didn't even mention the gold record. Got the name of the band
wrong too. Tsk-tsk-tsk." He bumped the microphone. "Show me
your tits, Alison, Perry won't care."

"Come on, Nicky," said Alison, turning away from the fence.

"Wait!" the intercom crackled.

Alison kept walking.

"Wait!"

Alison and Nick stopped. Looked back as the metal gates
slowly slid open, just wide enough for them to step through, not
far enough to take the Range Rover. As their footsteps crunched
along the gravel toward the house in the distance, Nick could
hear the gates grinding shut. Neither of them turned, but Alison
slipped her hand in his. They gave each other a reassuring squeeze
at the same time, as though on cue.

18

BEN TELARIS MADE his way to the waffle counter, told the beaner
in the chef's hat to make him another double order, and not to
skimp on the pecans, Pancho. Anderson was droning on behind
the microphone, thanking them all for coming to the regular
Tuesday breakfast meeting of the Orange County Business Lead-
ership Council and don't forget the charity softball game this
weekend. Yeah, yeah, you simple shit—Anderson was the only
person Telaris had ever heard of who had managed to lose money
on a McDonald's franchise. "I said a *double* order, Pancho. You
comprendo English?"

The Hispanic man behind the counter poured more batter

into the waffle trays. His eyes glittered with hate under the crisp white toque.

Telaris watched to make sure the beaner didn't spit into his waffle, his chest puffed out in the red sports coat with *Telaris Chevrolet-Corvette* in gold piping over the right breast pocket. Someone touched him lightly on the shoulder.

"Ben?" he heard Anderson chirp, "I've got a first-timer here who says he knows you."

Telaris half turned, still keeping his eye on the beaner.

"Good morning, Ben," the Angel said, "I don't know if you remember me—"

Telaris spun around to face him, his skin prickling with anticipation. He had forgotten to take his blood pressure medication this morning. His collar felt too tight.

The Angel reached out and shook his hand. He was wearing one of those fancy, blue-checked suits like some fag model in a magazine, all bright-eyed and bushy-tailed. "I'm John Calloway. We met a couple days ago."

"Yeah, I remember."

"Well, I'll leave you boys to mingle," said Anderson, waving to someone on the other side of the room.

Telaris waited until Anderson had moved off. "How did you find me here?"

"Your wife told me," said the Angel. "She said I just missed you. I tell you, the little woman makes a great cup of coffee. She has no idea what you really do for a living, did you know that? Probably for the best. I didn't really get to visit with your daughter though, she had an early class. Ah, sweet sixteen. She looks a lot like your mistress, Ben. About the same age, too."

Telaris moved closer, bumped the Angel with his bright red chest, hunkered down his bald, bullet head. "You come around my house again, I'll kill you," he hissed. "You hear me? I'll fucking kill you. I don't care how tough—"

"Take it easy, Ben. Your face is all flushed. You have to take care of yourself, you have financial responsibilities." The Angel kept an eye on the rest of the room as he spoke, calmly scanning the doorways. "Your wife said she and your daughter were going out of town. Palm Springs." The Angel had the same expression he had just before he fucked up Maynard. "She seemed very excited. Nice to see a family that stays together, plays together . . ."

Telaris felt like something was crawling on the back of his neck. "It's just a shopping trip," he said stiffly. "Don't get your bowels in an uproar."

"Señor? Your double waffle, señor."

"Ben? I think this gentleman has something for you."

Telaris turned, grabbed the plate, walked over to an empty table in the corner.

The Angel sat beside him, his back to the wall. He set two coffee cups on the table. "I got you decaf. Can't be too careful."

Telaris cut into the waffle with the edge of his fork, stuffed a big piece into his mouth, watching the Angel as he chewed. "You find out where Doc ran off to?"

"You shouldn't talk with your mouth full. Didn't your mother teach you anything?"

Maple syrup dripped from Telaris's fork as he gesticulated at the Angel. "You here to tell me anything, or you just come for breakfast?"

"I've already eaten, Ben, thank you anyway. I do have a few questions you might be able to help me with, though."

Telaris watched the Angel sip his coffee. He had pretty hands like a piano player. Shiny nails, probably never had a speck of grease under them. Telaris wanted to reach across the table, stab him in the eye with his fork. He could still see the cue stick poking out of Maynard's chest like a flagpole, moving with every breath. "You been to Doc's house? You checked it out?"

"It looks like he left with only his toothbrush and razor."

"Just like I told you. We checked it out early Saturday morning—"

"There was no sign of forced entry when I went there," said the Angel, looking down his nose at Telaris. "Did Lomax leave the door unlocked for you? Perhaps he baked a bundt cake too, a little snack while you searched his home."

"I had a key to his crib, he had a key to mine," seethed Telaris. "We *trusted* each other. Me and Doc rode together, life-on-the-line shit. We was blood brothers, understand?"

"Of course." The Angel nodded. Fucker didn't understand a thing. "You trusted him. That's why you called him three times on Friday. Once from home, twice from your office—"

"He was in charge of the cash delivery that night," said Telaris. "I wanted to make sure everything was . . . How did you know I called Doc? Who you been talking to? If my secretary's been yapping off, I'll bust her hump."

"I'm sure you will," said the Angel. "In the meantime, my inquiries have turned up a rather interesting anomaly. For instance—"

"What's an 'anomaly'?"

"A curiosity. Something that doesn't quite fit."

"Why don't you just say it that way then, quit fooling around with all these big words. You think that impresses me? You're as bad as Doc. All you college boys got something to prove." Telaris rested his elbows on the table, lit a cigarette. He could see Anderson shaking his head across the room. Fuck him and his nonsmoking rule. Telaris blew smoke at the Angel. "While you were coming up with your anomalies, my people found where Doc ditched his car. Long-term parking at LAX—"

"Lot F, stall D419," said the Angel.

Telaris covered his cough with the palm of his hand.

"Doc didn't take a plane," said the Angel, "that was just a ploy." He crossed his legs, watching the room as he talked. "Why do you think we insist on being repaid in currency?" He looked at Telaris as though he were speaking to a child. *"Bulk.* A million dollars in hundreds weighs twenty-five pounds. Nine million dollars weighs one hundred seventy-five pounds and fills four suitcases. Isn't that right?"

"It was a pain in the goddamned ass."

"Exactly, Ben. That much cash is too bulky to carry onto an airline, and no one would check all that money in at the baggage counter. No, Ben, you steal from us, your immediate problem is simply carting the loot around. Cash slows you down. Limits your options. That's the way we like it."

"Maybe Doc stashed the money," groused Telaris, annoyed that his information had been so quickly dismissed. "Maybe he just took off with what he needed and figures he'll come back when things cool off."

"Things will never cool off," said the Angel, "not until the money and Lomax are recovered. Never." He watched Telaris. "A photograph of Doc was shown to every ticket agent at all the airports. We checked car rental agencies, cruise ships, taxis, gas stations on the roads and freeways leaving the area . . ." He shook his head. "Doc is still here. He's found himself a little hole, rented a house somewhere under a different name, and now he's going to sit back with all that money, watch television, and wait to see what happens. That's what I would do, Ben. I'd think: After a while, maybe the Angel will start considering other possibilities. Maybe he'll look at my blood brother Ben—"

"I didn't take your money," said Telaris, "and if I did, I *sure as hell wouldn't wait around to have this conversation with you about it."

"That would be risky. Still . . . I find myself wondering why Doc would have left behind a motorcycle he was evidently very fond of."

"The Indian?" Telaris stubbed out his cigarette in the remnants of his waffle. "Doc left the Indian? No shit."

"Yes, he left the Indian," said the Angel, "and here's what I find so curious, Ben. He didn't have to leave it. It was at a shop being worked on, but it was ready—he could have picked it up Friday morning, *before* he stole the money. Yet he chose to leave it behind. A very rare motorcycle that he treasured. Strange, don't you think?"

"That's the anomaly you were talking about?"

"Yes, Ben. That's it."

"Doc's sitting on nine million dollars, he can buy any bike he wants," snickered Telaris. A wisp of smoke drifted up from the smoldering cigarette. He drowned it in syrup, emptied the dispenser, enjoying the Angel's momentary look of disgust. "You act like Doc planned this whole thing out—maybe it all came together for him at the last minute. He thought of all that money there for the grabbing and made his move."

The Angel looked at him with those ice-water eyes. "I guess that must be the answer, Ben. I'm ever so glad we've had this chance to talk."

After this was all over, after Doc had been found and the money turned over . . . somehow Telaris was going to find a way to wipe that smug smile off the Angel's face. He imagined himself sitting on the Angel's chest, pulling out his teeth with a pair of pliers. "Prospecting for gold," that's what he called it when he rode with the Evil Dead. Yeah, he'd like to go prospecting in the Angel's mouth. That would be a start.

19

NICK PRESSED THE doorbell only to hear a woman who sounded like Hillary Clinton shout, "Bill! Get in here!" inside the house. He looked at Alison. "Was that real?" She shrugged. They waited for a minute, then Nick jabbed the bell again. "Bill! Get in here!"

Nick banged on the door with the heel of his hand. The thick wooden door didn't budge. His hand hurt. He hit the door again. Harder this time.

"Don't play games, Elliot," said Alison. "You opened the gates—why not go all the way?"

"What a *delicious* idea," said Elliot, the speaker crackling.

There was a loud click. Nick pushed open the door and they stepped into a maze of dim corridors. The sound of running water filled the air, a skein of sound, cool and mellifluous. El-liot's voice over a succession of speakers led them through the twists and turns of the labyrinth—turn right, turn left, turn, turn, turn—their progress followed by the ubiquitous cameras.

The last turn opened into a huge room illuminated by soft, green light, as though filtered through dense foliage. The whole rear wall was a waterfall that plummeted from the high ceiling, cascading into a man-made pond. Mist shimmering in the air. The sound of the waterfall was hypnotic; at first Nick didn't no-tice the bed or the man lying at the center of it.

The bed was round, twelve feet across. Mint-green silk sheets dripped onto the floor. The man lay on top of the sheets, propped up by pillows, watching them—a pale, blubbery man in light green pajamas, rings on every finger, utterly hairless, bare feet languidly crossed at the ankles. He reminded Nick of a toad lounging on a lily pad.

"Come closer, Alison," said Elliot. "Let me get a look at you."

A row of computer screens and video monitors flanked the bed—Nick glimpsed empty corridors, the exterior of the house, CNN, porno movies, a *CHiPs* rerun. The sound was muted, ob-scured by the steady roll of the waterfall. A table on the other side of the bed held a milk shake glass filled to the brim. Straw-berry. Two straws. Large projection TVs were sited around the room, with the round bed at the epicenter. A football game was in progress.

"This is Nick," said Alison. "He and Perry were in the band together—"

"I know who he is," said Elliot. "I was having a little fun with you outside, Nick, but then, I've always considered 'fuckhead' to be a term of endearment." He tossed Nick a sheaf of computer paper. "I ran this off the Internet while you waited at my gate.

It's a complete record of every mention of your name. Newspapers, magazine interviews, TV transcripts . . ."

Nick glanced at the papers.

"Not much lately, is there?" said Elliot. "How soon they forget. Not me, though. You're the rock 'n' roller who never sold out, the hot-tub hubby. Rub-a-dub-dub, Nick, rub-a-dub-dub!"

"Ribbit?" said Nick. "Alison, did he say 'ribbit'?"

"Ribbit," Alison croaked. "Ribbit."

"Charming." Elliot sucked at the straw of his milk shake. "Maybe if you kissed me, Alison, I'd turn into a prince."

"Gag me," said Alison in her best Valley girl voice.

Nick walked over to the waterfall. He could see orange koi swimming listlessly in the eddies of the pool.

Elliot nodded at the televised football game. "About a year ago Perry sold me a recording of this quarterback having a conversation on a cell phone. Perry had snatched it with a radio scanner. Lousy quality as usual. Perry didn't even know what he had. He thought it was just another hotshot making a date with his by-the-hour boyfriend, but I *knew* that voice." He smacked his flabby lips.

"Elliot . . ." started Alison.

"There's no skill to scanning," pontificated Elliot, lying back on that big, round bed, "you got your thousand-channel unit gigging the ozone, hoping to snag something useful. Most people never do, but Perry could pull amazing things off the air: drug deals, collection agency harassment . . ." His pajamas rustled as he shifted his weight. "Perry was lucky, but he always sold too cheap. That's why I liked doing business with him."

"He wasn't lucky enough," interrupted Nick, walking back. "Something he taped got him killed. Him and my wife."

Elliot peered at Nick from under his heavy lids. "Really?" he said, dragging out the word, enjoying the possibilities. "Well," he yawned, "Perry always *was* careless." He waved a jeweled hand at his security monitors. "*I* believe in anticipating trouble."

"Have you been threatened?" Nick moved toward the bed.

Elliot winced. "Stop moving around. I don't like it."

"Did you and Perry get somebody mad? Is that what happened—"

Elliot smacked the bed. "I asked you to stop moving around," he said petulantly. "Stay put."

Nick moved closer. "I heard you were Perry's best customer. Do you know anyone who might have killed him?"

"Anyone?" Elliot guffawed. "The line forms at the rear." He swiveled, tracking Nick's movements. "I warned Perry. Keep your business quiet, I said, don't draw attention to yourself. He never listened. The show-off." He checked his monitors. "It's dangerous to know too many secrets. Some people take their privacy *much* too seriously."

"Can you blame them?" said Nick.

"You sound like a man with something to hide," murmured Elliot, wriggling back against the pillows, his head sinking into their softness. "The walls have ears, the hills have eyes. Taxicabs are wired for sound, recording every sigh and whisper in the back seat. O.J.'s phone call to his mother from the Bronco was taped by police helicopters—I had a copy before the mayor. Get used to it, Nick. Once you accept the fact that someone is always listening . . . watching, then you're free to be yourself."

"Free?" said Nick. "Look around. You're stuck here in the green grotto, pinned to your bed like a fat frog on a dissecting table—"

"Let's go," said Alison. "Elliot doesn't do anything unless there's a profit in it."

"Potential profit," Elliot corrected her. "Do stay, my dear. I've even prepared a brief entertainment for us." He picked up a remote control, clicked it. Alison's face came on the big-screen TV. She looked younger, eyes wide. An early screen test? "I've been putting this together for a few months," Elliot said, watching Alison's video image, slowing it down, "ever since Perry first brought you by." Alison in an Orange Crush commercial, playing beach volleyball. Alison in an evening gown, dabbing perfume behind her ears.

"Am I supposed to be flattered?" asked Alison.

"Here comes my favorite moment. Look, Nick," Elliot said, leaning forward, eager now. "She's about to say, 'And it's double-absorbent, with patented channels for those special days.' Alison, pray tell, what makes it special?"

Alison as a walk-on in a Tom Cruise movie. Alison taking a shower in a slasher film, the camera angle from the killer's point of view as she lathered her breasts.

"Alison, do you ever take a shower and *not* think of that scene?" said Elliot. "I know I don't." He sucked noisily at his milk shake, filling his cheeks. "I have a client who has taken a certain . . . interest in you. It's almost an addiction. He can't get enough of your voice, your image. He'll take everything of you that I can supply. If you had been more cooperative outside the gate, simply flashed a little titty for the camera—"

"What do you mean 'little'?" said Alison.

"This client would pay a great deal for more . . . personal tapes and videos," continued Elliot, slurping the last of the milk shake. He looked up at her, a drop of pink liquid hanging off his lower lip. "Nothing hard-core, I know you're adamant about that—"

"Forget it," said Alison.

"Don't dismiss the idea too readily." Elliot's tongue slid out, licked his lip clean. "You aren't getting any younger."

Nick saw her eyes flash.

"I . . . I'm simply suggesting," Elliot stumbled, "that from a business standpoint, you should make use of your assets while they are at their peak."

"My assets are fine."

Nick pulled the tape of Doc and Alison out of his pocket. "You said you were interested in anything Alison did. Listen to this."

Elliot snapped his fingers. Snapped them again.

Nick tossed him the cassette. He'd wanted to Frisbee it through his face and out the other side.

Elliot slipped the cassette into the studio-quality Nakamichi tape deck beside the bed. The waterfall instantly stopped as he hit PLAY.

"Do you recognize Doc's voice?" Nick said as the tape began. "Alison made other calls to him, so you should—"

"The classical-music lover," said Elliot, listening with his eyes closed. "He and Alison have a *lovely* chemistry—"

"Oh, please," said Alison.

"I mean it, Alison. I have those tapes in my personal collection. They're clearly a superior product."

"Those two push button tones at the beginning," said Nick, "did you notice them? Do your copies have tones like that?"

Elliot shook his head. "I don't buy raw tapes. Shhh," he hissed, listening intently. He waited until the tape was finished before opening his eyes. "The audio quality is terrible, truly *awful*, even for a snuff tape."

"So you think it was real?" Nick glanced at Alison, but her eyes were on Elliot, watching every move he made.

Elliot yawned. "I'm not a philosopher." He waved idly at the tape deck. "Whether or not that item is 'real,' as you so quaintly put it, is irrelevant." He pointed at one of the televisions, froze the porno video with a remote.

The still image on-screen was of a slender young woman being penetrated by a large, hairy man—the woman caught now by the remote, her head thrown back, her expression contorted, mouth wide.

"Is she feeling pleasure or pain?" asked Elliot. "Or is she faking it? Who knows?" He shifted on the bed, pajamas whispering against his flesh. "The only thing I'm certain of is that there's no commercial potential to your tape. The killing is too subtle and much too hurried." His eyes were shiny. "People pay a premium for sadism, and to command top dollar"—he lowered his voice, as though imparting great wisdom—"if you want the big money, you *really* need a female being murdered."

Nick stared at Elliot's puffy face. He was serious. Nick grabbed the tape back.

"Not so fast," said Elliot. "That tape has no commercial value, but it has a certain . . . collectibility. My client is interested in Alison, regardless of the quality—"

"Forget it," said Nick.

"I can answer for myself, Nicky," said Alison, watching Elliot, seeing something that Nick didn't. "What are you worried about, Elliot?" she said.

"*Moi?*" Elliot belched, patted his damp mouth with his palm.

"*You,*" confirmed Alison. "You're scared of something. Look at him, Nicky. Maybe he's scared that the person who killed Perry and Sharon is going to pay him a visit next."

"I'm quaking with terror," said Elliot, wriggling his hands. "Get me a diaper. I'm losing bladder control."

"You can't blame Elliot for being frightened," Nick said to her, playing along, trusting her judgment. "Perry had time to talk in that hot tub, and there's nothing like a gun pressed into your face to start a man chattering. Perry would have said anything to buy himself a few more minutes."

"If Perry got himself in trouble, that was his own doing," said Elliot, looking from one to the other.

"I'm sure you're right," Nick said. "Perry would *never* implicate you to try to save himself."

"Yeah," said Alison. "Perry was a selfless kind of guy."

"A prince," agreed Nick. "He'd throw himself in front of a freight train to save a tarantula."

"It's not fair that I should be held responsible for Perry's sloppiness," said Elliot.

"Absolutely not," said Nick. "Besides, you're safe in here. Got your cameras and everything to protect you. Of course, safety is relative, isn't it?"

"My daddy always said if somebody *really* wants to get ya, they're gonna get ya," Alison chirped happily.

Elliot swallowed. "Perhaps I can make some inquiries—"

"Don't bother," said Nick. "You'll be okay, Elliot. Heck, if someone broke in, you could show him one of your videos."

Elliot looked at Alison. "I'd want something very special in exchange for my help. I don't work for free. I'd want a command performance."

Alison laughed, the sound bouncing off the cool, green walls. "I don't take orders, Elliot. You know that."

20

THERE WERE TOO many flowers surrounding Sharon's casket, baskets and wreaths of lilies and white roses, their cloying smell so heavy that Nick could hardly breathe. It was almost ten o'clock; the chapel of the funeral home would be closed in another hour. He was ready.

He tugged at the collar of his shirt. The suit didn't help—he hadn't been this dressed up since he said "I do." The cycle was complete now. People had been filtering into the chapel for the last few hours, murmuring their condolences to him and heading for the door. Most of them were from the entertainment law firm where Sharon had been an associate, sleek men and women who checked their watches so casually that you barely noticed.

At least they had put in an appearance. Sharon's parents were on a photo safari in East Africa and were unreachable. Nick's mother, living in a Florida retirement village, said she hated to fly and she didn't really know Sharon all that well. She was sending a card.

The neighbors had shown up. Don and Donny had cried and invited him over for dinner and *Monday Night Football,* anytime. Krinol had been the first one at the chapel. He had darted in, laid a rose on Sharon's coffin, and left, unable or unwilling to even look at Nick. He had never tried to disguise his crush on Sharon, always asking Nick how "the music" was going with that smirk on his face. At least he had come to say good-bye to Sharon.

Even Calvin Thorpe had stopped by. He had prayed beside the casket, then shook Nick's hand, lingering with the handshake, holding on, as though gauging Nick's response.

Alison had stayed until just a little while ago, leaving to make final arrangements for shipping Perry's body to his family in New Jersey. She was the one who had selected a dress from Sharon's closet for the undertakers to put on her. Everybody said they had done a great job, whatever the hell that was supposed to mean. Fix her up, dress her up, burn her up. Sharon had wanted to be cremated, her ashes scattered off Catalina Island. They had discussed this when they were first married. Actually, Sharon carried the whole conversation; Nick wanted to wait fifty or sixty years before making funeral plans.

At least the music was good. The funeral home had a selection of Bach cantatas, traditional hymns, and New Age pop. Nick had brought a selection of Sharon's favorite cassettes: Neil Young, Aretha Franklin, Otis Redding.

A man in a gray, pin-striped suit waved to Nick from the entryway. He was a partner in the law firm. Nick recognized him from a Christmas party two years ago, Nick drunk, taking the

Yanni CD off the stereo, flipping it into the Santa centerpiece, demanding to know where the Supremes Christmas album was. Sharon had laughed—she still thought he was funny then. The partner—his name was Barry something, a stocky, middle-aged remora—glanced at Sharon lying in the coffin, then sidled over to Nick.

"Terrible, terrible," said Barry. "We're going to miss her down at the plantation. How are you holding up, Rick?"

"It's *Nick.*"

"You'll be fine," Barry said, not acknowledging the mistake. "Sharon asked me a couple of months ago if I could get you hired on at Warners. I've got some contacts in the A and R division, she thought they might be able to find you something. I've been trying, but . . ."

Nick stared at him. "What are you talking about?"

"I understand perfectly," said Barry, "but don't let your pride get in your way. Sharon said that's been one of your problems, Rick." He thumped Nick on the back. "I was very fond of Sharon. I'll call you," he said, striding away.

Nick watched him go—he didn't have the energy to do anything more. Alone now in the chapel, he sat down on one of the pews, stared at the coffin. He wanted to go someplace, pull the covers up and sleep for a few years. He heard the whisper of footsteps on the thick carpet, the sound barely registering through his fatigue.

A man in a blue suit stood there. A handsome man, poised and self-assured, with eyes blue as the sky on a perfect California day. He was different from the people who had come by earlier to pay their respects—they had acted uneasy around Nick, eager to leave. This man seemed perfectly comfortable in the chapel.

Nick shook the offered hand, felt the man's cool, feathery skin.

"I'm sorry for your loss," the man said, his voice muted and calm, with no sharp edges.

Nick could only nod. "Did . . . did you work with Sharon?"

"No," said the man. "I never had that pleasure."

"I see," said Nick. He didn't. The smell of the flowers was overpowering, filling the small chapel with the stink of lilies—he hadn't ordered them. Another useless tradition. "You must be from the funeral home," he said. "I told the director I didn't want to speak to any . . . what are you? Our local grief counselor?" Nick laughed, eyes squinted shut against the light. "Bereavement specialist?" He wiped his eyes. "Sorry. I'm a little . . . bereaved." Laughter bubbled out of him.

The man smiled back. "Would you mind if I sat with you awhile? We don't have to talk."

"Sure," said Nick, sliding over, making room for him on the pew, "you *have* to be better company than the attorneys." He rubbed his forehead, trying to ease the pressure. "You must have some pull around here. Why don't you tell them to crank up the ventilation? Either that or get rid of the damn lilies."

The man in blue smiled. "I'll see what I can do . . . Nick. You don't mind the familiarity, I hope?"

"I don't care." Nick laid his head back against the hard rounded wood of the pew, closed his eyes. Lyle Lovett came on the sound system singing "Family," a sardonic look at a series of deaths in the family, Lovett's mournful voice skating across the pain. Next up was the Pretenders' version of "Forever Young," Sharon's favorite cover of the Dylan classic. Nick preferred Dylan's howling original, but what the heck, it was Sharon's party.

"You must have loved your wife very much."

"Yeah," said Nick, his eyes still closed, "what the hell did I know?" He sensed the man turn toward him, watching him. Nick felt like a cloud adrift in a pure blue sky.

"That's a very odd answer."

"I guess in your business you hear mostly, 'Oh *yes*, I loved her very much,' then you pat the survivors on the back and tell them to hold on, that true love will never die." Nick opened his eyes. "Well, sometimes true love does die."

"I'll file that away."

"You patronizing me?" Nick sat up. "I don't appreciate that. Why don't you take off, counsel somebody who asked to see you. I didn't. You showed up, remember?"

"I'm very sorry, Nick. I didn't mean to offend you."

Nick rested his head in his hands. "That's okay. I'm a little . . . out of it. You must be used to this, huh? I wouldn't want your job for all the money in the world."

The man patted Nick's shoulder. "Money isn't really the appeal of the job."

There was something reassuring about the man in blue. He radiated a serenity . . . a peace with death and dying. Familiarity must do that. "I've never been in this situation," said Nick. "Nobody close to me has ever died. Just my father . . . I was only two years old though, that doesn't really count." He stared at Sharon's coffin, lid open. "I looked at her . . . but I didn't really look at her. Should I have? I mean, am I going to drive myself nuts in a few days because I didn't kiss her or something? Does that happen? It's like . . . it's over and done with, so what's the point? She's dead. Why would I kiss her now? Am I going to miss out on . . . closure, whatever the hell that is, if I don't do all the steps? Am I making any sense?"

The man squeezed his shoulder. He had a strong grip. "Death is my profession, Nick," he said softly, "but I don't pretend to know the answers to your questions. If you want to kiss your wife, feel free. If you want to close the lid, feel free to do that, too. One thing I *do* know, and of this I am certain: If death is describable, it is the absence of restraints—for the living as well as the dead."

"I appreciate that." Nick took a deep breath, slowly exhaled. "I'm also glad you use the phrase 'the dead.' That's honest. I hear the word 'deceased' and I see a tall, skinny man in a black suit rubbing his hands together, asking me if I want the burled walnut casket with the deluxe white satin interior." He cleared his throat, looked directly at the man, giddy from such intimacy with a stranger. "You're very good at what you do."

"That's very kind," the man said lightly, "but then, you're exhausted and emotionally distraught. I'm not certain how much I should trust your judgment."

"Yeah, and I've taken a blow to the head too."

"There you have it." The man's voice was cushiony now. "Have the police made any progress in their investigation? Do they have a suspect? The news account was so perfunctory. You must have so many questions."

"I have plenty of questions, but no answers." Nick wanted to spit. "They won't tell me anything."

"Nothing?" The man shook his head. "They must know how difficult this time is for you. A resolution, *any* resolution, would be a comfort. Even finding out the worst is better than not knowing—it's the loose ends that bedevil the mind."

"The cops don't seem particularly concerned with my comfort." Nick flicked the knee of his dark suit. Sharon had finally gotten to see him dressed up. "I'm surprised they let you wear a blue suit to work. I like it, don't get me wrong, but I thought you guys were locked into basic black."

"Well . . . I've always preferred blue myself."

"May God bless and keep you always,
may your wishes all come true,
may you always do for others,
and let others do for you,
may you build a ladder to the stars,
and climb on every rung,
may you stay forever young . . ."

"Are you crying, Nick? It's all right, I understand."

Nick shrugged off the man's hand. "I'm not crying, I'm mad . . . mad at Sharon, even angrier at myself. I feel like if she came back to life for five minutes I'd spend four of those minutes yelling at her, demanding answers, wasting the few moments we had." He shook his head. "I have this problem . . . I don't learn from my mistakes. If I was a rat in a maze they'd find me in a blind alley banging my head against the wall over and over again."

"Maybe you would be the rat that broke through the wall. The one who found a new way out."

Nick laughed, wiped his eyes. "I'd be the rat with the pounding headache." The music ended. He could hear the faint hiss of the remainder of the tape.

"I like that song," the man said wistfully. "'Forever Young.' Would that it were true." He winced. As though he had tasted something bitter. "Do you believe in God?"

Nick stared at him. "You're the second person in the last few days to ask me that. The other guy was a homicide cop. He was kind of a grief counselor too, but I think he was hoping to coax a confession out of me." He peered down his nose at the man in blue. "You're not trying to pull something like that, are you?"

"Confession isn't in my job description."

"That's good, because you'd be waiting a long time."

"Nick? You didn't answer my question."

Nick glanced at the coffin. "A couple of days ago I had a quick answer. Now . . ." He shook his head. "If there is a God, He doesn't care about us. If He did care, things would be different."

The man sighed and the sound blended in perfectly with the soft hissing of the blank tape. "Maybe God is doing the best He can. Maybe it's our mistaken idea that God is all-powerful that causes us pain and confusion. What if God has the best of intentions but He's old and feeble, with His best days far behind him?"

"I can see it now," Nick said sarcastically, "Old Man God shuffling around heaven in His bathrobe and slippers, carrying His teeth in a glass of water. *That's* comforting."

"It's just a suggestion," said the man. "A possibility."

"Then what good is God?" Nick demanded. "Might as well not be a God if He can't get the job done. Who needs Him?"

Nick didn't think the man's eyes could get any more blue, but as they watched him their color seemed to deepen and intensify, becoming a luminous cobalt blue.

21

"MARTOONI?" ASKED CLIFF. He held up a giant cocktail shaker, staggering slightly toward where Nick and Alison waited on the veranda overlooking the ocean. "I make a mean one," he said, four martini glasses wedged between his fingers.

Cliff Silver—"Silver, not Gold," he had said with a smile when he introduced himself at the door—was in his seventies but still fit, parading around in a white Speedo to show off his skinny muscles and leathery brown tan, his bare feet slapping along in black crocodile loafers. He had an intelligent, beaky face and a full head of hair the color of black shoe polish, brushed straight back.

"Dolores should be right out," said Cliff, putting down the

glasses on the patio table, filling them with a flourish from the cocktail shaker, not spilling a drop. He sat beside Alison, adjusted the umbrella so that he was in full sun. It wasn't quite noon.

Nick sipped his drink. It tasted like the high-octane fuel used by those dragsters that needed a parachute to stop. Alison winked at Nick, toasted him with her martini. The house was built high on the hills overlooking the Malibu coast, the water below a deep currency green. Even the fish had to be rich to swim off Malibu.

He watched Alison toy with her drink, making eye contact with him over the rim, the two of them sharing a private joke without a punch line. The breeze lifted the ends of her sunlit hair, tickling her neck, and he could hardly breathe she was so beautiful. He loved the way she lounged in her patio chair, one arm languidly propping up her head, posing for him. She looked like she didn't have a care in the world, but he knew better. Last night he had heard her crying in her room. He had knocked on the door, worried, but she'd called out that she was all right, said she just had allergies. Yeah. He had the same allergy.

"You met Dolores before?" said Cliff, draining his glass in one long, cold swallow. "No? You're in for a real treat. I was a good flack in my time, but Dolores Dahl, she wrote the book on Tinseltown. She could make or break a picture with a zinger— her column was carried in over five hundred newspapers. Louis B. himself used to tend bar at Dolores's Christmas party. Louella Parsons, Walter Winchell, they all faded out, but Dolores just keeps rolling along. She still gets valentines from Spielberg and what's that young kid's name . . . Tarantino. He called her 'the Last Dame.' She liked that." He poured himself another drink, peered coyly at Alison as he sucked the olive off its toothpick. "You are a real knockout. Do they still say 'knockout' these days? I hope so, because you do the word justice."

"Thank you kindly, sir," drawled Alison, stretching out her

long legs. She was wearing a short, cranberry-colored dress that matched her toenails. She said the dress was "nouveau-retro pop." It looked like a rerun to Nick, but he wasn't complaining. He liked the 1970s. On her, at least.

"Doesn't that accent just kill you?" Cliff said to Nick. "I've never done an honest day's work in my life, but I'd slave in a salt mine if she was cracking the whip."

"Don't believe him, blondie," said a gruff voice from inside the house. A tall, heavyset woman strode out into the light as though she were doing the sun a favor. "Cliff never met the pussy yet that could put him to work."

"Dolores, you wound me with the truth," said Cliff. He poured her a drink, offered it to her on bended knee.

Dolores took the martini, sat down beside Nick in a flounce of orange pineapple-print fabric, the muumuu billowing around her. She looked younger than he had expected, her skin soft and white, her steel-gray hair stylishly coiffed. The diamond on her pinky must have been five carats at least—she could use it to blind seagulls flying overhead. She sipped her drink, gargled the martini and swallowed. "Ahhh." She smiled. "Cliff, now I know why I keep your skinny ass around here." She winked at Alison. "Did he crank off some push-ups for you? I bet he did."

"Twenty-five," said Alison. "Guy's got a bod on him."

"What about handsome here?" Dolores said, appraising Nick like she was ready to wrap him up and take him home. "He looks like he packs a punch."

"I'll have to get back to you on that," said Alison.

"Don't wait too long," said Dolores.

"It's not like that," Nick said. "Alison and I are friends."

"How nice." Dolores had the unflinching eyes of a sniper. "Don't get me wrong, handsome, I liked Perry. He never came to visit that he didn't bring something: an old postcard of the

Brown Derby, a piece of cheesecake from Juniors . . . I miss the rascal." She suddenly leaned over the balcony, pointing. "There's Johnny Carson on his tennis court. See him down there?" She clucked her disapproval. "Work on your backhand, Johnny." She turned to Nick, leveled those eyes at him. "So, what can I do for you?"

"My wife was murdered with Perry," said Nick, "and we think one of the tapes he made was responsible. I heard that he sold a lot of tapes to you, or traded them . . ."

Dolores took another sip, not reacting. Nick could hear the *thwop* of a tennis ball being smacked back and forth, back and forth.

"We're not making any accusations," said Alison, "we're just asking questions." She wiggled her toes in the sunshine. "Perry sure would have loved the attention, all of us talking about him like he grabbed the cover of *People* magazine."

Dolores tilted the martini glass, finally nodded at Alison. "That he would." Cliff refilled her glass. Refilled his own while he was at it. "I liked Perry, but I bet he was one *hell* of a lousy boyfriend, am I right?"

Alison raised one eyebrow.

"It could have been worse," said Dolores. "You could have married him. Actors and rock stars, utterly useless when the applause stops. I should know, I married three of them."

"Four," corrected Cliff.

"Three," insisted Dolores, "the Cuban quickie was annulled."

"Do you think Perry might have been blackmailing anyone with his tapes?" Alison said.

"Blackmail?" Dolores threw back her head and laughed. Her chins bobbed. "Did you hear that, Cliff? The kids must have caught that Sirk festival at the NuArt."

Nick pushed away his drink. "Blackmail's just one possibility—"

"Hollywood is not a blackmail town," said Dolores. "Stars and serious players have ways to protect themselves, and unless it involves small children or large dogs, it's forgive and forget."

"Perry taped some pretty weird stuff," said Alison. "Important people too: doctors, news anchors . . ."

"You believe her, Cliff? Were you ever this naive?"

"Once, but it was a *long* time ago," said Cliff, bleary-eyed but still upright. "I still had my prostate."

"Let me tell you a true story, Alison," said Dolores. "A few months ago Perry gives me this tape, couple of guys yakking on the phone. One of them is a Beverly Hills entertainment attorney running down his biggest client, calling him a talentless schmuck who can't act with his clothes on. Very vicious, very funny tape. I played it at one of my parties and the two people laughing the hardest were the attorney and the client. Sharks love blood in the water, even if it's their own. Don't look so disappointed." She glanced over her shoulder. "Carmelita!"

"I am not deaf," said a slim Hispanic woman, coming out of the house balancing a silver platter—jumbo prawns arranged in concentric circles lay on a bed of cracked ice. She placed it on the table, sniffed at Dolores, and retreated back inside.

"Go on, Alison," urged Dolores, "Perry said you had a hearty appetite. I like that in a woman."

Alison smiled to herself, then attacked the prawns, squeezing lemons over their pink flesh, then popping them into her mouth. She crunched them between her white teeth, the sound loud and crisp in the quiet morning. Nick stared at her in amazement. She looked at him. "What is it?"

"You scare me sometimes," said Nick.

"That's the highest compliment a man can pay a woman,"

said Dolores. "Lauren Bacall scared the *shit* out of Bogie." She looked at Cliff. "What's the matter, you're not eating?"

Cliff shrugged his narrow shoulders. "Too much cholesterol."

Dolores shook her head, reached for a prawn, examined it with a sour expression. "I told Carmelita a million times, buy the prawns with the heads attached. That's the sweetest part." She nodded at Nick. "Cliff, who does he remind you of? What's that guy's name? You know . . ."

"Clark Kent?" offered Cliff.

"That's what I told him," laughed Alison.

"No, not Clark Kent," said Dolores. "You know . . ." She snapped her fingers. "Oh well, it'll come to me." She patted Alison's arm. "I'm glad I finally got to meet you—I told Perry for I don't know how long to bring you by."

"You *did?*"

"He always had an excuse," said Dolores. "You're a very talented young woman. Perry played some of your tapes for me. Very nice. Little rough around the edges, but you have a natural quality that's very rare. I told him I'd be happy to recommend you to some producers I know—strictly legit, big-budget boys. He said you wouldn't be interested."

"He said that?" fumed Alison.

"That's what he said. I didn't believe him, but that's—"

"Son of a *bitch.*"

"Relax, Alison," said Dolores. "Stress is bad for the complexion." She caressed her own flawless white skin.

"Do you still have any of Alison's tapes?" asked Nick. "Any of them with a man named Doc."

"Doc? No," said Dolores dismissively. "I didn't keep the tapes—erotic doesn't interest my crowd. Off the shelf or under the counter, it's too common, too easily available." She picked up another prawn. *"Influence* is the most valuable commodity in this town, precisely because you can't pick it up on Rodeo." She popped the prawn into her mouth, devoured it noisily, tail and all.

Alison watched every movement Dolores made, hanging on her every word. She noted the graceful arcs the older woman's hands made as she spoke, the length and color of her nails, the confidence in her voice, the sense that she knew the way the world worked and liked it just fine.

"I throw a party and people still come," said Dolores, "the *best* people—studio heads, stars, the top agents. You don't impress these kind of people with food or booze or sex. You got to give them what they can't buy themselves. That's where Perry and his tapes came in. Guilty pleasures are the sweetest, kiddo. The best tapes are the ones where you recognize the voices—a star complaining to her agent over her car phone, a talk show host hustling for a date, a supermodel making a liposuction appointment. Good healthy fun." She looked at Nick. "Sorry to disappoint you, handsome, but nobody gets killed over things like that."

"I could drop off some of my eight-by-tens tomorrow," Alison said to Dolores. "Maybe you could call some of those producers you mentioned. I'd be interested. *Real* interested."

Dolores sized her up, lingering, letting her wait.

It annoyed Nick to see Alison so desperate for her approval, but he knew he would have done the same thing in her place. He *had* done the same thing in her place, laughing at the crude jokes of major-market DJs, playing "Happy Birthday" from the stage of the Whiskey for their bimbo du jour, snorting coke with industry flacks, pretending to be impressed. Pretending it was worth it.

"We're having a screening next week of the new

Schwarzenegger film," Dolores said idly. "It doesn't open for a month but I have a friend at the studio. You should come. Bring Handsome with you. Sly will probably show—he's a crack-up, likes to give a running commentary over Arnold's dialogue. You'll wet your pants laughing."

"That would be great," Alison said.

Nick stood up, held out his hand to Alison. "Ready?" Alison gave him her "What's *your* problem?" look.

"I'll call you next week," Dolores said, wagging a prawn at Alison. She turned to Nick. "Why don't you take the boxes Perry stored in my garage. He's not coming back for them."

Nick stopped. "*You* have Perry's things?"

"Cliff, help Nick with the boxes," said Dolores. "That's a good boy. You two go fill up that Range Rover while Blondie and I finish these prawns and talk about her career." She reached for the platter. "Before you go, Cliff, mix us up another pitcher of martinis." She smiled at Alison. "Now, where were we?"

22

THE CAMERA CATCHES Alison as she walks out onto the back patio dressed in jeans and a Mr. Peanut T-shirt. Even with the 30X zoom it's only a medium close-up, the image soft because of the telephoto, the lens dappled with tiny spheres from shooting through the surrounding brush. Alison looks like a pointillist painting, a creature of shimmering light. Traffic can be heard in the distance, the faint sound of car horns mixed with the nearby twittering of birds.

Alison is drinking a cup of coffee, steam rising around her face as she sips. She isn't wearing makeup and there are circles under her eyes. She looks beautiful.

The hot tub has been covered with a blue tarp, hiding it from view. The camera bobbles slightly and a twig cracks. Alison turns, looks toward the camera. There is an intake of breath on the sound track. The camera steadies. No movement now. None. Rock-solid as Alison steps to the edge of the patio, seeming to peer directly into the lens. She finally tosses her head, takes another sip of coffee, and flings the rest onto the grass. Exhale.

She moves into the yard but away from the camera, bends down at the edge of a large garden and stares at the plants. The camera pans across the rows, showing tomatoes, zucchini, lettuce, cabbage, and a few stunted stalks of corn. She's on her hands and knees now, and the camera focuses on her hands pulling weeds from around the vegetables, tossing them into a pile on the grass.

In a series of extended shots we see Alison moving around and through the garden, pulling weeds, pinching bugs between her fingers, tending the rows. Her T-shirt is damp with sweat, her knees of her jeans stained a deeper blue from the dew.

She lifts her head, looks toward the house, listening. The camera follows her gaze but there is no one there. She has already turned back to the garden when the camera catches up to her again, sitting back on her haunches, her back straight, bare feet tucked under her.

She plucks a few fat leaves from a dark green plant, crushes them between her palms and inhales, her eyes closed to savor the fragrance. Mint maybe or basil. She wipes her brow with her forearm and smears dirt across her face. Her blond hair keeps falling into her eyes—she blows it back, puckering her lips. Alison is smiling, happy about something. A secret smile. For herself and for the unseen camera.

23

"THIS HERE'S A private club," the bouncer said to Nick, barring the doorway of Paparazzi with his XXL frame. "Rule is, men can't go inside unless they're a member." He was a sullen jock with a crew cut and a *Brock* name tag pinned to his L.A. Kings hockey jersey. "The honey wants to go in"—he jerked his head toward Alison—"that's okay."

Alison stepped forward before Nick could say anything. "Come on, Conan," she purred, "you look like a guy who makes his own rules. Give us a break."

The bouncer took in Alison's party outfit, a short red leather skirt, red halter top, and black motorcycle jacket. He looked toward the door of the club, then out at the Wednesday night traffic, thinking.

Paparazzi was a former Ferrari dealership on Pacific Coast Highway in Newport Beach, now repainted flashbulb silver, the plate-glass windows covered over.

"You going to let some pencil neck with a clipboard give you orders?" said Alison. "You're too good for that."

"You're right," said the bouncer, opening wide the door.

Nick could hear Tone Loc's "Wild Thing" pounding from the speakers as they entered the club, the ceiling vibrating from the dancers upstairs. He would have liked to go through the boxes of Perry's tapes from Dolores Dahl's place in Malibu, but Alison had other ideas. She had found some of her credit card receipts among Perry's things—when she checked, the cards had recent charges she had never made. Perry had evidently used the flimsies at Paparazzi four times in the last two weeks. She was curious to see where her money had gone.

Paparazzi had a long bar downstairs, the room circled by white leather booths. The room was half full, people standing around, smoking, watching each other. On the walls were autographed photographs of television and film stars—their faces were vaguely familiar to Nick, but their names escaped him. One of the *In Living Color* fly girls, a guest hunk from *Baywatch,* somebody from *Chicago Hope* standing beside Dom DeLuise at an auto trade show.

The club had been started last year by Haskell Weeks, an adolescent TV star during the eighties who had been unable to find regular work since his voice changed. Weeks had kicked off the opening with searchlights, limos, and a brief mention on *Entertainment Tonight.* Paparazzi had been news for a weekend, but the complimentary memberships offered to Bruce Willis, Madonna, and Brad Pitt had been ignored. Instead, the club was populated by bit-part actors and over-the-hill athletes, faded stars, and local wannabes.

Nick and Alison looked around, then headed for the bar.

The bartender was a bosomy redhead with heavy black eye-shadow. She smiled at Nick. "What can I get for you?"

"Beer," said Nick. "Whatever's on tap."

"Mineral water, slice of lime," said Alison.

The bartender set down their orders, turned to Alison. "You look familiar. Were you on *All My Children* a while ago? You had amnesia?"

"I've done a few commercials," Alison said, stirring her drink with her fingertip, the ice cubes tinkling.

Nick sipped his beer. "We're friends of Perry Estridge."

"Perry?" The bartender nodded. "Champagne cocktail. Silly drink for a man, but he was cute and he tipped large. Somebody told me he got himself killed. Too bad."

Nick licked foam off his upper lip. "He was in here last Thursday. Were you working?"

"Every night but Monday. We're closed Mondays."

"Was Perry acting funny?" asked Alison. "You know, de-pressed or scared or anything?"

"You cops?" The bartender laughed. *"Four-eyes and the Babe*—sounds like a canceled action series with lots of car chases." She wiped the bar. "Perry was the same as usual. Singing along to the oldies. Dancing with the pretty girls. He always kissed my hand when he left." She shook her head. "Only per-son who ever did that."

"Those pretty girls," said Nick, "did any of them have boyfriends? Husbands maybe?"

The bartender shrugged.

"Who was Perry hanging out with Thursday?" asked Alison.

The bartender nodded toward a corner of the room. "See the

one with the ski jump hairdo? Name's Tad," she said sourly. "Anytime Perry walked in the door, Tad got thirsty. I don't know why Perry put up with him."

Nick saw a skinny character with a narrow face and a mile-high pompadour talking with two young women, a blonde and a brunette. He stood there in his ironed jeans, pearl-button shirt and ostrich-skin cowboy boots, holding a drink in one hand, the other resting on the brunette's ass.

Tad followed their progress across the room, his eyes on Alison. "Come on over," he invited her. "I'm just getting to the good part." He glanced at Nick. "Why don't you get me a fresh drink, my man? Double Jagermeister."

Nick laid his hand on Tad's neck. "I'm not your man," he said softly. "I don't want to embarrass you in front of your fans. Maybe there's someplace we could talk."

"S-sure," sputtered Tad. "Ladies"—he waved to the two women—"I'll be right back. We're just about to finalize my new recording contract. Don't go away now!"

"I'm going to ask around on my own," Alison said to Nick. He started to argue with her, but she kissed him on the cheek and said she'd catch up with him later.

"Do I owe you money?" said Tad. "My residuals are due—"

"You don't owe me money," said Nick as Tad led the way up the stairs. They stepped into the strobe-lit dance room, disco fever blasting out at about 120 decibels. "This is your idea of someplace to talk?" shouted Nick.

Tad checked his reflection in the mirrored walls. His head bobbed in time to the music, his pompadour so stiff that it barely moved. He stared at Nick, eyes narrowing. "Nick?"

"Do I know you?"

"Fuck, man, don't you remember me?" Tad looked pained.

He glanced up, distracted by the images of the dancers projected on the ceiling, transmitted from cordless video cams carried through the crowd. "My band opened for you and Perry in San Jose once. Don't you remember?"

Nick shook his head.

"Rudy and the Hardrockers. I was Rudy!" Tad shouted. He pulled Nick into one of the small dark rooms off the dance floor, closed the door behind them. It was a little quieter. Tad watched the crowd through the glass windows while he talked. "We played mostly Led Zep covers. Then I was in SkullFire, a death-metal band; now I'm doing this rockabilly revival, Tad and the Crackers—"

"Spare me the résumé. I heard you and Perry hung out some."

"*That's* why you're here? Shit, I thought you were looking to start a new band. I mean, rockabilly is okay, but between you and me, this hair gel is killing my follicles and these cowboy boots pinch my feet. So if you're looking for a rhythm guitar—"

"Was it business or personal with you and Perry?"

"You got a cigarette?"

"I don't smoke."

"Then I guess I don't either," Tad said with a smirk.

"Was it business or personal?"

"Hey, man, I don't draw distinctions."

Nick could see the dancers watching their video selves instead of their partners. It was the first chance for most of them to see their image writ large, the last chance for some. "Did Perry ever tell you that someone might be looking for him?" he asked. "Someone he was worried about?"

"I heard he got popped while fucking some bimbette. That's the way I want to go, man." Tad's face was bathed in the reflected glow of a red spotlight. "You're organizing a musical trib-

ute, aren't you? That's why you're asking all the questions. I'm
ready, man. Nostalgia sells beaucoup. I know a chick from *L.A.*
magazine will still take my call—"

Nick jerked on one of Tad's earrings and he howled. Nick
hung on. It wasn't that he was particularly angry at Tad, he just
hated Hall of Fame tributes and reunion tours with fat, bald gui-
tarists playing their one hit over and over again. Maybe he *was*
a little angry at that 'bimbette' crack.

"Let me go, man," squirmed Tad. "Come on, Nick, let me
go."

"Why was Perry spending so much time with you?" said
Nick, hanging on to the earring. "He was broke but he was carrying your bar tab. Why?"

"Owwww."

"What made *you* such good company?" said Nick.

"I had a long memory! Okay? I was never more than an
opening act, but I remembered when Perry was a headliner. Same
as I remember you. Let me go, man, *please?*"

Nick let go. Another wasted evening. Tad was a rented side-
kick, paid off in cadged drinks and cigarettes.

"That *hurt,*" whined Tad, rubbing his earlobe. "You can't
go around beating up on people, man. You're not even on the
charts anymore." He touched his pompadour, reassuring himself. "You should buy me a drink, Nick. I think my ear might be
infected."

"Did Perry ever mention any . . . tapes he made? Party
tapes?"

A leer spread across Tad's face like an oil slick. "You into
that too? Yeah, Perry was still a star with a tape deck and a telephone. Haskell loved Perry's stuff—he comped Perry his initia-
tion fee and a year's dues in trade for some choice samples. After
hours we used to—"

"Are a lot of people at the club into tape games?"

"A few," Tad said, dancing again. "Inquiring minds, you know? I guess that's part of the reason Perry came around. It was like Battle of the Bands some nights—tapeheads would bring by their best stuff, but Perry always won. He had this new chick working with him lately. I heard her once, she sounded *so* tasty . . ." He turned.

Alison stood in the doorway, a sour expression on her face.

"Whoa," said Tad.

Alison closed the door behind her, walked over to Nick. "Bartender told me that Perry was buying rounds of drinks all last week with my credit card, telling everyone he had made a 'major career move.' Bastard. Let's go home. I hate this place— it's the elephants' graveyard."

Nick stroked her hair, wishing he could kiss away her hurt. He looked at Tad, who was watching everything with his small, dim eyes. "Ask around," Nick ordered him. "See if Perry had gotten himself into trouble with the tapes he made."

"Why do you care, man? Perry doesn't care anymore."

"Find out if anybody has a tape with a guy named Doc on it."

"Doc?" Tad stared at the ceiling videos. "I know him." Nick grabbed his arm and Tad cried out, pulled away, retreating to the corner of the room. "What did I do, man?"

"How do you know Doc?" Alison said, her voice soothing.

Tad stayed in the corner, looking from one to the other, confused. "If it's the guy I'm thinking of, he came to the club a few times . . . must have been six months ago. He had some awesome crank. The three of us got seriously tweaked."

"He knew *Perry?*" said Nick.

"Sort of. They first met each other here. Doc really got off on Perry's tapes, called him an artist, a performance artist, which is bullshit, if you ask me, but Perry ate it up. What's the matter?"

"Nothing." Nick pushed back his glasses. "Was Doc a member?"

Tad patted his pockets for a cigarette. "No. Doc always came on Wednesdays. That's open house. He just came a few times—"

"What did he look like?" said Nick.

"I don't know . . . kind of tall, real skinny . . . from the crank, I guess." Tad kept patting his pockets, looking for a cigarette. "Doc was a real wiseass though, I remember that. Like he was smarter than me. I hate that, man."

"Would you recognize him if you saw a picture?" said Nick.

"Is this worth anything, man, because I think I should be paid for all my trouble and my ear *still* hurts—"

Nick handed him a twenty. "Did Doc ever say where he lived? Do you know his phone number? Or what kind of car he drove?"

Tad shook his head like a metronome. "I don't think he had a car. He was into that biker thing. Big chopped-out Harley. I don't know, man, that *Wild One* shit went out with Mickey Rourke and Gary Busey, you know what I mean?"

"Do you know his name, by any chance?"

"His name is Doc," said Tad. "That a trick question?" He picked a crushed butt off the floor, rounded it out between his fingers, lit it, dragged deep and started coughing. "That's better." He looked at Nick. "All I know is Doc is just like the rest of them." He jerked a thumb toward the dancers. "Everybody wants to be in showbiz."

"What does that mean?" said Alison.

Tad stared at her. "Doc kept bugging Perry to call him up, put him on tape."

Alison glanced at Nick.

"Doc kept saying he could talk the talk," Tad jabbered on, "but Perry said he preferred working with the '*vérité* factor'— what is that, anyway?" He shrugged. "Doc was pretty bummed. Maybe that's why he stopped coming around?"

Nick and Alison looked at each other. Yeah. Time to go home. Doc must have convinced Perry to put him on tape, probably paid for the privilege too. After all, Perry was an artist. Alison had been right about the "murder" tape: it was bogus. Doc was trying to put something over on Perry, to impress him, but the only person Doc had fooled was Nick.

Alison gave Nick a sad smile in the flickering strobe light. She took no joy in being right.

Nick handed Tad a business card. "Leave a message with my service if you hear about somebody who was mad at Perry." He watched Tad mouth the numbers, then slipped him another twenty. "Sorry about your ear."

Tad tucked away the bill. "Perry said you had it made—wife who works, nice house . . ." He stared hungrily at Alison. "Me, I never get a break. I bit the head off a bat before Ozzie, but he got all the press. Same thing with Kurt Cobain—I was wearing a dress onstage in 1985. Nineteen eighty-five, man! Nobody even noticed." He turned to Nick. "My problem was I never had the right connections, never blew the big shots. I blew the losers."

24

"What did Dolores say?" asked Nick.

For an instant Alison looked like she wanted to throw the phone at him. "She said the director is on location. She told me, 'Don't worry, honey, there will be plenty of industry people at the party next week.' " She shook her head. "I'm damn tired of waiting, Nicky."

Nick dragged a long-handled net across the surface of the swimming pool, skimming up leaves and dead insects, ejecting them onto the flagstones with a flick of his wrist. He had spent the last hour doing the exact same thing. It was early afternoon, Thursday, clouds drifting across the sun, a chill in the air.

He and Alison had stayed up late last night after coming back from Paparazzi. The two of them sat outside, watching the stars. It felt like an ending. Not a happy ending, but the end of the bad times. The worst of the bad times anyway. They had done everything they could. If one of Perry's tapes had gotten him killed, him and Sharon, then Calvin Thorpe was going to have to figure it out.

Around two A.M. Alison had decided to go for a swim. She had tried dragging him toward the pool, but he had begged off. As he went inside, he heard her splash into the water, and he remembered the sight of her diving into the lake after the car wreck, remembered her graceful nakedness, the rain beating down . . . Nick had almost turned around last night and joined her. Almost. Next time, he told himself. Sure.

Nick scooped up the last of the debris in the pool. It was clean now. He watched the water with a sense of satisfaction out of all proportion to the task completed. He didn't really need to bother skimming the pool—Sharon was the swimmer. He needed to be doing something though, preferably something mechanical and mindless. Something that showed results. Leaves drifted down from the surrounding trees into the pool. He sighed, dipped the net into the water again, starting over.

The phone rang in the house. "Let it ring," said Nick, but Alison dashed into the house. She came back onto the patio a few moments later. "It's Elliot," she grimaced, handing him the portable phone. "You talk to him."

"Nick?" said Elliot. "You there?"

Nick let his silence speak for him.

"I wanted . . . wanted to see how things were going with you two," sputtered Elliot. "I've been doing my best to help—"

"What's wrong?" said Nick.

"No ... well, *yes,* I am a bit concerned—" The telephone crackled. "Are you using a cell phone?" Elliot said.

"No, a portable. You're coming in loud and—"

"You *ass,*" barked Elliot. "Haven't you learned anything? I'll call you right back. Make sure you use a land line."

Nick heard the connection end. He glared at the telephone, walked back into the house. The phone rang. He tossed the portable on the couch, picked up the extension in the living room. "What do you want, Elliot?"

"You're using a wired unit?"

"Yes." Nick rolled his eyes at Alison.

"I don't think my caution is odd, under the circumstances," said Elliot. Nick heard him lick his lips. "I haven't read anything more about the murders in the papers. I was hoping you could tell me how the investigation is proceeding."

"You have it backward," said Nick. "You're supposed to call when *you* have something to tell *me.* Good-bye—"

"Wait!" Elliot's voice cracked. "Don't hang up! We're in this together, you know. One hand washing the other."

"I don't want you washing anything of mine, Elliot."

"Nick?" whispered Elliot. "Beatriz, the woman who cooks for me ... she's usually quite reliable, gets here every morning at seven. She didn't ... she didn't show up for work today. I called her house and there was no answer. Her husband is usually home during the day. ... I'm sure there's a simple answer, *la migra* perhaps, but I'm feeling a little ... isolated. You must find that amusing," he said, "but I require certain ... human services."

Nick could hear layers of conversation over the phone: porno moans, cartoon squalks, cheering crowds. Elliot must have had all his televisions on at once.

"The hydrotech man came to service my waterfall and tend to the fish today," said Elliot, speaking faster now, hurrying. "He was the same man who comes every week. I *recognized* him, but Nick . . . I couldn't bring myself to let him in. I couldn't even speak to him. He stood out there buzzing at my gate and I just sat here watching him with my surveillance cameras until he gave up and left."

"I don't think you have anything to worry about," said Nick. "Alison and I spoke to a guy named Tad last night—"

"This is all so unfair," Elliot said bitterly. "I wish I had never gotten involved with Perry. Sloppy people—"

"Is there anything you want to tell me?" Nick said.

"So many secrets," Elliot said softly, "you have no idea . . . Dirty laundry piled high as the sky," blubbered Elliot, "and no way to sort it out. I've done nothing but listen to my tapes ever since you left, hours and hours . . ."

Nick looked outside into the yard, listening to the fear in Elliot's voice, wondering. "You want me to come by again? Maybe if we both sat down and listened to what you've got we could figure it out."

Elliot's flabby breathing hissed from the receiver.

"Elliot?"

Elliot cleared his throat. "I appreciate the offer, Nick," he said, brusque now, "but I need to make some inquiries first, *cautious* inquiries. This requires a delicate touch, and you are a crude and abrasive individual. No offense—"

"Of course not."

"Your approach is too direct, that's all I'm saying, and such tactics attract attention." Elliot slurped something. Another milk shake probably. "I'll see what I can do. Call me if you think I need to take more . . . drastic precautions. I'll give you a special number. My private line." He repeated the number twice. "You *will* call me, yes?"

Nick hung up without answering. He looked at Alison. "Are you almost through checking out Perry's stuff?"

"Get real." Alison looked frazzled, wisps of hair out of place. "You should see all the junk he had boxed up—tapes, clothes, weird electronic gear, *records* for God's sake. Who has a turntable? I feel like I should just send it all to his parents, but the shipping would be . . ."

Nick put his arms around her. "Why don't you wait?" He brushed back her hair. She smelled good. "Let's go out to dinner tonight. I know this great rib joint in Santa Ana—"

"I'm just so . . . *pissed* off at Perry," Alison said.

"I understand. You feel abandoned—"

"I'm not mad at him for dying, Nicky," Alison said, pushing him away. "What do you think this is, *Oprah?*"

"So much for Mr. Sensitive."

"Sensitive doesn't suit you—stick to kickass." Alison paced around the living room. "I don't even care that much about him ripping off my credit cards, that's just Perry. I'm mad at him for not telling me about Dolores Dahl. I can't forgive him for that, no way." She kicked a pillow that had fallen off the sofa, sent it bouncing off the wall. "That bastard liked having me sweat for every lousy commercial and Chevy Chase walk-on. He was scared I was going to pass him by, that if I got a few good parts I wouldn't need him anymore."

"Can you blame him?" Nick said. "You were leaving him even *without* getting your big break. He was hanging on with—"

"What are you defending him for?" she snapped. "He fucked you over as bad as me. Worse even."

"What does that mean?"

"You know what I'm talking about," Alison said coolly.

Nick took a deep breath, trying to match her forced calm. "You think Perry and Sharon were in the hot tub when the killer found them? You think they were going at it?"

Alison stared at him with those deep, blue eyes.

"Then you didn't know Sharon," said Nick.

"I knew Perry."

"Takes two," said Nick, unbending. "Maybe Sharon and I had our problems, and maybe she was going to divorce me, but I can't see her fucking Perry behind my back. Not her. Not a chance."

Alison's eyes shimmered with tears.

"What is it?" said Nick.

Alison shook her head.

"Tell me," said Nick.

Alison looked away, out toward the swimming pool, watching the leaves drift down from the trees. "I wish someone believed in me like that," she said softly.

25

—but I'm feeling a little . . . isolated, said Elliot. Rewind. *—I'm feeling a little . . . isolated.* Rewind. *—isolated.*

The Angel looked out at the lights blinking in the twilight, from the cozy houses inland to the oil platforms off the coast, a Morse code of flashing lights, red and blue and green and yellow, blinking out a message that no one could understand. No one at ground level anyway. The Angel had a better view, high above the surrounding streets and homes, standing out on the balcony of the penthouse suite watching the sunset. He had the whole top floor of the hotel. Nothing above, just the way he liked it.

—feeling a little— Rewind. *—little—* Rewind. *—isolated.*

Oh yes, the Angel could see things clearly from way up here. Red brake lights along the 405 freeway. Like the sign says, "Slow Down and Live!"

"You must *really* like what that guy is saying," said Jacklyn, the busty blond hooker, "the way you keep playing it over and over." She stood in the doorway to the balcony, watching him, one hand on the doorframe as though she needed something to hang on to.

"I find it interesting," said the Angel. He had planted tiny RF transmitters in the telephones at Ben Telaris's home and business, at Remlinger Cycle Design, and at Nick's house. The dullness and repetition of people's daily lives never ceased to amaze him. There was something about this call though. It tickled something in him. The Angel held up the recorder. —*feeling a little . . . isolated.* He looked at her. "That about sums it up, doesn't it?"

"I don't get it," said Jacklyn.

"He means like the human condition," said Fran, the slim dark hooker. "Right?"

The Angel stared at her. She looked back at him from a nest of shaggy curls, her eyes alert. She could be a problem.

He had requested two young punkettes, blank girls raised on television and screechy music, healthy young animals with flat bellies and perfect complexions and no curiosity, none that touched him anyway. He preferred ones who neither spoke English nor understood it, all the better to ensure his anonymity. Fran was too smart for her own good, but her complexion was flawless. Perfect skin was an absolute necessity—a blemish was like a tear in the sky.

"Why don't you come back inside, honey?" said Jacklyn, hefting a bottle of champagne, ice dripping onto the carpet. The tips of her spiky blond hair were dyed purple. She reminded him of a sea anemone.

"I'm not your honey," said the Angel.

"Do you mind if I join you?" said Fran, stepping out onto the balcony before he could answer. She wore a wispy pale blue dress, gauzy and transparent—the dress lifted in the updraft of the patio, exposing her brown thighs. Her wrists were sheathed in fine silver bracelets that jingled as she moved, making music, muted by her flesh.

Jacklyn wore a bright red vinyl skirt and a red half-bra that barely covered her nipples. Blood-red lipstick outlined in black. She stayed inside the suite, hesitant. "I got a fear of heights," she said, her voice a baby girl pout. "I had a boyfriend once who did construction . . . he told me they were always fucked up when they built these high-rise hotels. He used to carry a bong in his tool kit. So maybe they welded the braces, maybe they missed a few if they were in a hurry. Who was to know?" She peeked out the door. "Wowie. It's a long way down."

The Angel, turning away from her, looking out at the lights again. —little . . . isolated. He felt Fran's hands caressing his shoulders as she stood next to him, her fingers moving lightly across his blue suit. —isolated.

"If you'd prefer two different girls it's easily arranged," said Fran. "You don't seem very excited by me or Jacklyn. They said you were a VIP, so if you're not happy—"

"Don't take it personally," said the Angel.

"How else should I take it?"

"You're perfect," the Angel reassured her.

"No," said Fran, admiring his beautiful face and form, "you're the perfect one."

The Angel waved a hand toward himself dismissively. "This old thing?" he teased. "It's just something I slipped on . . ."

Fran watched him.

"I'd like you to stay," said the Angel. "You and Jacklyn."

"That is so sweet," Jacklyn said, still hugging the edge of the balcony. She drank directly from the champagne bottle, and it bubbled over, ran down the neck of the bottle. "Whoops!" she giggled, licking the bottle; she was a feral child with a new toy. "You're not from around here, are you?"

"No," said the Angel. "I'm not."

"I can tell."

Fran took the Angel's right hand, kissed each one of his fingers, laid it on one of her tiny breasts. Through the diaphanous fabric of the dress, her nipple stiffened against him, growing long and thick as his thumb. She closed her eyes, swaying against him.

The Angel could feel the blood howling through him as the night soared overhead.

Jacklyn stepped out onto the balcony, a little unsteady from the champagne and the great height, the sound of traffic echoing from far below. She stood behind him, peeling off his suit jacket, as Fran slowly unknotted his necktie, the two of them working in tandem.

The Angel pulled off his tie as Fran began unbuttoning his shirt, her bracelets clicking together. He fingered the tie, felt its cool silk sliding through his grasp as he watched her, her head bent forward slightly, her dark curls shielding her face from view.

Jacklyn was right behind him, gently grinding her pelvis against him. She reached around, undid his belt, then began to unzip his fly, doing it slowly, tooth by tooth, the metallic progress steady as a metronome.

A high-performance jet fighter was flying in from off the coast, headed back to Mira Mar after night exercises. The Angel listened. Smiled. It was an F-15 Eagle. State-of-the-art Mach 2.5 killing machine.

The Angel knew the F-15 well. He owned one. He had stolen it from a Jordanian air base, flown it out himself while the rest of the wing scrambled after him. It filled the Angel with sweetness remembering the twisting, low-level chase, the wind howling around him as he pulled the stick back. He had eluded the Jordanians somewhere over the Bekaa Valley in Lebanon, wagging his wingtips in the moonlight . . . He loved the Middle East. So much opportunity there.

During the Gulf War the Iraqi air force had moved their prize fighter planes into Iran. Safe haven from Allied air superiority, they thought. The Iranians, ancient enemies of Iraq, had decided to retain most of the planes after the war. Some they kept for themselves. Some they sold for hard currency. The Angel now had a Mig-29, and a French Mirage 2000 parked next to the F-15 inside a hangar at his private airfield in South America, along with a team of mechanics and crates of spare parts. Fuck the Academy. He had his own personal air force now. There were times flying over the Amazon jungle, almost grazing the top of the rain forest or doing power rolls under the stars, that the Angel felt immortal.

Fran made little crying sounds at the back of her throat as she engulfed his penis, her curls tickling the tops of his thighs. Jacklyn stayed behind him, rubbing herself against him, whispering the filthiest suggestions into his ear.

She might as well have been speaking a foreign language for all the good it did her. The Angel was airborne and climbing, strapped into the cockpit of the F-15, pressed back into the seat by the acceleration as he pulled back on the stick, fifty thousand pounds of thrust hurtling him forward into the dark dark night, leaving thunder and desolation in his wake. The earth below was in full retreat.

26

NICK SLID THE curtains shut, metallic rings slithering across the rod, covering the large windows overlooking the swimming pool. It was dark outside, darker inside now, safe from prying eyes smoking cigarettes in the distance. He felt comfortable in the darkness, walking across the room, barefoot, wearing just a pair of shorts. No shirt, no shoes, no service. That was fine with—He banged a knee against the sofa, cursed softly. So much for the blind man navigating smoothly through familiar territory. Nick barely recognized his life anymore.

He finished the beer in one long swallow, flipped the empty bottle but missed the spinning longneck. It bounced on the carpet but didn't break. His reactions were shot. He was tired. A little drunk. Excuses, excuses. He could see a line of light under Alison's door, the television in her room whispering. He couldn't bear to sleep in his room . . . but he wasn't ready to knock on that door.

He lit a few candles, the bare minimum, made it over to the stereo in the living room, hand outstretched, and riffed through his CDs. Little bit of Sly and the Family Stone to cool out the rough spots. Yeah. He plugged in his headphones, cranked it up, shuffling to the music.

He swayed awkwardly, eyes half closed, listening to Sly. The take-no-prisoners approach to love had never sounded so good. He stumbled, off balance, and almost fell. Sharon had once asked him how it was possible for a person to have perfect pitch but be unable to dance. It was funny at the time. Funny to her anyway.

Fuck her. Great, Nick. Dissing the dead. Well, why not? She wasn't going to hear him. No one else was either. He danced on in the darkness, candles flickering against the night.

He glanced at Alison's door as the music wrapped around him, staring at the ribbon of light that separated her from him, a zone of transit. He shook his head but didn't turn away from her door—he just cranked the music up louder, loud enough to make his ears ache in the headphones, loud enough to blot out all thoughts, all desires, each and every one. Liar.

The candles guttered down, fighting for life, flaring high one last time—in the sudden light Nick saw Alison curled up in the big leather reading chair in the corner. She was dressed in a long black slip, invisible in the darkness, only her eyes watching him. Nick was frozen by her stare, embarrassed, unable to move.

She uncurled from the chair slowly, moving toward him, eyes locked on his, as she took off his headphones, dropped them on the floor, and embraced him. They danced to the music at their feet, pressed tightly together, the slip rustling between them. Her fingernails dug into his back, guiding him smoothly across the carpet, dancing in the dying light.

There was only this moment and the heat between them . . . no memories, no past, no future . . .

She kissed him, drove her tongue inside his mouth, and he kissed her back, tasted barbecue sauce, smoky and hot, and she broke away from him, stalked to the curtains and threw them open wide.

"Don't—"

She flung open the windows, pushed out the screens, sent them clattering onto the patio.

"You shouldn't have done that."

"We need some fresh air in here," she said, drinking up the cool breeze that blew in. "I could hardly breathe with all this *stuff* around us." Her hair lifted around her shoulders and she shivered with pleasure. "Isn't that better?"

The night was scattered with stars, the edges of the trees aglow in the moonlight. The pool . . . the pool was bottomless, black as ink.

Alison lit fresh candles. She stuck them all over the room, two and three at a time, wax dribbling everywhere. There was too much light. He blew out some of them but she laughed and relit them, added even more. The living room looked like a church or something.

"Stop it," he said, grabbing at her, but she shook him off.

"I want to see you," she said, her laughter ebbing. "What is it? You still think there's somebody out there?" She faced the open window, arms thrown wide. "Come out, come out, wherever you are!" She waited, the wind rippling her slip, then turned to him. "See, Nicky, there's nobody there." She smiled. "Just us."

Nick glanced out at the darkness. "Blow out the candles."

She stared at him, the candles flickering in the breeze, shadows everywhere. "You're not afraid of somebody out there, are you?" She shook her head. "You want to keep it dark so you can't see me too clearly. You want to be able to pretend you're here with her."

"No . . . that's not it."

"I thought we weren't going to lie to each other, Nicky."

"Go to bed," said Nick.

"You'd like that, wouldn't you?" She pushed, hands thumping against his chest, challenging him. Her eyes burned into him. "Look at me, Nicky."

"I know—"

She pushed him again. "I'm the one who's here with you. Not her. Me."

"I know who—"

She slapped him across the face. "Look at me!"

"Hey!" He grabbed her arm as she swung at him again.

She pulled free. "If you want to fuck me, you're going to have to look at me," she growled, pushing him again. Her nails left marks on his bare chest. "Look at—"

He pushed her back, pushed her harder than he intended and sent her sprawling. As he bent over to help her up, apologizing, she tripped him and he cracked his head on the coffee table.

She was on him in a second, her bare thighs straddling his chest, slapping him across the face. "You *want* to fuck me." Slap. "First time you saw me you wanted me." Slap. "I *know* that look, Nicky."

He grabbed her hair, tried to pull her off but she bit his arm and he howled, tore himself free, tried to get away but she grabbed him by the throat, clawing at him.

"Stop it!" he grunted as they rolled around on the floor, her legs locked in the small of his back so he couldn't get any leverage. Alison was hot against him, squeezing the air out of him, spots boiling in front of his eyes . . . "Stop it!" he cried, trying to rise. "I don't want to fight you!"

She clung to him, teeth bared, their faces inches apart. "You don't want to fight? No? Then what do you want to do, Nicky? Huh? What do you *want* to do?"

He peeled back her fingers from his face as she squeezed him between her strong thighs, pushing the breath from him until he was dizzy. The breeze blew the curtains into the room, sweeping their sweaty bodies with cool air.

She slapped him. "What do you want to do, Nicky?" Slapped him again. There was blood in his mouth now.

He got to his knees, her legs still wrapped around him, lifting the both of them off the floor. Her slip was bunched around her waist as she ground against him, twisting so they both fell over again.

She was on top of him now, her fingernails poised over his eyes. She reached into the wide leg of his shorts, grabbed his penis. "Why are you hard, Nicky? Why is that?" She slapped him. "Why, Nicky?"

"Because I want to fuck you! Okay?"

"Yeah?" She pulled his shorts down, whipped them off and threw them over her shoulder.

He embraced her but she pushed him back onto the floor.

"Yeah?" she demanded.

"Yes!"

Her eyes shimmered as she nodded. "Yes." Tears ran down her cheeks, molten fire in the candlelight. "Yes."

He gently pulled her down toward him and kissed her tears, licked them away.

"What took you so long?" she whispered into his ear, grabbing the base of his penis, groaning as she guided him inside her.

There was a phone ringing somewhere but Nick wasn't going to answer it. He was still half asleep, lying on the rug with Alison beside him, her leg thrown over his, skin to skin, wrapped in each other's smells. Nick fought to stay asleep, to ignore the persistent ringing. It sounded like a nightmare echoing inside his head.

The answer machine finally picked up. Nick heard his own voice, then the recording beep.

Silence.

He tensed, wide awake now, waiting for the caller to say something. To say they must have the wrong number. To ask for someone who wasn't there. He waited for the caller to break the connection.

Silence.

Alison was awake now too. "Nicky?" she whispered. They shared fear now, the way they had shared everything else tonight. The living room was lit only by the last two flickering candles, but he felt as though someone could see every goose bump on their bodies.

Silence.

He carefully disengaged himself from her, moved toward the phone. He could see her sitting up now, a soft shadow watching him. He picked up the phone.

Silence.

Nick didn't say anything.

There was no such thing as perfect silence, the complete absence of sound. There was always . . . something else. A sense of place, of boundaries and dimension. A signature. The silence on the line was familiar. It was the same silence Nick had heard after

Doc was killed. The silence of someone listening. Waiting. Dead silence.

"Who is it, Nicky?"

The connection was still open, the silence colder than the breeze that blew out of the night. The line went dead. Static boiled around them.

27

Nick heard footsteps as he dreamed of making love with Alison. A sweet dream too. The footsteps were disconcerting though, ranks of marching feet clomping through their groaning lust, Alison licking the sweat off his neck as he shuddered against her—

Breaking glass.

Nick jerked upright, falling halfway out of the sofa bed, tangled up in Alison's long legs, sheets strangling him. The 9mm was somewhere under the mattress but he couldn't find it and Alison was moving slowly, rubbing her eyes—

Calvin Thorpe stepped through the shattered sliding glass door from the patio, dapper in a three-piece pin-striped suit, his shoes crunching over the shards. Only his narrowed eyes betrayed his surprise at seeing them together on the sofa. "What happened to you, buddy?" he said, staring at Nick's nakedness. "You look like you been in a fight with a cat. All scratched up . . . You should get a tetanus shot." He looked at Alison. "Oh." He took off his hat and tiny bits of glass fell from the brim. "Morning."

Alison smiled as she wrapped the sheet around her bare breasts. If she was covering up to protect Thorpe's sensibilities she could have done a better job.

Nick snatched up his shorts from the floor, angrily pulled them on. It was *his* house. He didn't owe Thorpe or anyone else an explanation for why he and Alison were in bed together . . . He wished he had one anyway. "Didn't your mother ever tell you to knock first?" he fumed.

"Careful now," Thorpe warned him.

Nick was about to spit back a warning of his own when he realized Thorpe was trying to protect his bare feet from the broken glass.

"I did knock," said Thorpe. "That's what broke your door. Glass was already cracked. Sorry." He spread his hands. "I rang the front doorbell but nobody—"

"It doesn't work—" Nick stopped as two cops walked in. They faced Thorpe but their eyes were on Alison.

"Upstairs," Thorpe ordered one of them. "You take downstairs," he said to the other.

"What's going on, Calvin?" asked Alison.

Thorpe stared at Nick and Nick knew exactly what he was thinking: You tell *me* what's going on, buddy. Only two days since Sharon's funeral . . . not much of a period of mourning. He unfolded a legal document, handed it to Nick. "Search warrant."

He looked sad. "Just sit back, the officers know what they're looking for."

Nick tossed the papers onto the couch. "You could have waited until later to pull this crap."

"Warrant specifies anytime between six A.M. and ten P.M.," Thorpe said placidly. He checked his watch. "It's already six-oh-six. I let you sleep in."

"You didn't need to go legal on us, Calvin," chastised Alison. "We're all friends here."

"No, we're not," Nick said.

"If you'd like to go get dressed," Thorpe said to Alison, "I'll make sure you have your privacy." He turned away. "Logan!" The cop poked his head out from the laundry room. "Escort the lady to her bedroom."

Nick and Thorpe watched her leave, the sheet wrapped around her, trailing behind like the train of a wedding dress. Thorpe waited until she had disappeared into her room, then turned to the open sofa bed, flipped up the mattress, and slid it smoothly back into the frame. Without missing a beat, Nick threw the cushions onto the sofa, put them in place, and the two of them sat down. Perfectly executed morning-after choreography.

"Okay, Thorpe," said Nick. "What's going on?"

Thorpe rested his elbows on his knees, holding his hat in his big hands, smoothing the gray suede Borsalino. "You feeling better today?" he said, working his way around the brim. "No more headaches? Dizziness? That's good. A man needs all his faculties." He glanced toward the guest room. "New morning, new beginning."

"It's none of your business—"

"One of the nice things about police work," rumbled Thorpe,

"it's *all* my business." He looked at Nick with a pained expression. "You think what happened here last night, this business with you and Alison . . . You think it evens the score between you and your friend Perry?"

"Another nice thing about police work," Nick said, "is you can talk shit and nobody punches your lights out."

"Oh, there's been some that's taken a swing at me." Thorpe picked a piece of glass from under his hatband, laid it carefully on the coffee table. "Just once though. They never come back for seconds."

"Here I thought you were a turn-the-other-cheek guy."

Thorpe smiled. "I'm a Christian, not a fool." He picked up one of the small pillows from the couch. It smelled like sex ripening. He laid it back down. "Would you mind if I shared something personal with you?"

"Spare me."

"My wife walked out on me a year ago," said Thorpe, as if he hadn't heard. "Left me for another man. A real estate salesman with hair plugs. I didn't believe it at first. She left me a note taped to the refrigerator, used the stationery I bought her for our anniversary. One of the uniforms spotted them driving around all lovey-dovey . . . He was afraid to tell me, mumbling all over himself, must have taken fifteen minutes to get it out of him." He creased the crown of his hat with a fingertip. "He was right to be scared too . . ."

Nick listened. He couldn't help it.

"I embarrassed myself for that woman. I begged her to come back, no questions asked." He shook his head. "You should have seen me, crying like a baby one minute, threatening her the next." He smoothed the pillow. "Juries can be very lenient when it comes to crimes of passion, Nick. I loved my wife. I still do, but the things I thought about doing to her, to him . . . I'd get *so* angry my teeth would ache."

"One question," Nick said gently. "Did you ever find your wife in a hot tub fucking this other man? Banging away so hard that water was splashing over the sides?"

Thorpe looked at him. "No. I never did." He waited.

"Me neither," whispered Nick.

"I see," said Thorpe.

"Does this conclude the personal-revelations portion of our programming?" asked Nick. The two of them were sitting so close Nick could see the faint stubble on Thorpe's burnished, blue-black skin. It was barely light outside, but he must have been up for hours.

"I'm getting a lot of . . . suggestions from the brass to make an arrest," said Thorpe. "The bosses think that a top-to-bottom search of the house and grounds may yield something that was overlooked the first time. You're going to have to vacate the premises for a few days."

" 'May yield *something*'? Like what?"

"You look worried, Nick."

"Wrong again."

"I don't want to turn on my TV and see you headed for the border in a white Bronco," Thorpe said slyly. "That only works once, and you're no football hero."

"You still haven't told me what you're looking for."

"No one laughs at my jokes," sighed Thorpe. "Maybe it's my delivery." He shrugged. "Ah well. The coroner's report was inconclusive, Nick, but we did find something interesting snagged in a crack of the hot tub: a red nylon thread. A jacket fiber probably, that's what they told me. Very faint traces of gunpowder residue on the fiber."

"I don't own a red nylon jacket."

Thorpe reached into his suit jacket, took out a photo and handed it to Nick. "I can't take credit for finding this. Officer Harris—remember him, the patrolman you throttled that first night we met? He's taken a real interest in this case, put in lots of unpaid overtime. He found this printed in a back issue of *Los Angeles* magazine." He crossed his legs as Nick stared at the glossy.

It was a group shot, a color picture taken at a CD party two years ago, Nick standing around with the members of Fever Dreams, a mediocre rock 'n' roll band, a vanity project bankrolled by the lead singer's mother. Nick had done the best he could with them, but the CD was terrible. The party, however, was great. Chartered eighty-foot yacht, tiger prawns and French champagne, brandy snifters of cocaine. It was the eighties all over again. That wasn't why Thorpe had brought the photo. It was the tour jackets. Fever Dreams was never going to play Europe but they had the jackets, just in case. Red ones. Red nylon.

Nick shivered. The air was still damp from last night. That was it. "I didn't keep this jacket. It was ugly."

"That's what I told the brass," Thorpe said earnestly. "I told them we checked your closets that first night. I would have remembered. Still . . . maybe we missed something."

"Isn't there a way to test the thread you found in the hot tub against the ones used in the jacket?" asked Nick.

"Yes, there's a fiber profile we can match," said Thorpe. "Harris is trying to find a band member, or anyone else who might have a Fever Dreams tour jacket. It's not easy. The band evidently disintegrated some time ago, but Harris is very motivated. I don't think he likes you—"

"Nicky?" called Alison.

"We'll be vacuuming your closets and carpets for fibers," said Thorpe. "You'd be surprised what we can come up—"

"Nicky, come in here," called Alison, excited. "Quick!"

Nick ran toward the guest room, Thorpe close behind. He saw Alison on one knee beside the telephone, the cop standing beside her. "What is it?"

"We've got him, Nicky," Alison said, talking rapidly, "we've got his number." She pointed to a small brushed-aluminum box dotted with electronic diodes that was next to the telephone. The box had a dual-line adaptor so that both it and the phone could plug into the wall jack. "I found this in with Perry's things that we got from Dolores Dahl. I hooked it up yesterday because I thought it was . . ." She glanced at Thorpe. "I thought it was one of those blue boxes of Perry's that let you make free long-distance calls, but it wasn't, so I figured tough luck, but it's *better* than a blue box—"

"Slow down." Nick kneeled down beside her. "What is this thing?"

"Did you tell Calvin about the call last night?" she said.

"What call?" said Thorpe, hovering over them.

Nick winced at the sound of dresser drawers being pulled out and dropped onto the floor of the upstairs bedroom. "No one spoke when I answered the phone, but I think the call was made from the same room that Doc was in the last time Alison talked with him."

"How did you come to that conclusion?" chuckled Thorpe. "Pay attention, Logan," he said to the uniform, "this should be interesting."

Nick shifted, uncomfortable.

"Go on, Nicky," said Alison, "tell them."

"Every room has a distinct sound signature," Nick explained to Thorpe, "based on its size, furnishings, whether it's carpeted or uncarpeted . . . The answer machine recorded the call last night. My equipment here isn't sensitive enough, but if I was to take it into a studio, I think the silence on last night's call would match up with the silence on the tape of Alison talking with Doc."

"Isn't he *great*, Calvin?" Alison kissed Nick on the cheek.

"Yes, Alison, Nick is something else," said Thorpe. The uniform guffawed, but a glance from Thorpe shut him up. "This 'Doc' who calls you at all hours of the night," Thorpe said to Nick, "isn't he the one you thought got murdered while you were listening on the phone? No wonder you don't look so good, buddy—you just lost your alibi. Don't be sad, it was a lousy alibi anyway."

"Nicky didn't say it was Doc on the line," said Alison, "he said somebody was calling from Doc's place."

"At the bowling alley you weren't so sure that Doc had been murdered," Thorpe said to her. "What changed your mind?"

"Doc never called me. *Never*. That's not the way the game is played." She tapped the metal box. "Check it out, Calvin."

Nick bent to see too, his head brushing against Thorpe. There was a digital readout on the screen of the box: a phone number and time of day. Another number, another time.

"The first number is the call yesterday afternoon from that reporter," Alison said to Nick, "but look at the call at three forty-seven A.M.—"

"The last two digits are the same as the tones I heard on the Doc tape," said Nick. He was stunned. "Local prefix too." He picked up the box. "What is this thing?"

Thorpe took the box from him, examined it, wire dangling to the telephone. "This is a bootleg caller-ID unit," he said, impressed. "It tells you who's calling before you answer the phone. Works even on unlisted numbers." He hesitated, then put it back down. "They were illegal in California until just a few weeks ago."

"Would you do me a favor, Calvin?" said Alison. "Find out who this last number belongs to. That's Doc. Find out where he lives, and check in on him. Maybe Doc is alive and well, sitting in his living room watching TV and having a good laugh at our expense." She squeezed Nick's hand. "Maybe Doc isn't laughing at all. Would you check, Calvin? Would you do that for me?"

Thorpe was already writing the number in his notebook.

28

ALISON ANSWERED HER cell phone on the second beep, pulling it from her purse with a practiced motion. "Yeah, Calvin," she said, watching Nick pace, "he's here with me."

Nick stopped for a moment, then went back to pacing around the small office while Alison sat on the couch talking with Thorpe. He hadn't been able to sit still since they left the house a few hours ago. He glanced out the window, half expecting to see the deserted parking lot swarming with cop cars. Alison's Range Rover was alone on the cracked asphalt.

They were holed up at the office of Alison's agent, their overnight bags tossed on the floor beside the green Naugahyde couch. It was midafternoon—the agent had taken off for her regular long weekend in Palm Springs, leaving the key in its usual hiding place. The office was a cluttered two-room suite with ugly furniture and discount oil paintings, a five-gallon bottle of Arrowhead water in one corner. The office complex was in receivership—most of the tenants had moved out, but it did have a fancy Newport Beach zip code.

"Is Nicky under arrest?" Alison said coolly. "Then you don't need to know where we're staying." She nodded. "I'm not mad at you, big guy, my daddy just taught me to stick up for my rights." She laughed. "No, he didn't tell me to stick up for Nicky's rights, I came up with that all by myself." She winked at Nick. "Uh-huh. You've got my number, let me know as soon as we can come back to the house." She lowered her eyes. "Thanks for trying, Calvin, we appreciate it." She broke the connection, flipped the phone shut.

"Well?" said Nick.

"Calvin says they've made a good start searching your house and they haven't found anything yet," said Alison. "I think he was happy about it."

"That's what *you* think."

"Why don't you sit down?" said Alison. "Relax."

Nick checked out the window again. "Your pal Calvin thinks I killed Sharon and Perry. He's not really looking at anyone else, he's just going through the motions—"

"He's just doing his job, Nicky."

"Quit defending him, will you? I've been his main suspect ever since you told him I went back into the house for my business cards—"

"Don't start that again—"

"I'm surprised he hasn't arrested me already. If he finds anything at the house even *vaguely* incriminating that's it. Investigation is over. Case closed."

"Calvin's not going to arrest you for something you didn't do," said Alison.

"Dream on."

"He ran that number from the caller-ID box like I asked him," argued Alison. "He even went by the address to check it out, but there was nobody home."

"I'm not surprised," said Nick. They had called the number five times since leaving Nick's place. No answer. No answering machine. No nothing.

"The phone number belongs to a Jeffrey Lomax, 'Doc,' according to his neighbors," said Alison. "Calvin said there wasn't any sign of forced entry at the house, and the car that's registered to Lomax isn't in the garage, so maybe he's on a trip. The neighbors said that he's often gone for days at a time—"

Nick stopped pacing. "Calvin didn't go inside?"

"Course not," she laughed. "You need a warrant for that, and there's no grounds. Calvin said he peeked in the windows but didn't see anything suspicious. No overturned furniture, no blood or dead body. Calvin promised to keep asking around, but—"

"What's the address?"

"He wouldn't tell me." She looked at him. "What?"

"I want to go to his house. Check it out for myself."

She leaned off the couch toward him. "Can't you just kick back for a while? Maybe we were wrong—"

"I wrote Doc's number down from the caller-ID box," said Nick, taking a crumpled piece of paper out of his pocket. "With your phone skills we should be able to get his address."

Alison sat cross-legged on the couch, watching him. She

looked like a primitive idol, the kind men were sacrificed to. Willingly.

"This is important," said Nick, handing her the paper. "I *need* to know."

Alison sighed in resignation. "What do you want me to do?"

He told her.

"I'll try it," she said, flipping open the phone, "but I warn you, after we get back from Doc's house, *I'm* the boss."

"So what else is new?"

Alison dialed Information. "Op-operator?" she quavered, her voice sounding like a young teenager. "I need the address of 822-0906." Pause. "Unlisted? I *need* the address. My brother is there and it's getting late and I called and called . . ." She started to cry. "I can't help it!"

Nick took the phone. "Operator, this is Calvin Thorpe"— he winked at Alison. "I drive a cab for Southcoast Taxis. I'm here to pick up this young lady but she lost the address. . . . I *know* it's against your policy . . ." He lowered his voice. "This little girl is standing on the corner of a lousy part of town and I don't know where to take her. I know that's not your problem but she's *blind*, lady. Couldn't you make . . . That's right, blind." He gave the phone to Alison.

"My brother is staying with his friend Jeff Lomax, operator, L-o-m-a-x, but I don't . . . Yes, I'll hold." Pause. "Thirteen fifty East Harrison Place, Laguna Beach. God bless you, ma'am." She hung up, looked at him. "You got potential, Nicky."

He kissed her. "Let's go."

An hour later they were sitting in Alison's Range Rover on the outskirts of Laguna Beach, lined up bumper to bumper on Laguna Canyon Road. Nick was poring over the Thomas Brothers map book trying to find the most direct route to Doc's house.

Alison glanced at the dashboard gauges. The radiator temperature was edging toward an eruption. "You really should buy this car from me, Nicky. You need a car. I'll make you a good deal."

"You couldn't *give* me this car."

Alison crept forward five feet before she had to hit the brakes. "This car would do wonders for your image." The temperature gauge was spiking. "People would think you were back on top if you were driving this machine. Make me an offer."

"You want to pull over, let the success-mobile cool off for a few hours, or you just want to keep driving and see if you can blow the engine, put it out of its misery?"

"It's *supposed* to run hot," said Alison. She slammed on her brakes, almost hit the car in front of her. "Good brakes too." It wasn't working on him. "I'll never get used to Southern California traffic," she said. "I grew up in a little town about a hundred miles from Dallas. Two traffic lights, four filling stations, one speed trap."

"When I was growing up people still talked about 'rush hour,' " said Nick, "like there was a distinct segment of the day when traffic was bad and you could schedule your trip around the congestion. Now, it's always rush hour. Every minute of every day. You live in second gear. Turn right at the flashing yellow signal. People adjust though. They get cell phones and lumbar-support seats and dashboard fax machines. They listen to books on tape and Howard Stern on radio. They *cope*. Which is too bad. If they didn't adjust, things would have to change—"

"Don't be such a party pooper," said Alison. "Being stuck in traffic isn't so bad. It's sure better then living in some jerkwater town where you can get anyplace in five minutes but there's no-place you want to go."

"Who's the one wearing out her middle finger every time somebody tries cutting in on her?" said Nick.

Alison checked her makeup in the rearview. "We all cope in our own way, Nicky.

"Uh-huh." Nick looked up from the map book. "Take the next right. Straight up this hill. We're almost there." He glanced at the temperature gauge. "We may actually make it."

29

DOC LIVED ON a ridge of expensive homes overlooking Laguna Canyon on one side, the sun setting into the Pacific on the other. The canyon view was marred by erosion and drought. Last fall's windblown fires had scorched the earth, racing up the slopes toward the houses, cacti exploding from the heat. Half the block had been lost in the conflagration, houses burned down to the concrete slabs, the empty swimming pools now strewn with beer cans.

Alison parked down the street from Doc's house, the radiator of the Range Rover hissing angrily. Contractors had started rebuilding, but in a few years the fires would return, started by kids or derelicts, blown by the hot Santa Ana winds. Insurance would cover the loss and the process would begin again. There was a sense of futility to the cycle, but the view was too good to give back to the rabbits.

Doc's house was a small white Spanish-style structure with a red barrel-tile roof, arched windows and an attached garage. Nick pressed the doorbell, then listened to it echo in the quiet house. A phone rang inside. He turned and saw Alison with her flip phone.

"Just checking," she said. "I wanted to make sure the operator had given us the right address."

Nick looked at the house next door but the curtains were pulled, the sound of the television leaking out into the evening. He strolled around the side of the house, his feet sliding on the steep slope overlooking the canyon, pebbles rolling over the edge. He tried to imagine Thorpe doing this but he couldn't.

"Be careful, Nicky."

"Yes, dear." Nick clung to the side of the house as he edged around back. The wooden deck overlooking the canyon was cracked and rotten—he could see a sheer drop through the planks. His foot went through one of the boards and he had to grab on to the railing to stop himself.

"Nicky?"

"I'm all right. Stay where you are." Nick was breathing hard when he got to the back door, peered through into the kitchen and saw dishes piled in the sink, beer bottles on the counter. He tried the door. Locked. Big surprise. Time to make a decision. The smart move was to turn around and go for a long drive with Alison and let Thorpe handle the investigation. He remembered the call last night, the silence on the line, insinuating itself into his life. . . .

"Go around to the front," he called to Alison. He waited until she left, then kicked in the door. He had never been one for making the smart move.

He listened before stepping over the threshold. His nose wrinkled at the smell of rotting food as he walked through the kitchen. There was a television in the living room, a cargo-hatch coffee table, and two leather couches studded with cigarette burns. A diploma from Princeton was on one wall, hung upside down. At the center of the room was a black Harley with the engine manifold disassembled, parts neatly laid out on the oil-stained carpet. He opened the front door and ushered Alison in, checking the street behind her.

"I heard something when I was outside," Alison said. "It sounded like a door breaking."

"Really?"

Alison eyed him. "Maybe the back door was a little stuck?"

"That must have been it."

She glanced into the kitchen, noted the door splintered out of its frame. "I think you fixed it now."

They walked through the house, checked the bathroom. No razor. No toothbrush. The soap was dry. It was dark outside but someone had left the lights on.

Alison stopped in front of a small, framed photo in the hallway—a tall, sharp-eyed man with a goatee and red hair down to his shoulders straddled a black motorcycle, sneering directly into the camera, his arm around two bare-breasted women. Proud to be bad, yet somehow above it. She tucked the photo into her purse.

Nick put on his Walkman, listened to the Doc tape on the headphones as they moved from room to room, trying to visualize the scene. He heard Doc break off his conversation with Alison, a loud thump, like someone being hit, then what sounded like shattering glass. No, it was heavier than that. He played that part again. Not glass. More like pottery breaking. Then Doc pleading, *This is so fucking . . . inappropriate, bro.* Nick felt sick to his stomach.

Alison opened a door. Nick had thought it a closet but it led down a long flight of steps, thickly carpeted. The light was dim down there. Murky. He put the Walkman away, started down, keeping to the sides to avoid any squeaks. He sensed Alison behind him, motioned her to stay. She flipped him the finger.

The air seemed thicker as he descended. He stopped and Alison stopped behind him. The house creaked faintly on its supports. The wind whispered through the ventilation ducts. He filtered out these familiar sounds, listening for any other noises, listening . . . listening. There was another sound. Breathing. Calm, regular breaths from below. No fear from whoever was down there, waiting for them at the bottom of the stairs.

Nick pointed down to Alison, warned her not to move. She nodded, her face suddenly pale. She waved at him, urging him back. He kept going, listening after every step. He wasn't sure of the exact location of whoever was waiting for them. The breathing was coming from near the bottom of the stairs, but left or right . . . ?

Alison touched his arm. He turned and saw her indicating a light switch on the wall, the switch turned off. They communicated by hand signals, a desperate pantomime.

Nick readied himself six or seven steps from the bottom, glanced behind him at Alison, nodded and squeezed shut his eyes as he launched himself into space. As he sailed down Alison hit the lights. Nick opened his eyes as his feet hit the floor, whirled and saw a man in a blue suit blinking in the sudden bright light. Nick threw him against the wall, heard his head thump hard against the paneling. He took the man's wrist, pulled it behind his back, locking him up. The man wasn't struggling but Nick kept the pressure on. Alison was down the stairs now.

"You're hurting me, Nick," the man said placidly.

The man's voice was familiar. Nick placed his forearm against the man's throat, bent his face backward for a look. "This guy was at Sharon's funeral," he said to Alison. "He told me he was a grief counselor—"

"I did not," insisted the man. "You assumed that's who I was. I merely did nothing to dispel your misapprehension."

Nick squeezed harder. "Who are you?"

"Would you mind easing up a bit, Nick?" said the man. "You seem to be crushing my windpipe."

"Who are you?" Nick tightened his grip.

"Think of me as your guardian angel," the man gasped, still not struggling. "Nick? My windpipe?"

"I don't need a guardian angel," said Nick.

"Nicky, you're killing him! He hasn't done anything."

Nick backed off his throat but increased the pressure on the man's bent-up arm, lifting it between his shoulder blades. The Angel should have been in agony but he didn't react. "What are you doing here?" demanded Nick.

"I could ask you the same question," said the Angel.

"You were waiting for us." Nick twisted the man's arm still higher, wanting to hurt him, to make him cry out, but the Angel just grunted. "You called me last night, *didn't* you?"

"I called several people last night." The Angel's voice was unhurried. "You were the only ones who came to visit. Who were you expecting to find here, Nick?"

Nick drove the Angel into the wall again. He patted down that blue suit, expecting to find a gun, but there was just a set of car keys and a wallet. He flipped open the wallet. There was a few hundred dollars in large bills, three sets of American Express

Platinum Cards and driver's licenses, all with different names. Nick tossed the Angel back his wallet. He straightened his glasses, disappointed. He wished there had been a gun. Wished there was some legitimate identification. Most of all, he wished the Angel had put up a fight.

Alison was looking around the finished basement. There was a king-size bed at the far end facing a full-length mirror.

The Angel smoothed his suit, then pulled out a comb, ran it through his hair. There was blood in the comb. "You surprised me with that move on the stairs, Nick. That doesn't happen very often." He wiped off the comb with his handkerchief, slid it back into his jacket, and looked at Nick. "How did you know I was down here?"

"I heard you breathing."

"You're serious?" The Angel looked impressed.

"Nicky? You should see this."

"I've given you no cause for alarm," the Angel said. "I haven't threatened you. I haven't attacked you—you're the one who assaulted me. Where does all that anger come from, Nick?"

"Go ahead," said Nick.

The Angel walked toward Alison, shaking his head. "He heard me breathing," he said to himself.

Alison stood before a dual cassette deck and a rack of tapes next to the bed. The deck was attached to the base of a portable telephone, ready to tape the calls.

Then Nick saw what Alison had noticed: the wall jack for the telephone had the same dual-line adaptor that Perry's caller-ID box plugged into. He looked at her. She nodded.

"What is it?" the Angel said. "What do you see that I don't?"

Alison was going through the pile of cassettes, reading labels. "Here's Doc and me. And here. And here." She looked at Nick. "He was recording our calls from this end, just like Perry was at the other. Doc must have had a caller-ID box so he would know beforehand who was calling. He wouldn't have wanted to lose a moment."

Nick imagined that it was last Friday: Doc lying on the bed talking with Alison, lights turned down low, masturbating to her voice, maybe watching himself in the mirror, suddenly surprised, caught in the act by someone he knew. "Bro." Someone who had killed him, then picked up the phone and listened, heard Alison and Perry as he stared at the caller-ID box with Nick's phone number blinking . . .

"Caller ID? That's interesting," said the Angel. He threw his cuffs, straightening his tie where Nick had throttled him. "One can always learn something. I enjoyed our discussion about the nature of God at the funeral home, Nick. When I went to your home that evening, one of your neighbors was kind enough to tell me where you were."

"How did you know where I live?"

"The last call Doc received was made from your house," said the Angel. "The very last one." His cold blue eyes lingered on Alison. "Naturally, I was curious what had been discussed."

"Did you take his caller-ID box?" said Nick.

"Pay attention, Nick. I didn't even know about the box until a few minutes ago," said the Angel. "I used . . . other means to trace Doc's ingoing and outgoing calls." His eyes glittered. "Someone must have known I would come calling, and removed the unit. Someone is going to be punished for that."

"Why are you looking for Doc?" asked Alison.

"Why are *you*?" said the Angel.

"You first," said Alison.

"I guess it can't hurt . . ." The Angel smiled at her. "Doc disappeared right after your call. He left with some money that didn't belong to him."

"Doc didn't disappear," said Nick. "He was killed."

The Angel didn't react, not in any way that Nick could pinpoint, but there was a certain . . . stillness in the room. "I've considered that possibility," the Angel said at last.

"You're considering it again right now, aren't you?" said Nick. "You're thinking that maybe somebody else ran off with your money. A guardian angel who gets fooled . . . he's not really up to the job, is he?" Nick enjoyed seeing a line of consternation crease the Angel's forehead. "If someone did kill Doc, who would be your most likely candidate?"

The Angel just stared at him.

Nick reached for the phone. "I'm going to call Thorpe, Alison. Get him and his forensics crew—" The Angel was right beside him. Nick had no idea he could move so fast.

"Hang up the phone," said the Angel.

Nick slowly stood. The Angel was four or five inches taller but less muscular. Nick would hit hard and keep hitting. No rules. No mercy.

"Would y'all stop swinging your dicks at each other?" said Alison, tapping her foot in frustration. "Tell Nicky what he wants to know. Share and share alike."

"Well put." The Angel inclined his head to Alison. "There *is* a business associate of Doc's . . . I've had doubts about him."

"Does he have a name?" asked Nick.

The Angel ran a thumb down one of his lapels, watching Nick. "What did Doc talk about in that last call? Did he seem at all . . . concerned?"

"This isn't right." Alison was staring at the bed. There was a nightstand on each side, a gray lamp on one of them.

Nick glanced at her. "You're redecorating?"

"There must have been another lamp," said Alison. "It's a set. You can tell." She looked at Nick. "Can't you tell?"

"No . . ." Nick jerked as though he had been struck. *"That's the sound we heard—"* He had thought it was pottery breaking on the tape.

Alison was already on her hands and knees, crawling around, running her fingers through the fibers. Nick joined her.

"If you're looking for blood traces, I've already done that," said the Angel, annoyed. "I sprayed the whole house with luminol; it's a chemical that reveals even minute amounts of bodily fluids under black light—"

"Damn!" Nick got up, a ceramic sliver stuck in the palm of his hand.

Alison plucked out the sliver, brought it over to the lamp. It was the exact same color. "They broke one of the lamps when they were fighting, then cleaned up later," she said, "just like on the tape."

The Angel wiped Nick's hand with his own bloodstained handkerchief. Red on red. Blood brothers. Nick tried to pull away but the Angel held him tight. "What's the matter, Nick?" he said as Nick struggled futilely. "Afraid of a little blood?" He looked over at Alison. "Now then, what tape might that be?" he asked innocently.

30

SOMEONE WAS BANGING on the front door of the office. "Would you get that?" Nick asked Alison, spilling coffee grounds on the rug of the suite's interior room. It was almost nine-thirty Saturday morning but he was still half asleep. She had already gone for a run on the beach, called Thorpe and told him where they were staying, then dived back into their makeshift bed on the sofa.

He stood there in a pair of camouflage-print boxer shorts filling the coffee maker and watching her pull on her clothes. More knocking. Thorpe had made good time on the drive over. Nick couldn't wait to tell him what they had found out last night at Doc's house. He was less eager to admit to breaking into the house. Oh, well. Thorpe could always use it in a sermon.

"Hang on to your britches, Calvin!" yelled Alison, crossing the room, adjusting her green running shorts and tank top. Welcome to Sherwood Forest. Nick heard the door open. "I sure hope you brought some fresh fruit— Oh."

Nick put down the coffeepot. Oh?

Alison walked back into the room with three bruisers wearing baseball uniforms. The men lumbered through the doorway, their big arms splitting the short sleeves, baseball bats in their hands. Alison fired a warning glance at Nick, not that she needed to bother. He knew what those bats were for.

"Hey guys," Nick said cheerfully, "Thorpe said he was bringing a few other cops over for breakfast, but I didn't think you were coming direct from softball practice. Sit down, I'm just making coffee."

A brawny mesomorph with a swastika earring and a Louisville Slugger on his shoulder looked toward the doorway. "Ben? Whadda we do?"

Nick followed the mesomorph's gaze, saw a fourth man, a beefy balding man with crafty eyes and tufts of hair wafting up from his collar. Nick shivered, his hands involuntarily balling into fists. Ben wasn't wearing a baseball uniform. He wore a red nylon jacket. Probably missing a thread, a match for the one Thorpe had found in the hot tub. This had to be the "business associate" of Doc's that the Angel had told them about.

"Ben?" said the mesomorph.

"Wise up, Pinball," Ben said to the mesomorph. He nodded at Nick's boxers. "Nice cammies. You boys should take a lesson from G.I. Joe." He peered at Nick. "You saw it coming right away, didn't you, bro?"

"You're not my brother," Nick said tightly.

"See what I mean, boys?" rumbled Ben. "Told you he was smart." He smiled as the three other bikers fanned out across the small room. The one called Pinball peeked through the blinds at the nearly empty parking lot. "Where are my manners?" said Ben. "This gangly turd here is Joker," he said, indicating a twitchy man with dilated pupils, "and that's B-Boy with his cap turned backward like a faggot. You already met Pinball, and I'm Ben." He winked to Nick. "I figure we start out friendly and take it as far as you want to go."

Nick wasn't about to introduce himself. "Spiffy uniforms," he said, aware of Alison on the couch, her hand near her purse with the flip phone. "Next time tell the boys to avoid wearing steel-toed biker boots, though. It blows the ensemble."

"The uniforms ain't meant to fool you," Ben said, "not for more than a second anyway—it's for the neighborhood-watch types who see all of us big uglies jumping out of a van and might get curious. Instead, they spot the Pony League uniforms and go back to watching *Wheel of Fortune*."

"Yeah, and this way you get to carry bats," said Nick.

"There's that, too." Ben grinned. He suddenly grabbed Alison by the hair, jerked her away from the purse.

Nick rushed him. He didn't take more than two steps before a bat slammed into his midsection. He heard Alison cry out as he fell to his knees, gasping, holding on to the floor as he tried to stop the room from spinning. He picked up his glasses, put them back on. He could see Joker's hands in front of him, grease rimming his nails, the knuckles jailhouse-tattooed with the words *Fuck you*.

"That's enough, Joker," said Ben.

Joker unwound from his hitting stance, tapped the top of Nick's head with the bat like it was home plate. "Sure, Ben," he said, his bony face creased with disappointment. "Remember though, I got first ups."

Ben let Alison go. Blond hairs drifted onto the carpet. "Know why Joker gets first ups? 'Cause he's the one spotted you two coming out of Doc's crib with the Angel. He followed you. We've been watching the house ever since Doc took off. You think we're stupid?" His thick neck flushed. "You must be another college boy."

"What do you want?" said Alison. "Just tell us."

"I like her attitude," said Ben. "No bullshit heroics like G.I. Joe, just 'What do you want?' A real pleaser, huh, Joker?"

"Great tits too, Ben."

The bikers laughed. It sounded like rocks being broken. Nick glared at Ben. He noticed. "Look at this guy, Joker," said Ben, eyes narrowing. "He's got a real hard-on for me. What did I ever do to you, G.I. Joe?"

"Maybe he can see into the future, Ben," said Joker.

Ben chuckled. "Maybe. He patted Nick on the back. "B-Boy, help him into that swivel chair. It's the first inning."

Nick whirled, slammed the heel of his hand into Ben's face—it was a glancing blow, Ben backpedaling. Before Nick could follow up, Joker rapped him in the side of the head with the bat and Nick went down again. He was still dazed when B-Boy threw him into the chair and strapped his left wrist tightly to the arm of the chair with one of those studded-leather bondage belts the heavy-metal bands favored. Nick could smell sweat and beer and dirt, felt B-Boy's belly nudging him as the biker started on the other side, cinching Nick's right elbow down with another belt. Just the right elbow. He was helpless in the chair, but his right hand and forearm could still swivel freely.

Ben watched, rubbing his cheek where Nick had hit him. He looked happy.

"You comfortable?" asked B-Boy. "Strap's not too tight?" He gently laid his cap over Nick's face, then punched the cap, sending the swivel chair skidding backward. More laughter.

Alison grabbed a pen off the desk, stabbed Pinball in the chest and raced for the hallway door. She almost made it, but Joker caught her, dragged her back into the inner office, groping her breasts while she clawed at him. He threw her across the couch, his hands and face scratched up.

Pinball came after her but Ben called him off. "Look what she done to me," pleaded Pinball, blood staining his shirt.

"I don't blame her," said Ben. "If it was me, I'd have shoved it in your eye." He turned back to Nick, pushed the swivel chair up against the desk. "You see what I have to deal with? The smartest one in the whole bunch was Doc, and he goes and fucks me. There's mornings I wake up and say to myself, 'Ben, crime don't pay.' "

"Come closer, Ben," said Nick. "I can't hear you."

Ben kept his distance. "I like your style. Ah well," he sighed. He cleared off the desk with a sweep of his arm, the red nylon jacket flashing past, knocking papers and the Rolodex onto the floor. "Put your right hand on the desk."

Nick hesitated.

"Don't go chickenshit on me now, G.I. Joe," Ben said. "You two been showing some serious colors." He nodded at Alison. "*Both* of you. I like that." He looked at Nick, his tiny eyes sharp as tenpenny nails. "Come on, you look like you got quick reflexes . . . Besides, if you don't want to play, the blonde's gonna have to."

Nick slid his free hand out.

"Step up to the plate, Joker," said Ben.

Joker stood on the opposite side of the desk from Nick, holding the bat over his head like a meat-ax.

Nick jerked his hand back.

"Don't do that," said Ben, his face suffused with an excited glow. "We got rules to this game: You're allowed to move your hand side to side on the desk, but you can't pull it away. Every time I ask you a question and I don't like the answer, Joker takes a swing at your hand. Just your hand. You got that, Joker? That last time wasn't funny—my wife kept asking me what got splattered all over my shoes."

"What if Joker misses?" asked Nick.

"Three strikes he's out," said Ben. "Then B-Boy is up."

"I'm *always* last to bat," complained Pinball.

"This is quite a game," said Nick. "Has anyone in my position ever won?"

"Well," said Ben, "it's not really that kind of game."

Nick laid his hand on the desk. It trembled.

"There you go," said Ben. "First question—"

"You're not going to get away with it," said Nick.

"People been telling me that my whole life"—Ben grinned—"and I'm still here."

"Yeah, but where are you?" said Nick.

Ben glared at him, unzipped his red jacket halfway down, warming up. "First question. What's the Angel doing keeping company with you two? The Angel don't ride bitch, he's strictly solo. What's he need you two for?"

"The Angel scares you, doesn't he, Ben?"

Wham! The bat crashed into the desk an inch from Nick's hand, splintering the wood. Nick hadn't seen it coming, he'd just reacted.

"Strike one," said Ben.

"If the Angel doesn't get you, the cops will," said Nick. "Then there's me, Ben. You're surrounded."

Ben barked laughter. "I love this guy." He rested his big hands on the end of the desk, just beyond Nick's grasp, close enough for Nick to see a piece of gristle caught between his yellow teeth. "Second question. Does the Angel know where Doc is hiding?"

"Oh, he's getting close," said Nick.

Ben nodded. "What about the money? Does the Angel think Doc still has the money with him?"

"The Angel knows better," said Nick. "So do you, Ben."

Wham! The bat slammed into the desk. It must have grazed Nick's pinky, because the end of his finger was flattened, the nail split and bleeding. Nick didn't feel it at first. Then he did, a wave of pain crashed over him and he almost threw up, blinking back tears.

"Strike two," called Ben. "Foul tip."

"U.S.A.! U.S.A.!" B-Boy chanted, hefting his bat, cheering Nick on. "Keep that hand moving, G.I. Joe!"

"Just a second." Joker peeled off his baseball shirt, stretching bare-chested, taking practice swings in the air. His muscular torso was sheathed in smooth pink burn scars. He looked like a newborn Gila monster. "Okay," he said, positioning himself, knees flexed, ready.

"You did the job yourself, didn't you, Ben?" Nick gasped. "These cretins would have just gotten in the way."

"Hey Ben," said B-Boy, peeking through the venetian blinds, "somebody parked next to their Range Rover. There's some big . . . Shit, Ben, it's that big nigger cop that was looking in Doc's windows yesterday."

Nick took a deep breath, started to yell a warning to Thorpe, but Joker jabbed him in the chest with the bat, knocked the wind out of him.

"I know what a cretin is," snarled Joker. "It's like a retard, right?"

31

CALVIN THORPE WAS standing outside his car, checking his notebook for the office number, when he heard Alison call his name. He looked up toward the third-floor windows of the office complex and waved. He started toward the stairway, carrying the paper grocery bag of oranges, strawberries, and bananas, carrying it from the bottom so that it didn't break. He had included a couple of containers of nonfat yogurt for himself. He was going on a diet and this time he was going to stay on it.

Alison had been excited when she called early this morning, going on about how she and Nick had new information that would "make your mouth water, Calvin." Well, Thorpe had some new information for her and Nick too.

Thorpe bounded up the stairs, eager to see the two of them. They were quite a couple: Nick volatile and brooding, a tough customer, but there was something about him that Thorpe liked. Alison . . . she was smarter than Nick, soft and playful as a kitten but with claws to match.

He remembered yesterday morning, walking in on them in the living room. Clothes everywhere but where they were supposed to be. He smiled to himself. There was a time he would have been unnerved at the intimacy between Nick and Alison so soon after the murders, but he had seen their mutual attraction that first night, all of them standing in the rain over the dead. Sometimes death actually hastened passion, hurrying them toward each other's arms, fleeing from oblivion.

He walked down the hall, found the office number he had written down. He knocked on the door, then opened it, bumped it wide with his hip as he carried in the bag of fruit. "Alison? Nick?" He walked toward the inner office. Something smelled bad, like dirty socks. "Where are—"

Something hit him on the back of his head and Thorpe stumbled, the bag falling, oranges rolling across the floor. The breath roared out of him as he was hit again. Thorpe ran forward, covering his head with his hand, reaching for his pistol in its waist holster.

Nick was sitting at a desk in the office, trying to speak but his mouth wrapped with masking tape. Alison was slumped on the couch, groggy. Nick struggled to get up from the chair, his eyes on Thorpe, warning him. Thorpe ducked, just missed being brained, taking the blow from the baseball bat on his shoulder, numbing the whole arm.

The creep who had hit him reared back with the bat but Thorpe kneed him, lifted him off the ground, sent his cap flying. The man groaned, his cap slumping to the floor. Thorpe drew his pistol but before he could turn, someone else smacked him from behind, a bat smashing into his hand, sending the gun skidding across the floor.

Thorpe lowered his head, charged this new assailant, a huge side of beef with a swastika earring. Thorpe drove him backward across the office, the man off balance, the swastika earring spinning between them. He gave the man a final shove, sent him careening through the window, glass breaking, the man screaming as he fell.

Thorpe was hit again, this time a chopping blow to the kneecap. Pain exploded behind his eyeballs as he staggered, dropped to one knee. That's when he was hit again with a baseball bat. A home run to the side of the head. Right out of the park. Thorpe saw a flash of red out of the corner of his eye, then he was falling slowly, leaflike, taking his time, settling down onto the carpet with warm blood rushing over his ear. He heard Alison calling his name again and again. He wanted to tell her he was all right, but he couldn't get his mouth to work.

It must be spring cleaning because someone was beating the carpets—thud, thud, thud—getting out all the dirt. There were two sets of feet standing over him, flailing away. All this cursing. There was a lady present too.

Thorpe's head was at a weird angle. He could see Nick tearing at a leather strap that was holding down one of his arms, using his teeth, finally breaking free. Go, kid, go. The creep with the backward cap was still bent over on the floor. Alison sat up on the couch, reached for her purse.

Nick rushed toward Thorpe, ripping the masking tape away from his mouth. It looked like he was holding one of his hands funny. The men beating the carpet stopped. Thorpe was glad. The sound of it was making him sick to his stomach.

A man without a shirt moved away from Thorpe and swung

at Nick, but Nick scuttled out of reach, holding his side like he was in pain. The shirtless man backed Nick into a corner, bat raised high. His skin was covered with scar tissue the color of bubble gum. Double bubble.

There was a loud noise. Another. Then another. Nice tight pattern. The scarred man folded up like an old highway map, bending at the knees and waist, flopping onto the floor.

Alison was on the couch, holding a pistol ... a 9mm. It looked good in her hand. She was pointing it at the man in the red jacket when a wastebasket banged into the wall next to her, sent papers everywhere. She flinched, shooting wildly as the man in the red jacket and the one with the backward cap dashed out. The one with the cap was running funny from where Thorpe had kicked him.

Thorpe could see Alison follow them out the door as Nick bent over him. She came right back and picked up the phone.

"Calvin?" Nick looked terrible, his face swollen, one eye going purple. "Can you hear me, Calvin? Blink if you can hear me."

Thorpe blinked. It was the least he could do. Things were beginning to hurt. His knee. His back. His head, God his head was killing him. What hurt worst of all were his feet. Which was strange. He knew he hadn't gotten hit in the feet. Maybe the man in the red jacket had been standing on them while he worked him over with the baseball bat. Thorpe had known all along that it wasn't the carpet that was being beaten. You do what you can to put your mind at ease.

"Did you call 911?" Nick said to Alison.

"Calvin?" Alison was right beside him. She was crying. Something about a pretty woman crying ... it made her look even prettier. Wonder why. "Calvin? Please don't die. I've called for help. You just hang on. Okay?"

Thorpe blinked. He didn't do such a good job of it this time.

"Calvin!" shouted Nick. It looked like a shout, the way his mouth worked, but it didn't sound very loud. "Calvin! Stay awake! Listen to me! There's an ambulance on the way!" He turned to Alison. "He's going into shock," he said to her.

Alison leaned over him, so close that her hair tickled his face. Nice. She gently wiped his face with a cool, wet cloth. That was good too.

"Calvin!" Nick took his hand. "Calvin! Do you . . . do you want me to pray for you?"

Alison looked at Nick like he was speaking Japanese.

Thorpe managed to raise an eyebrow.

Nick blushed. "I'm trying to help."

"Where the hell is the ambulance?" said Alison. She went to the window. "Hey Calvin, that guy you tossed is still on the pavement. Way to go. Calvin?" She picked up the phone. "Nick, isn't there some kind of special police code that means 'Officer down'?"

"I don't know," said Nick. "I'm sure there is, but . . ."

It's 998, thought Thorpe, 998.

"Calvin!" said Nick. "Don't fade on us now, we're almost there. That bastard in the red jacket, he was the one who killed Sharon and Perry. He killed the man on the tape, too. Jeffrey Lomax. Doc. Can you hear me? Blink, Calvin. Calvin!"

Thorpe knew about it. A friend at DEA had called last night, told him that while Jeffrey Lomax didn't have a police record, the DEA had him in their "known associates" file of Ben Telaris, a major drug supplier. Telaris didn't have a chance. As soon as Thorpe took a little rest, just a little nap, he was going after Telaris. He couldn't wait to see the look on the doper's face . . .

"Calvin!"

Shhhhhhhhhhhhhhhhhhhhhhhhhhhhhhh.

32

Alison was waiting for Nick when the elevator doors at the ICU opened. She stopped him before he could get out, gently took his arm, and pressed the down button.

A cop yelled from down the hall, sprinted toward them, but Alison just waved as the door closed. She took the bouquet of flowers from Nick, inhaled their fragrance, then tossed them in the corner.

"Those are for Thorpe," Nick said testily.

"Calvin's not going to be smelling anything for a while," said Alison, impatiently punching the down button again.

The doors opened and three nurses stepped in, talking nonstop until they got off a few floors later. When they left, the flowers were gone.

"What happened?" said Nick. "Why can't we wait in ICU? Is Thorpe . . . Is Calvin dead?"

"He's still in a coma—"

"Then why can't we—"

"Damn it all, Nicky, you're going to get *arrested* if you go up there," said Alison. "Harris, the young cop you tossed around the night Sharon and Perry . . . Harris is telling everyone that we set Calvin up, lured him to the office so he could be murdered. Harris says Calvin told him this morning that he was close to breaking the case wide open."

"Son of a bitch." Nick chewed his lower lip as the elevator beeped out the floors. "Why would they bust us?" said Nick. "I mean, you *killed* that scumbag Joker. You saved Calvin's life." He looked at her. "You saved my life, too. How does that fit with the ambush theory?"

"It's not me they're after, Nicky."

"Oh." Nick was having a hard time thinking. Just when he thought the worst was over . . . "Are you sure, Alison? I gave a statement to this new detective who's taking over the case . . . what's his name? Stanz. He didn't even wait until I came out of X ray. Sitting there asking me questions while the tech is telling me not to move a muscle. I told Stanz to find Ben with the red jacket if he wants to get a pat on the snout from the chief. He seemed really interested—"

"It was an *act*," said Alison. "I gave him a statement too, a complete description of Ben and the other one. He hardly looked up from his notebook the whole time. He's just going through the motions until he gets the paperwork from the DA." Her voice softened. "I wish Calvin was still in charge of the case. I know you thought he had it in for you, but at least he was waiting until he had something solid against you."

Nick could still see Calvin pushing Pinball through the third-story window, could still hear the whooshing crackle of the glass breaking—sweet music. "I miss him too."

The elevator doors opened into the lobby and Alison darted ahead. She had changed into jeans and a T-shirt before the cops had taken them to the hospital. Nick was wearing baggy shorts and a tank top. With the bandages layered around his torso he looked like he had on a bulletproof vest. It still hurt every time he took a deep breath. He was lucky—that's what the ER doctor said. Just three cracked ribs and a crushed finger. Nick stared at the splint on his right hand. That was going to slow down his guitar playing. There goes the Grammy.

"What's so funny?" said Alison.

"Nothing."

They took a cab back to the agent's office in Newport. There was something forlorn about Thorpe's Pontiac parked beside the Range Rover in the parking lot—the Buick was like a big old dog waiting for its master to return. Maybe he wasn't coming back.

Two cops were sitting around guarding the office, smoking cigarettes and drinking Pepsi. Scaring off the bad guys. Alison sweet-talked the cops into letting them take their overnight bags but Sharon's 9mm had already been removed, kept for evidence. When they left, Alison gave each of the cops a kiss on the cheek and an autographed photo of herself in a bikini from the agent's file cabinet.

Nick insisted they first drive to Doc's house. Maybe the Angel would still be there. Maybe one of the bikers was still staking out the house. He still had hopes of getting to Ben before anyone else did, finding out if there were any other games that small-eyed bastard knew how to play. When they got to Doc's house, though, it was swarming with cops. Alison had told the detective about Jeffrey Lomax in her statement, told him about the Angel, too.

"Now what do you want to do?" said Alison as they stopped at a traffic light on Pacific Coast Highway in Laguna. They could see the usual cutthroat pickup basketball games on Main Beach, elbows flying for the watching throng. One of the players was tripped as he went up for a layup and landed hard. Nick heard applause. The light turned green. Alison headed North on PCH as the fight broke out. "Nick?"

"Let's go to Huntington," said Nick. "I want to check in with Rebar, see if his friend Gwyneth managed to get the 911 tape. We can stay at his place. No one will find us there."

"Why don't we just get a motel?"

"Why don't you just drive?"

"Why don't you kiss my ass, Nicky. What do I look like, your chauffeur? Why are we going to crash at this Rebar's house?"

Nick shook his head, looked out at the passing scenery. "Someday, I want to get on a plane and go someplace where the man is still king of the castle. Where you don't have to explain anything—"

"It's called Bubbaland," said Alison. "It's a dirty little country where nobody has all their front teeth, and the height of humor is lighting farts at halftime. You can grab the next plane there if you want, I'm staying here."

Nick held his head in his hands, finally looked her way. "If I told you that I had a brain tumor, would that get me off the hook for what I just said?"

"No."

"If I said my vocal cords were taken over by a Martian control device implanted during an alien abduction when I was a teenager—"

"Don't make jokes about that, Nicky. I saw this video on Fox . . . it looked real to me."

Nick laid his head back in his hands.

"I'll write it off to temporary stupidity," said Alison.

"I want to see Rebar because of his girlfriend, Gwyneth," admitted Nick. "She has connections with lots of cops. This new detective didn't even react when I told him about Ben. Maybe Gwyneth can ask around, find out something—"

"What if she does, Nicky? You want to find this guy *yourself*? After what he just did to us?"

Nick stared at her. One of them was crazy. "Yeah," he said slowly, *"especially* after what he did."* He punched the windshield, the splint flying off his finger. "You think I trust the police to handle—"

"Don't give me that crap, Nicky. You don't *want* the police to handle it. I saw your face in the office, when those bikers were swinging away at your hand. You were scared . . . but you were getting off on it."

"I almost wet my pants."

She shook her head. "I'm worried about you, Nicky. I'm worried about myself if I stay with you."

Nick smiled. He liked the sound of that.

Alison kept driving. At least they were headed in the right direction. "Where in Huntington?" she said at last.

"Far end of the beach," said Nick, "almost to Sunset." He watched her stern profile slowly soften. "Thank you. Driver."

Alison fought back a smile. "You're still an asshole."

"I love you too." He meant it as a snappy comeback but it sounded serious. Sounded good.

Alison kept her eyes on the road. "Was that another one of those brain tumors?"

Nick didn't answer. He must have dozed off, because they

were passing the oil fields around Huntington Beach when she shook him.

"Are we there yet?" asked Alison.

"Little further," said Nick, sitting up, pain shooting through his side. He shook out some of the pain pills the doctor had given him, chewed them down. Yuck. "It's right past where we met up with Perry's agent walking on the beach. See those houses on the edge of the sand? There's a parking lot . . . Make a left at the next light. Let's stop at that market first, I need some more adhesive tape for this hand. We can pick up some food and beer, too. If we're going to be uninvited guests, we might as well be uninvited guests bearing gifts."

Rebar's front door was off its hinges, leaning against the doorframe. Nick knocked anyway. "Rebar?" He could hear music playing inside the house. "Rebar?"

The music was turned down. Nick heard someone shuffling toward the door, sand underfoot. Rebar peeked through the space between the canted door and the frame. "Hey, Nick," he mumbled. "What are you doing here?"

"Can we come in?" Nick looked at him. "You all right?"

"Yeah, sure, come in."

Nick slid the door against the wall and he and Alison followed Rebar back into the house, the young man shambling toward the living room, holding on to the wall for support.

The living room windows had been opened to the beach, sand billowing through the screens, coating the floor and everything else with a fine, gritty patina. Fast-food wrappers floated on the breeze. A rusty hibachi tilted next to the sliding glass door, a couple of burned cans of Spaghettios on the grill. A cracked surfboard was in the middle of the room, piles of food-crusted paper plates strewn across its neon-orange surface. A barbecue fork was stuck into the nose of the board.

Rebar flopped down in a brown corduroy beanbag chair, scratched his buzz cut, head lolling. He was wearing a wrinkled paisley kilt and a purple vest, his bare arms tattooed with medieval scenes of knights and dragons, wizards and princesses. A body-heat fairy tale.

"What's wrong?" said Nick.

Rebar looked at Nick, bleary-eyed, then at Alison, then back to Nick. "I called you yesterday, but you weren't there." It sounded like an accusation.

"You want a beer?" asked Alison. "Orange juice?" She took the grocery bag from Nick and set it down beside Rebar. "Apple?" She held out a Red Delicious.

Rebar took the apple but didn't take a bite. "She's gone, man," he said to Nick. His chin quivered.

"Gwyneth?"

"Who else, man? Who fucking else?"

"Where did she go?" asked Nick. "I need to talk with her."

"Good luck, dude. You find her, tell her she can come back anytime. She calls me, I'll come get her."

"Why did you call Nicky?" asked Alison.

"I miss her voice inside my head," Rebar said to Nick. "It's a beautiful sound, man, better than any music I ever played. I'm more alone now than ever. What am I going to *do*, man?"

Alison popped open her flip phone, punched in the number of the hospital. She got the main switchboard, asked for ICU. She started to sit down on the couch, then thought better of it. No way were they staying here tonight.

Nick had bent down beside Rebar, talking softly to him. "Why don't you take a shower and we'll go out for dinner. You'll feel better after—"

"I don't want to feel better," said Rebar, standing up, going over to the portable stereo, rummaging around in the stack of tapes and CDs.

Alison closed the flip phone. "Calvin is still in a coma," she said to Nick.

Nick shook his head.

"Here." Rebar tossed Nick a cassette. "Here's a copy of that 911 call you wanted. Gwyneth told me to tell you you're welcome. That's why I called you yesterday."

Nick stared at the cassette. It was a little anticlimactic now. He already knew who killed Sharon and Perry. He slipped it into Rebar's stereo. Why not?

The tape hissed and crackled. *This is 911,* said the operator. *What is the nature of your emergency?* There was the drumbeat of rain drowning out the caller's voice. Nick remembered the sound of the rain that night, pounding on the roof of the Porsche, remembered standing in the rain staring down at Sharon's body, the tiny hole in her back where the life had leaked out. . . . *Please speak up, sir,* said the operator. A door slid shut, the phone booth door, the caller's voice clearer now, but still clouded by the storm.

Nick adjusted the graphic equalizer on the stereo, boosting the high-end vocals, trying to filter out as much of the extraneous noise as he could. Rebar had a good system, but the quality was still mushy. He heard the caller give Nick's address to the operator. There was a blast of static. Lightning maybe. Then the caller's voice, clearer now, saying, *Listen bitch, this is a situation that requires police attention, so beam your ass over there.* Dial tone.

Nick rewound the tape, listened to it again, fiddling with the controls. There was something about the caller's voice . . . a tone . . . an inflection that was vaguely familiar.

"What is it, Nicky?"

Nick rewound the tape.

33

THERE WERE THREE parking valets in white dinner jackets at the entrance to Tulane's estate, standing in front of the gate, watching Alison and Nick pull up in the Range Rover.

Before the Range Rover came to a complete stop, there was a valet at each door. "Name, please," said the one with a clipboard.

"Nick Carbonne." He looked at Alison. "Plus one."

As the valet ran his finger up and down the guest list, Nick could hear music pounding from the house. He saw a couple stumble out of the front door of the mansion, laughing, almost falling down the steps. Their faces were painted with polka dots. The man wasn't wearing any pants.

"Sorry, Mr. Carbonne, you're not here."

"I talked to Tulane an hour ago." Nick watched the polka dot couple. The woman was literally leading the man by his penis. He could see Alison smiling, out of the corner of his eye.

"You're not—"

"Why don't you call him?" said Nick.

It took four calls into the house before the valet got Tulane on the phone. A few moments later Alison handed the valet the keys and they were let in the gate. As they walked up the driveway they saw the polka dot couple sprawled on the grass, surrounded by lawn jockeys, an army of silent sentinels, one hand thrust forward in salute, watching the couple having sex, the two of them making cat sounds as they worked.

"Nice party, Nicky," said Alison as they passed the couple. "I guess this time you're gonna dance with me."

Tulane was a twenty-two-year-old rock star who had hit it big with his second album, very big. Nick had helped him with the production of his first album, even laid down some tracks in the studio himself. Tulane was an average guitarist but he had a sexy voice and a lean, white-trash charm that had sold over eight million albums domestically. A high school dropout, he had bought the three-acre estate in Lemon Heights from a Stanford software entrepreneur who had gone bust. Paid cash.

The music got louder as they climbed the steps to the house. Must be Tulane's new album. People were milling around inside, smoking, guzzling Tulane's favorite booze, Southern Comfort, straight from the bottle. Empties and crushed Moon Pies littered the floor, the chocolate-and-marshmallow concoction ground into the Oriental carpet. Someone had thrown a chair through one of the stained-glass windows. Velvet paintings of Elvis and Tammy Wynette beamed down blissfully from the walls, the king and queen above the throng.

A Confederate flag covered the dining room table, a silver

platter heaped with dull white powder at the center. It didn't look like coke. Coke was evil but it looked like clean snow on a new morning. This stuff just looked evil. A skinny blonde lurched into the table, hoisted a fingernail of the powder first to one nostril, then the other. Nick asked her if she had seen Tulane, but she just stubbed her cigarette out on a high-backed chair and wandered away.

A man with a tiger-striped face offered Alison a joint, his mouth frozen into a crooked grin. She started to take it, then waved him away. She looked at Nick. "You're a bad influence, Nicky. Thanks."

People wandered past with their faces painted like lions and leopards. He asked a woman with a boar's snout and painted tusks if she had seen Tulane.

The boar woman grunted, her eyes dilated so they were all pupil, suddenly grabbed his crotch.

Alison knocked her hand away from him.

The boar woman bellowed, stared at Alison, the sound dying in her throat. She edged away.

"What's downstairs?" said Alison.

"Recording studio, game room, swimming pool, gun range—"

"Let's go," said Alison. "That's where the boar queen came from."

They fought their way downstairs, going against the current, a steady stream of lions, tigers, and zebras coming up, snorting, pawing the steps, laughing, grab-assing each other, their eyes wild in the light.

The swimming pool was filled with people, some half dressed, some naked, paint dripping off their bodies. Music pounded from the speakers, too loud to talk to anyone. Nick checked the faces, but he didn't see Tulane.

The recording studio was crowded too, maybe twenty or thirty people dancing, their nude bodies painted with animal patterns. Another table heaped with dull white powder was in one corner. Nearby, a short man in a loincloth was painting a chubby girl, dabbing on leopard spots while she did a slow turn.

Nick heard pounding on the thick glass of the control room. He turned and saw Tulane waving at him.

"Nick! How you doin', boy!" said Tulane as Nick and Alison walked into the control room, closed the door behind them. Tulane was tiger-striped, whiskers etched across his cheeks. "What happened to your hand?"

"I banged it on a desk," said Nick.

"Got to be more careful." Tulane checked out Alison. "Why don't you and your galfriend let Lulu paint you up?" He indicated a tall woman with dreadlocks bent beside him, her body painted lioness yellow, her fingernails long and curved. She held Tulane's testicles in one hand as she carefully tiger-striped his penis. "You tried the Lovetron?" He nodded at a heap of white powder on the mixing console. "It's dynamite, boy." He looked down at Lulu, grinned at Nick. "Goes right to your johnson."

"I need to use your soundboard," said Nick, shouting over the music. "I got a tape I want to check out."

"What do you think of my new album?" asked Tulane. "I really wanted to use you, boy, but the suits at the label—"

"Album sounds . . . good," said Nick. The album was badly mixed, way too much bass, and Tulane's vocals were flat. "You mind if I work on this?" he said, taking the 911 cassette out of his pocket, slipping it into the B deck. He flipped a switch and cut off the control room speakers. The only sound was Tulane's breathing as Lulu finished striping his penis. In the studio, Nick could see the dancers moving faster and faster, but the heavy, soundproof glass kept the album at bay.

Tulane watched Nick put on headphones. "I thought you called because you wanted to come to the party."

"Not tonight," said Nick.

"Lulu come up with the idea of having this zoo party," Tulane said proudly. "Next week we're doing Dead Rock Stars night. You're invited."

Nick looked at Alison, who was trying not to laugh. "Thanks," he said to Tulane as Alison put on a pair of headphones and sat down beside him. He switched on the computer, booted up the DINR audio-manipulation program and started the tape. Nick could see Tulane and Lulu behind him, reflected in the glass, snorting fingernails of white powder.

What is the nature of your emergency? asked the 911 operator, the sound wave on the computer screen jumping with the sibilance in her voice. The audio quality of Tulane's equipment was dramatically better than Rebar's home unit, but the tape was still only marginal, the sound of the rain beating down on the phone booth muting the caller's words. *Please speak up, sir,* said the operator.

"What now, Nicky?" said Alison. "I can't hear anything."

Nick rewound the tape, replayed the call, this time isolating the background noise between the vocals with the DINR program: the hiss and hum, the static, the rain. He hit the LEARN button and the computer sampled the specific audio signature of the noise, the characteristic frequency, and stored it in its memory. Nick replayed the call and this time the computer filtered out the signature. Much better. He replayed it again, fine-tuning the signal, bumping up the vocal range. He could make out the caller's words now:—*isn't* my *problem, lady.* It wasn't Ben's voice, not him or any of the other bikers.

"Wow," said Alison.

The lights in the studio had dimmed. Through the glass, Nick could see that the dancers had reached a new level of excitement, lions, tigers, and bears, oh my, soundlessly groaning and grunting, mouths contorted, filling themselves with skin.

Alison put her hand on Nick's arm. She lifted his headphones off one of his ears. "Let's hurry up, Nicky. I want to get out of here." She sounded nervous.

Nick followed her gaze. Saw Lulu lying on an equipment table, clawing at the air as Tulane's tiger stripes slid into her, his head thrown back, roaring.

Nick let the rest of the call run, the computer smoothing out the background. *Listen, bitch,* said the caller, *this is a situation that requires police attention, so beam your ass over there.* There was a contempt in the caller's voice that permeated everything. He was surprised the operator hadn't just hung up, disregarded the call. *Listen, bitch.* No hint at what the caller must have seen at Nick's house, no sense of outrage, disgust, or sorrow. *—so beam your ass over there.* It was the mocking, supercilious tone of the caller that was familiar to Nick, that had prompted this visit to Tulane. He still couldn't place it.

A strobelight was flashing in the studio, the striped and spotted bodies jerking spasmodically, freeze-framed in lust. The table of white powder had been overturned, the animals grunting as they sucked it up off the floor. Zebras were fucking lions, tigers fucking gazelles, predators and prey mixing it up under the strobelight flicker. Somewhere William Blake was smiling. An ocelot pressed her breasts against the window of the control room, licked the glass.

"Can we go now, Nicky?" said Alison. "Nicky?"

Nick had to tear himself away from the sight of the ocelot grinding her shaved pubis against the glass in front of his face. "What's your hurry? I thought you were the one who was ready for anything."

"I'm ready for anything I want to do," she said, glaring at the ocelot, "but I don't want to do *this*. About a month ago, I was at a party where everybody was snorting this stuff . . . It turned into a bad scene fast. I want to get out of here. You done?"

"Almost." Nick rewound the tape again, closed his eyes as he listened. There. Right after the lightning flash. Something. He rewound it six digits on the counter. There. What *was* that?

Tulane and Lulu were grunting in the corner, the tiger and the lion scrambling around on their hands and knees.

"Listen to this," Nick said to Alison. He replayed that section of tape, heard the crash of lightning, then an instant of relative silence immediately afterwards, a faint sound within the silence, inaudible without Tulane's studio equipment. "What is that?"

Alison shook her head. "A bell? Like a Hare Krishna might wear? I don't know . . ."

Nick replayed it, the two of them listening.

The scene in the studio was deteriorating rapidly. The animals were fighting now, paint smeared across faces and flanks, writhing in the strobelight flicker, heads thrown back, their screams muted by the soundproof glass, somehow made more terrible by the silence. They watched as a lion woman was dragged off kicking and biting, saw a green snake man held down, blood smearing his scales. Eden was over and done with, the law of the jungle had reasserted itself.

"Don't look," Nick said to Alison, turning away, "you'll just get distracted." He rewound the tape, notch-filtered out the lightning flash. Played it again. "I *know* that sound," he said, trying to place it.

"Me too," Alison said softly. "Just a few days ago . . ."

"Dog tags," said Nick, feeling a warm wave flow through

him, the calm before the storm. He knew where he had heard that distinctive sound before.

"A soldier?" said Alison. "I don't think so, Nicky."

Nick smiled. "That's not what I meant. Dog tags. Like Lassie. Rin Tin Tin." They both jerked as a giraffe crashed against the door to the control room, clawed at the lock.

"Let her in, boy," Tulane called from between Lulu's legs. "The more the merrier."

34

"WAKE UP, NICKY." Alison was shaking him. "He's closing up," she whispered, scooting down in the driver's seat.

Nick rubbed his eyes, stretched, his knees banging against the dash of the Range Rover. The lights of the Circle K across the street blinked off. Bradley, the clerk they had questioned last Monday, stepped outside and locked the front door behind him. He pulled a bush jacket around his shoulders, tried the door. The small wirehaired dog at his feet shook himself, license tags tinkling.

It was the sound of the dog tags that Nick had recognized on the 911 tape. He had needed Tulane's studio equipment to hear the tags, but it was the smugness in the caller's voice that had originally nudged Nick's memory at Rebar's place. It wasn't Bradley calling 911, but there was the same speech pattern, the same nasty, supercilious tone that Nick knew he had heard before.

It was three A.M., the stars peeking through the clouds, and a dampness in the air that made Nick feel stiff and sore. The baseball bats might have had something to do with it too. Alison had suggested they go to a motel after fighting their way out of Tulane's zoo party, but he couldn't wait to learn more about the 911 call.

"Do you want to talk to him now?" asked Alison, watching Bradley check the street, then pull a Twinkie from his jacket and gobble it down. He unwrapped another one and tossed it to the dog. The dog leapt for it, caught the creamy treat in midair. "He's leaving, Nicky."

"Let's wait," said Nick. "I don't see a car . . ."

They waited until Bradley and the dog walked across a vacant lot and headed down an alley, before getting out of the car, following at a distance, not talking, staying in the shadows between the streetlights. The dog wasn't on a leash, keeping up with Bradley's pace. It was quiet, hardly any cars on the street, the jingling tags rattling the silence. Bradley and the dog left a trail of junk-food wrappers in their wake—Twinkies, HoHos, Ding Dongs—the two of them sugar-shocking their way home.

Nick and Alison gave Bradley plenty of room, cutting through a darkened strip mall offering take-out teriyaki, Spanish-language videos, and discount computers. Some skateboarders had set up a makeshift ramp in the mall parking lot using wooden pallets and cardboard. Nick stopped for a moment to watch them jumping into space, knees bent, hair flying, free of gravity. Temporarily.

Bradley veered across the street to The Heights, a run-down

two-story apartment building with cracked aggregate-concrete steps and a front yard of green-painted pebbles. He waited while the dog added a fresh turd to the collection on the pebbles, then unlocked the corner apartment and went in. A light was already on inside.

"Now what?" said Alison. "Don't do anything stupid, okay?"

"Thanks for the vote of confidence," whispered Nick, moving closer, hearing voices in the apartment. They scooted around the side of the building, weeds and trash crunching underfoot as they edged toward the window. The blinds were slightly raised— Nick felt Alison's hair brush against his cheek as they peeked in, seeing Bradley and somebody else sitting on a couch in the dimly lit living room.

They walked back to the front of the apartment, unsure of what to do. Nick was about to try the direct approach and ring the buzzer, when they heard the dog whining and scratching furiously at the door. Nick heard Bradley's voice inside, demanding to know what the dog's problem was. The door opened. "Get out, you—"

Nick pushed Bradley aside, stalked into the apartment, Alison right behind him. The dog licked Alison's hand. The guy on the couch jerked upright—Nick saw a reedy, young intellectual wearing a Leatherface sweatshirt over white jeans, an arrogant mouth twisting with fear. He threw up his hands. "I surrender!" He looked like a slightly older version of Bradley.

Nick turned away from him, staring instead at the big-screen television that dominated the room.

The picture was grainy and dark, shot from a distance with a telephoto lens, but he could still recognize Alison's face in candlelight, her hands clutching the carpet, her head thrown back, groaning as Nick drove himself into her from behind.

Alison stood watching the television, her head slightly tilted, like a film critic evaluating a new release.

"We have no drugs," said the guy with the Leatherface sweatshirt, his voice the same petulant whine that was on the 911 tape. "No guns. Take the money and credit cards, cowpoke, ride off into the sunset."

"They're not here to rip us off, Phillip," Bradley sneered. "Wake up and smell the Starbuck's. It's *them.*"

Phillip squinted at them in the television twilight, finally nodded, recognizing them from the shadowy video. "You have no right to barge in here," he blustered. "Get out before I call the police."

"Yeah, you probably have the number on your speed dialer," said Nick, leaning into Phillip's pinched face. "I know you called in that 911, motherfucker," he said softly.

"What if he did?" snapped Bradley. "That's what a good citizen is supposed to do."

"My little brother misspoke," demurred Phillip, hands still trembling. "I don't know what you're talking about."

Nick had noticed the family resemblance, but there was an important difference between the brothers. Bradley was hostile and insulting, but at least he was upfront with his attitude, blatant as a spitting cobra with its hood spread. Phillip was more covert—an arrogant little man with furtive eyes under a mousebrown thatch of thinning hair. He looked like one of those skulking protomammals that fed on dinosaur eggs.

"How did you bust Phillip for the 911, Kojak?" Bradley asked Nick. "*He* must have screwed up—I don't give you credit for that much brains."

Nick ignored him. "What did you see that night?" he said to Phillip. He watched the man's Adam's apple bob, his neck directly over Leatherface's upraised chain saw. "What did you see at my house?" Nick growled. "One way or the other, Phillip, you're *going* to tell me."

"It . . . it was a very rainy night," said Phillip. "I should have stayed home. Damn dog didn't want to go. He wanted to stay with Bradley at the market, stay nice and warm, but I insisted. Rainy nights can be good for filming, gives the scene moody atmospherics. You ever see *Seven Samurai*?" Phillip asked. "Kurosawa? Climax takes place during a torrential storm. Perfect touch." He tucked his legs under him, his white jeans starched and raspy. "Besides, everybody stays home when it rains, and leaves their curtains open . . ." He looked at Nick. "Damn dog. I should have listened to him."

Nick held his gaze. Phillip had dirty eyes. He must use the dog as an excuse if he got caught peeping—he could always say the dog ran off or he was taking the dog out for a walk. Nick leaned closer. "Did you actually see it happen, or did you get there after the fact?"

"All that rain . . . there was nothing I could do," said Phillip. His face turned sullen. "We have a waterproof housing for the camera. Supposed to be waterproof anyway, it sure cost enough—"

"Did you see her die, Phillip?"

"Oh." Phillip shrugged. "Yes." He stared at the television, the images of Nick and Alison reflected on his shiny face.

Nick turned. He saw Alison astride him on the screen, her breasts swaying in the candlelight. He looked around and everyone was watching the television, their eyes bright.

"Not bad, huh?" Bradley gushed to Alison, sitting on the arm of the chair. "See how I establish the scene, going wide, then look here . . ." The camera zoomed in on Alison's fingers clutching the carpet. "That's my signature," he preened. "You get the audience in the picture, then zoom to a tiny piece of action and their mind fills in the rest."

"I like it," said Alison, watching her nails claw at the rug onscreen. "Adds a whole new tension to the scene." She sounded serious. "You do your own editing?"

"All in-camera for *me*," bragged Bradley. "If I had a shotgun mike I could have picked up the scratching of your nails as I racked the zoom."

"Little brother thinks he can turn shoddy camera work into a career," said Phillip. "He should have stayed wide—"

"Fuck you, Phillip," said Bradley. "You can't even hold a shot steady."

Nick walked to the VCR and removed the tape. The screen went snowy gray, filled the room with a harsh, pixilated light.

"Hey!" said Bradley. "That's not your property—"

"It's not yours," said Nick. "You trespassed on our lives. You didn't ask permission, you just—"

"So, according to you, if I film the Pacific Ocean, the video belongs to the Coastal Authority?" snickered Bradley. "Is that your reasoning?"

"I know how you feel, Nicky," said Alison, "but I'm kind of a trespasser myself. Don't get me wrong, I think *we* should keep it . . ." She smiled at him. "Our first time. Wow."

"Yeah, wow," said Nick. Was he the only one who believed that some things deserved to remain private? That an intimacy shared with strangers was an intimacy lost? He looked at their bemused faces and felt very old.

Nick strolled around the room. The building was shabby but their apartment was neat and clean, their video equipment top of the line: Sony thirty-five-inch stereo monitor, Mitsubishi stereo

VCR. The video camera they had used had to be professional quality to have recorded by candlelight, particularly using the telephoto lens. Nick indicated the bookcase lined with videotapes. "Are all these of people fucking? Is that what you do? Sneak around peeping, making your punkass videos? Amateur porn—"

"What are your intellectual qualifications to judge our work?" said Phillip. "My brother and I are video guerrilla artists. Beyond *vérité*. Beyond deconstruction. We're beyond the edge— your limited imagination couldn't begin to grasp the significance of our work."

"You saw Sharon and Perry being murdered and didn't do anything to stop it," said Nick. "I can grasp that." The brothers didn't answer. "Did you film the murder, too, Phillip? A serious artist like yourself, you wouldn't have just watched. You'd have made the most of the opportunity."

"Indeed." Phillip nodded. "We're planning on submitting it to Sundance." He beamed. "It'll make *Reservoir Dogs* look positively limp by comparison."

Alison looked shocked. It was about time.

"I'd like to see the video," Nick said quietly. It wasn't a request.

"That's not possible," said Phillip.

"Do it, Phillip," said Bradley.

"Don't tell me what—"

"Look at him, Phillip," said Bradley. "He's a thug who thinks he's in the right. John Wayne in *The Searchers*. Belmondo in *Breathless*. Bruce Willis in anything."

"Cancer Man in *The X-Files*," said Phillip, pulling back from Nick.

"Nothing more dangerous than a moron on a mission," said

Bradley. "Do *you* want to deal with him, Phillip? Show him the video. Make him happy."

Phillip got up and went over to the VCR.

"How did you know where we live?" Nick asked Bradley.

"That's my specialty," Bradley said proudly. "Anytime a babe comes into the market and uses a credit card, I keep the flimsy. Name and address. Sharon walked in a couple of weeks ago, bought a six-pack of dark Beck's, a half-gallon of low-fat, and a copy of *Spin*."

"This is how you pick your . . . subjects?" said Nick. "All these videos?" He indicated the bookcase lined with tapes. "Random selection?"

"Nothing random about it," said Bradley. "Sharon smiled at me. Asked me how it was going." He shook his head. "I liked her." He glanced at Phillip as the older brother took a tape from the stack and queued it up. "I wanted to film her first, but it was *his* turn to go out."

Alison sat beside Nick on the couch, took his hand. Nick tried to maintain an emotional distance from the shadowy image on-screen, Perry and Sharon in the hot tub, their faces obscured by steam. The date and time flickered momentarily in the lower right-hand corner: 22:18. Nick and Alison were just leaving the party in L.A., saying good-bye to the band. Nick had his alibi, but it didn't make him feel any better. The sound track of the video surged with rain. "Was . . . was this where you came in?" said Nick.

"Yes," said Phillip. "Lucky timing, huh? Got there right as the action was beginning. Like Cartier-Bresson said—"

Lightning flashed, briefly illuminating the scene. Sharon was crying as Perry turned away, pleading with someone off-screen. The camera was trembling.

Nick put his arm around Alison, squeezed her tight. His lungs felt heavy; it was an effort to breathe, but he couldn't stop himself from watching. He stared at Sharon's bare shoulders, remembering the softness of her skin. He noted how she kept her distance from Perry in the tub, then felt disgusted with himself for noticing.

Alison cried out as the gunshots burst from the speakers, flinching as though *she* had been shot. Nick felt hot tears running down his cheeks as Sharon hurdled from the tub and across the patio toward the lens, the camera jerking, trying to keep up with her. Nick was yelling for her to run, run, run, knowing she wasn't going to make it, unable to stop himself from urging her faster. She collapsed at the edge of the flagstones, rain splashing across her nude body, the pitter-patter of a million tiny violations . . .

The camera jiggled, caught a flash of red as the killer approached, his face out of the frame. The screen went white. Alison clung to Nick, weeping.

Phillip turned off the VCR but left the TV on. No one said anything for a long time.

"Phillip," Nick asked finally, "when you called 911, why didn't you just tell them what had happened? You just said that there was an 'incident.' No specifics. Why?"

There was a faint beeping coming from Alison's purse.

"Why didn't you tell them?" asked Nick.

Alison wiped tears from her eyes, fumbled with her purse.

"Oh," said Nick. "I get it." He wasn't angry. He was tired from lack of sleep and stress and being beaten up. Most of all he was tired of being right. "If you had told 911 that a murder had taken place the cops might have hurried, and you needed time to get back to the house from the Circle K. You filmed the cops rolling up, didn't you, Phillip? Must have been quite a sequence, all those light bars flashing in the rain, neighbors coming out of their houses in their bathrobes . . . Did you get me arriving on the scene? Great video, right, Phillip?"

Phillip looked at Bradley.

Bradley looked at Nick. "Fucking award winner."

35

"HELLO, ALISON," SAID the Angel, speaking into his cellular phone. "I'm sorry to wake you but . . . Oh. You're certainly up late. Or up early." He checked his watch: almost four-thirty. "Is Nick there with you? I'm glad to hear it. Two by two, that's the way of the world, isn't it?"

"Not at some of the parties I been to lately," she drawled.

The Angel watched a tiny insect crawl across the steel compressed-gas cylinder resting beside him and onto the back of his hand. "I hope I'm not . . . disturbing anything, but you did give me your mobile number. May I speak with Nick?" He smiled as the insect took flight, iridescent wings fluttering into the night.

The Angel settled down on the hill overlooking Ben Telaris's exclusive neighborhood as he waited for Nick to come to the phone. The dry scrub crumbled under his blue suit pants. The storm last weekend had been quickly sucked up by the sandy soil. Southern California had been a desert before the coming of man—it was still a desert everywhere the water sprinklers couldn't reach, locked into a cycle of drought and flash floods, mud slides, and brushfires. Ah, the cycle of life, the terrible swift sword of Mother Nature.

Not in this development, of course. There was plenty of water to go around here. The large houses were surrounded by ripples of green turf dotted with security-service signs, the grass lush and spongy underfoot, teeming with life. Less than one hundred yards away from all those swimming pools and landscaped gardens, the surrounding hills were brown and crisp as straw. Scorpions lived there.

The Angel was perched above it all, his vision unobscured. He could see everything from this spot. Find the pivot point and use it, that was both his strategy and his philosophy.

"What is it?" said Nick.

"Your phone manners, Nick," clucked the Angel, "mind your manners. This is your lucky day."

"Yeah?"

"I appreciated your letting me hear that tape of Alison and Doc," said the Angel. "I'm going to return the favor at sunrise today."

"I don't want any favors from you."

"I can understand that. Still, I think you'll enjoy what I have planned. Where are you now? Don't bother answering, just make sure that you're at Anaheim Stadium in an hour. I'll call you then. Sunrise is just before six, so be ready to move fast."

"What's this about?" said Nick.

"It will be worth the trip," said the Angel. "I've never lied to you before, have I?" He hung up before Nick could answer.

The Angel scanned the deserted streets with a pair of low-light binoculars. The neighborhood below was still quiet, but the biker that Telaris had stationed in one of his new Corvettes had fallen asleep in the last hour, slumped over the wheel, that ridiculous backward cap fallen off onto the seat beside him.

The Angel hefted the compressed-gas cylinder onto his shoulder, wrinkling his suit jacket. It weighed over a hundred pounds but he moved effortlessly down the steep hill and across the backyards, not approaching the house directly, taking a roundabout course over fences and hedges, moving silently toward Telaris's lavish rambler.

He left the compressed-gas cylinder beside one of Telaris's well-tended orange trees at the back of the house, picked himself a juicy one, inhaling the orange fragrance as he carefully made his way around to the front. The biker slept peacefully in the Corvette parked in the driveway.

The Angel watched the man snore as he peeled the orange in one long spiral strip with his fingers. He ate the orange slowly, savoring the sweet juicy taste, licked his fingers clean. He glided toward the open driver's-side window, reached in and grasped the man's head—one hand on his chin, the other on his crown. "Wake up," he whispered.

The biker's eyes flew open, widened for an instant before the Angel twisted sharply, breaking his neck.

The Angel gently laid the man's head back against the seat, then rubbed his hands with the orange peel to cleanse them of the man's pungent body odor. He walked back to the rear of the house, moved the compressed-air cylinder next to the central air-conditioning intake, opening the valve of the tank with a *hisssssss*, feeding in the gas.

Butyl acetylene was light, colorless, and highly flammable,

odorless in its natural state; a distinctive rotten-vegetable smell was added at the refinery for safety's sake. *Usually* added. The gas in this cylinder was odorless.

He squatted beside the air-conditioning unit, listening to the gas hiss, imagining the volatile fumes wafting through the rooms on quiet little fingers. There wasn't nearly enough gas to fill the sprawling, ranch-style home, merely enough to rise to the ceilings in a thin layer no more than an inch or two thick. It would be enough. It would be plenty. It would be glorious.

A light went on in the house next door and the Angel froze, waited. A few minutes later the light went off. The Angel gathered up the now empty cylinder and was on his way, up the hill, moving quickly now, eager for the dawn. He stowed the tank in the trunk of his parked car, then went back to his spot overlooking Telaris's house and called Nick.

"We're at the stadium," said Nick, answering on the first ring.

"I hope you didn't break any traffic laws getting there," the Angel teased him.

"Now what?" said Nick.

The Angel gave him Telaris's address. He repeated it twice, even gave Nick directions. "You and Alison should hurry, Nick. You won't want to miss this."

"Have you found the man who killed my wife?" demanded Nick. "Is that what this is about?"

"Very good, Nick, no wonder I like you. Intelligence is a gift from God. Be honest now—haven't you ever wanted to give the gift back?"

"I want him," said Nick.

"I know just how you feel."

"Keep the money he owes you," said Nick. "Let me have *him.*"

"The money is irrelevant," the Angel said dismissively. "Money is merely symbolic; it's the *debt* that counts. This world exists in an equilibrium more fragile than you can possibly imagine, Nick. A debt unpaid upsets that balance, looses chaos and uncertainty—the oceans turn to dust, rain the color of blood, the sky falling . . . I could never allow that. Hurry now. You know where to go, you don't want to be late." The Angel smiled. "I take such vast pleasure in the restoration of order. It's almost a sin." He broke the connection.

The sun was a sheer slice edging over the Santa Ana Mountains to the east, its dim light not reaching the neighborhood. Not quite. The Angel still had time to sit and contemplate the fruits of his labors. He sat on the hillside for several minutes, not moving, not thinking, letting the breeze blow through him. He took a deep breath. Ahhh. It smelled like rain. Not now, not today, but there were clouds gathering in the distance.

The Angel picked up the phone again, this time punching in Telaris's number. It rang seven times before he answered, his voice thick with sleep. "Good morning, Ben," the Angel said cheerfully. "Time to die."

Telaris cursed and hung up.

The sun was higher now, streaking the night sky with orange and yellow, revealing the arc of heaven for all the world to see. There was nothing like it. The Angel loved sunrise and he loved it best at fifty or sixty thousand feet up, seeing the sun coming around the rim of the earth through the canopy of an F-15, setting the world afire. Supersonic sunrise. There was nothing in creation like it.

He waited until he spotted Alison's Range Rover driving slowly down the nearby streets, Nick sticking his head out the window, checking addresses.

The Angel took the small radio transmitter out of his pocket, checked to make sure it was set to the proper frequency. Then he called Telaris again. It was adding insult to injury, but the Angel had long since come to terms with his own cruel sense of humor. It was an indulgence he allowed himself. A last vestige of his humanity.

Telaris picked up the phone. He didn't say anything but the Angel could hear his raspy breathing.

"Ben?" said the Angel. "Do you have any marshmallows?" He pressed the radio transmitter, instantly activating the six microreceivers that he had placed in the light fixtures when he had visited Telaris's wife a few days ago. The microreceivers were barely bigger than a match head, and they sparked for barely a second, but it was enough.

The ceilings of the house boiled with flames, fire rolling down the walls, sucking up the oxygen, and setting the draperies ablaze. The house was now a vast torch, fed by the butyl acetylene, delivering up its possessions. Through the telephone, the Angel could hear Telaris shrieking over the sound of the firestorm.

The Angel watched through the binoculars as the Range Rover screeched around the corner, racing toward the house, which glowed now with a lovely orange light, every room ablaze. Windows all over the house were cracking now, popping out of their frames from the heat, one after the other. The Angel could hear what sounded like Ben beating at the front door, kicking at it from inside as he struggled to get out. Someone seemed to have put superglue in the deadlocks.

Telaris would be racing from room to room, his night turned to brightness raging, inhaling fire into his lungs with every breath. The Angel listened again to the telephone but all he heard was a roaring, like the howling of a great hot wind.

Alison drove the Range Rover in front of the house and Nick leapt out, just as the picture window in the front exploded.

Telaris stood in the living room, beating at the jagged shards of glass with a kitchen chair. He staggered to the windowsill, tried to climb out through the flames, but the glass cut him, the metal frame so hot it was melting. He lunged over the window, tearing himself open in his desperation to escape.

The Angel trained his binoculars first on Alison, saw her shock and horror, watched as she turned away. Nick waited on the sidewalk as Telaris crawled toward him, pajamas ablaze. Nick took a step toward him, as though to help, then stopped.

Telaris held out his hand to Nick, then crumpled onto the front lawn. Onto that cool damp grass. He raised himself up on one knee. The Angel had been wrong—Ben wasn't wearing pajamas. It was his *hair* that was on fire. Mats of hair on his legs and arms, coarse, black hair on his back and belly burning in the morning light.

The Angel could see pity and pain and a profound sadness flicker across Nick's face as he watched Telaris, saw his shoulders slump with the ache and weariness of journey's end, but the Angel saw no joy in Nick's gaze, none at all. Ah well.

Telaris looked around, blind, more of a blister than a man now, still searching for the Angel, knowing he was out there watching. You had to hand it to Ben. Sitting on the hill, the Angel silently applauded the man's fierce defiance. Dying well was the best revenge.

Lights were going on in houses up and down the block.

36

NICK AND ALISON peeked in the door of Thorpe's hospital room. Thorpe waved feebly from the bed and they scooted inside before one of the nurses could spot them. The room was in the intensive care unit, and technically restricted to immediate family.

Thorpe was in a body cast, an IV bottle dripping into his left arm. It was Thursday morning, five days after he had been attacked by Ben Telaris in the office of Alison's agent. Thorpe hadn't regained consciousness until Monday.

Alison bent over the detective, kissed him gently on the cheek, her lips brushing the bandages that covered much of his head. "How you doin' there, big man?" she said, her voice husky, putting on a brave front, holding back tears.

Thorpe beckoned her closer. "You bring me anything to eat?" he whispered in her ear. "They're trying to starve me to death in here."

"I got a German chocolate cake on order," she promised, "just need the go-ahead from your doctor." She sat on the edge of the bed, holding his hand.

"Hey, Calvin," said Nick, standing a little way off. Thorpe beckoned and he took a hesitant step. "We won't stay long. We were worried about you . . ." He hung his head. "I wanted to thank you for what you did at the office, taking on those bikers like that."

"You put up quite a fight yourself," Thorpe whispered, voice dry. "You and Annie Oakley here."

"I'm sorry I didn't do more," said Nick. "I tried—"

Thorpe waved him silent. "Didn't you hear?" he croaked, "the DA was the *real* hero, I'm just a prop for the TV cameras."

The district attorney had called a press conference yesterday trumpeting the successful closing of a "particularly vicious double homicide." The DA cleared his throat while the cameras rolled. "The killer," he announced, "one Ben Telaris, after severely injuring one of our best detectives"—here he indicated the photo of Thorpe next to the podium—"was murdered, apparently by his confederates early Sunday morning, just hours before our officers were going to arrest him." While he would have liked to try Telaris himself, the DA joked, "sometimes the criminal element save the taxpayers money." That sound bite led the nightly news.

"At least the DA showed your picture," said Nick. "Sharon and Perry were just referred to as 'innocent victims.' "

Thorpe beckoned him closer. Nick pulled a chair up to the

side of the bed. "I never really thought you did it," whispered Thorpe. "I had to do my job, buddy."

Nick patted his hand. "No hard feelings, Calvin."

Thorpe stared at him with those dark eyes. "It was bad at Telaris's house, that's what one of the uniforms told me. He said Telaris looked like a burned pot roast." Thorpe shook his head. "After what he did to me . . . what he did to *all* of us"—he winced, shifted slightly—"I can't say I'm sorry. The Good Book says forgive and forget, but I'm not a saint."

"Neither am I, Calvin," said Nick.

"I don't know about you two, but I'm just happy that we're all alive," said Alison. "That's as close as we're going to get to having the last laugh. I'll settle for that."

"I'm not laughing," said Nick.

The door opened and an attractive, buxom woman walked in, stopped when she saw them. She had long, straight hair and a smooth mocha complexion, and was dressed in an elegant cream-colored suit with dark brown piping. She looked at Thorpe, then at Nick and Alison. "Can I help you?" she said, her eyes wary.

"Friends," whispered Thorpe.

"I'm Alison," she said, standing up. "This is Nick. Calvin was working on our case when—"

"So *you're* Alison," said the woman. "Calvin told me you were a pretty young thing, and I see that he told the truth. He told me about you, too, Nick—I'm glad he didn't have to arrest you. Calvin is fond of you." She calmly offered her hand. "I'm Eunice Thorpe. It is a pleasure to meet you both."

Alison shook her hand but Nick just stared. "You're Calvin's wife?" he said, confused. "Did you . . . did you come back after you heard that he was in the hospital?"

"Come back?" Eunice Thorpe looked at him like he was crazy. "Where do you think I've been?"

Calvin was coughing. Maybe it was a laugh. Alison passed him his glass of water.

"Calvin said you had walked out on him," said Nick, glancing at Thorpe. "He said you left him for another man."

Eunice Thorpe had a rich, rolling laugh that crinkled her eyes and made the room seem festive.

"Calvin?" said Nick. "What's going on here?"

"You told this boy I ran off with another man?" chuckled Eunice Thorpe. "Don't you go putting ideas in my head, Calvin." She set down her purse, fluffed the pillow under his head, kissed him long and slow.

Alison nudged Nick.

Eunice Thorpe sat on the bed, smoothed Calvin's hair. "Who did I run off with, Calvin? Wesley Snipes? Luther Vandross? How about that Forest Whitaker? Yeah, he's the one—I *do* like a man with some meat on him."

Thorpe wagged a finger at her.

Eunice Thorpe looked at Nick. "Calvin tells you his wife left him. That way you and Calvin have something in common. It worked, didn't it, Nick? Just a little?" She crossed her legs. "Sometimes Calvin's wife is cheating on him, so he understands the jealous suspect who murdered his own wife. Other times Calvin's wife has died. Killed by a drunk driver, if the suspect is a drinker. Overdosed, if the suspect is a doper." She dabbed the corners of Thorpe's mouth with a tissue. "Once you were even gay, weren't you, Calvin? You remember that?"

Calvin nodded, laughing.

Alison joined in. Nick didn't.

"I am surprised at you, Calvin," teased Alison, "but if you ever decide to bag this police thing, you've got a real future in show business. There's always a need for good character actors."

"Does this mean he's not a lay preacher, either?" Nick said.

"Preacher?" Eunice Thorpe had to hold her sides. *"Preacher?* That's a new one, Calvin. You're branching out."

"A man can't rest on his laurels," whispered Thorpe. He stretched out his hand to Nick but couldn't reach him. "Come on, Nick, where's your sense of humor?"

"Everything is fine, Nicky," said Alison. "We're together, that's all that counts." She put her arms around Nick, kissed him.

Nick hesitated for a bare instant, remembering the Angel's gleeful insistence on the world's fragile equilibrium; then Nick kissed her back, kissed her gently, wanting to lose himself in her hot embrace, to touch something that was real and certain and sure.

37

NICK WAS TALKING with Sharon, raising his voice to be heard over the sound of rain outside, the wind howling like it was wounded. Nick was telling Sharon that he had found out who had killed her. That he had seen the man die with his own eyes. Watched him burn. Ben Telaris was dead now. Just like Sharon. They both knew she was dead, but neither of them wanted to bring it up.

Rain, rain, go away, come again another day. Nick told her that he wished things had been different between them, wished he could take back things he said, things he didn't say. Sharon smiled. It was the same smile he had fallen in love with, the last thing that remained after all the arguments and silences, more lasting than their wedding vows. Till death do us part.

Nick said he wished that she had told him she was going to leave him. Maybe he would have asked her to stay. Maybe . . . She looked at him, raised an eyebrow. He heard thunder. Right. Maybe he wouldn't have done a thing to stop her.

He asked her if she knew about him and Alison. No response. None was needed. He was sorry about many things . . . so many things, but that wasn't one of them. Alison. Now he was smiling. Rain, rain . . . washing Sharon away, piece by piece. He could see right through her now. He reached out for her but it was way too late for that. Sharon said something to him but he heard only thunder. No . . . it wasn't thunder. It was a telephone ringing.

The answer machine picked up. "Alison? Are you there?"

Nick opened his eyes. Alison was already sitting up on the sofa bed, the sheet sliding off her. He felt goose bumps where their skin touched. Alison fumbled the receiver to her ear. "Elliot? What are you doing calling me so late?"

"It's barely nine," said Elliot. "Turning in a little early these days, aren't we? You must *really* be tearing up the bed, hmmm?"

"What do you want?" said Alison.

"I've spent the last few days trying to reach you," chided Elliot. "Your bitch of an agent says she no longer represents you, and your clone phone has been disconnected. I never expected to find you *still* playing grunt tag with Nick . . . Hello? Alison? If you're too busy to talk just say so. I'm doing *you* the favor."

"That would be a first." Alison tickled Nick's back with her nails.

It had been two weeks since Nick and Alison had watched Ben Telaris burning on his front lawn. They had spent the time driving to the beach, or just lazing around the house, making love. Nick made a few desultory efforts to find work, but he didn't want to think too much about the future —when she was leaving, when he was going to start sleeping upstairs.

Unlike him, Alison had called Dolores Dahl every morning, left a succession of messages on the machine, the calculated gaiety in her voice sounding increasingly forced. Cliff had finally called back, tipsy, the crash of the Malibu surf in the background—he said Dolores was at Betty Ford for a 'tune-up' but would make sure that Alison got an invitation to the next screening party. "Honest injun, babe," he had signed off.

"The gentleman we spoke about on your last visit," said Elliot, "the big fan of yours, he's interested in meeting you. Don't hang up. He's a rather famous director, strictly A-list . . . you would recognize his name if I said it."

"Who is he?"

"Ask me no questions, darling," said Elliot. "He begins shooting his latest film in Europe next week and wants you to read for a part. He's leaving tomorrow, so if you're interested you're going to have to do it tonight."

"I don't know . . ."

"Up to you, I'm just networking. Let me know if you do any more jack-off tapes, I can always—"

"What's his name, Elliot?"

"My lips are sealed," said Elliot. "That's the way he wants it and he is a very, *very* good client. *Ciao*—"

"Wait!" Alison looked at Nick. "Is he there now?"

"Any minute," said Elliot. "I've got some satellite-feed Larry King outtakes that he's interested in. Come by if you want, but he probably won't stay past midnight."

Alison heard a dial tone.

The Range Rover took the twisting curves up toward Elliot's house atop Lookout Point, wheels churning mud, the headlights making little headway against the rain and dark.

"You going to say anything, Nicky?"

"I don't trust Elliot. You do. What else is there to say?"

"It's not a matter of trust, this is the way it works in Holly-wood," she said, her eyes on the narrow road, shiny in the red glare from the instrument panel. "A studio honcho sees you on the street or at the gym and your life changes just like that. Fast as a snakebite."

"Interesting phrase," said Nick as the windshield wipers slapped back and forth.

"Sharon Stone was doing walk-on bimbo parts when Paul Verhoeven picked her for the lead in *Basic Instinct*. It *happens*. You should know that, Nicky—one day you were just another band in L.A., next day you're hearing your songs on radio. You got your big moment, Nicky, I'm still waiting for mine." Her knuckles were white on the steering wheel. "This director who wants me to read for him tonight might have been the same one that Dolores Dahl told me about—I got me a second chance, Nicky, I'm sure as shit not about to let it pass."

The headlights caught a black Mercedes parked outside the chain-link fence at the crest. Alison hit the brakes, the Range Rover skidding into the Mercedes. "Whoops." Alison glanced at the camera atop the fence.

"The gate's ajar," said Nick, uneasy. "I thought Elliot was paranoid about security." One of the floodlights atop the fence was out too.

"The director must have left it open," Alison said eagerly, pushing wide the door. "Race you!" She dashed through the rain, feet splashing through the puddles as she ran.

Nick caught up with her on the doorstep, the two of them laughing, wet and steamy, Alison butched out in a black motor-cycle jacket with the collar turned up and tight black jeans, her hair slicked back. Nick was wearing a T-shirt, shorts, and the same wrestling-team jacket he had worn on the night that Sharon and Perry were murdered. He had hesitated before putting it on, but it was his favorite jacket. He used to think it was his lucky jacket, too.

Alison rang the bell while Nick wiped his glasses. They heard Hillary Clinton blaring: *Bill! Get in here!* No answer from the intercom.

Nick tried the door. It opened. He stood there on the threshold. "I don't like this."

Alison rushed through, shaking rain off of her jacket, flinging back her hair. She looked at him. "You coming?"

Nick followed her down the narrow hallway. Right turn. Then a left. Deeper into the labyrinth. They passed barred windows which trembled in the storm, panes cracked, the frames crumbling. Nick kept looking at the speakers overhead, waiting for Elliot to give them directions, but there was only an occasional squawk. A succession of cameras followed their progress, red lights blinking.

"Now what?" said Alison as they came to another split in the hallway. "Do you remember from last time?"

Nick listened. There was the sound of rain beating on the roof and, far away, the waterfall in the main room, separated from them by innumerable passages. "Which way, Elliot?" he said to the camera, exasperated. "Either tell us, or we're leaving."

"We're not leaving," said Alison. "Maybe this is part of the screen test," she whispered, showing her best side to the camera. "Woman in jeopardy, like Julia Roberts or Sandra Bullock? My character has to show a cool resourcefulness—"

"Elliot's toying with us," said Nick. "He gets us out of bed, out of the house and into the rain, now we're wandering through his little maze while he watches and listens. How do you know there *is* a director waiting for you? Maybe Elliot is just making a video of you to sell—"

"Is it so hard to believe that some movie big shot could be interested in me, Nicky?" Her face was tight and angry, eyes flashing. "You think I'm happy carting my portfolio around to every production company in L.A., buttering up middle-aged talent coordinators with grabby hands. You think I like driving the 91 freeway after midnight in that piece-of-shit car sounding like it's ready to throw a rod?"

"The Range Rover has mechanical problems?" Nick said innocently. "I was just about to make you an offer. Gosh, I'm glad you told me."

Alison shook her head, finally gave him a tough smile. "You are *such* an asshole."

"I was hoping you hadn't noticed."

"I'm not blind, Nicky." She peered down each of the corridors. "I think it's a left."

They took the left, followed it another twenty feet, then around a sharp turn, through a door, and into the dim emerald-green light of the main room, the mist from the cascading waterfall sparkling in the air like snow in a glass globe. Elliot lay on his round bed, propped up on thick, fluffy pillows, watching them.

The speakers suddenly crackled with Alison's voice: *It don't matter what you like, buster. What matters is what I like. Git some, that's my philosophy of life.*

Alison looked at Nick. The waterfall was louder now, rolling down one whole wall of the room, splashing noisily into the koi pool.

What about you, boy? Alison said on the tape. *Are you afraid to go after what you want? How long are you going to be happy sitting in the dark, fantasizing? You're the quiet type, I can tell, and that's too bad. Be* bold. *Faint heart never won a fancy lady.*

Nick stared at Elliot. There was no response from the man on the bed. Nick moved closer. The tape was louder now, hissing and popping—the sound of bacon that first morning after the murders . . . Nick waking up, hearing Thorpe's bacon frying on the griddle.

You're touching yourself, Alison teased on the tape. *I didn't tell you that you could do that. Imagination is a dangerous thing, get you in trouble fast. You like that idea, do you? No more safe and sane for you, lying there with the covers pulled up around your chin—no, you're going to be one of them wild boys living out on the edge where things get nasty. You got big ideas, I can tell. I know you, boy, better than you know yourself.*

Nick was close enough to Elliot now to see the tracks of his tears down his cheeks. No . . . they weren't tears. Someone had shot out Elliot's eyes.

Nick ran back to Alison, grabbed her and dragged her toward the door they had come through. It was locked.

You want to play with me, though, you best be bold, purred Alison.

38

"IS THIS BOLD enough for you, Alison?" It was Doc's voice. Nick recognized it from the murder tape, that same phony, prep school coo.

"Doc?" Alison looked around at the speakers, confused. She hadn't seen what had happened to Elliot. "Doc?"

"Mais oui, le docteur est ici," cackled Doc.

Nick tugged at the door, beat against it with his fists. He saw movement out of the corner of his eye, turned as a tall, gaunt man strolled through a door on the opposite side of the room, a pale, jumpy redhead with freckled skin and a thin mouth, wearing pressed gray slacks and a buttery cardigan. Ichabod Crane with a *GQ* makeover.

"So this is the new boyfriend," Doc said to Alison as he glanced at Nick, his eyes bright with hate. "I thought you would have dumped him by now." He twirled a revolver with his index finger, gunfighter style, daring Nick to make a run at him. "One can only associate with the lumpen proletariat so long before the experience ceases to charm." His smile was sharp and thin as a fishhook. "I speak from experience."

Nick watched Doc spin the revolver, the back-and-forth action hypnotic in its simplicity. Sleight of hand was always simple, fooling you with just a bit of misdirection. Once you accepted the false premise that Doc had been murdered, you never caught up. "Congratulations, Doc," said Nick, fighting down his fear. "You had everyone fooled. You had *me* fooled anyway."

"Fooling you wasn't really a consideration, asswipe," said Doc. He looked at Alison, smoothed his sweater, minding his manners now. "It *was* a temptation to remain safely out of sight though, but I had to come back for my girl. Money isn't everything."

Alison calmly stood there, hands on her hips, head high. Nick didn't know what she was auditioning for, but she was going to get the part.

"You thought I was all talk." Doc preened for Alison. "That's all right, you can admit it. I'm *glad* you dismissed my feelings for you. It spurred me on—now look what I've accomplished."

"I am impressed," said Alison.

Nick was taken aback by the cool admiration in her voice.

"You should be." Doc kicked over one of Elliot's televisions, the picture tube imploding with a dry pop. "You wanted boldness, I've given you boldness. I've risked everything for you," he swaggered. "You have no idea of the chance I took."

"Yeah, we've met the Angel," Nick said.

The pistol shook in Doc's hand. He almost dropped it. "I'm not afraid of the Angel."

"I can see that," said Nick.

"I *used* the Angel," Doc bragged to Alison, breathing hard. "Playing with fire . . . that's what I did." He was waving the pistol now. "I knew the Angel would track you down eventually . . . The Angel is very thorough, he had to be curious about the last person who called me. I almost left the caller-ID box at my place, but I didn't want to make it too easy for him." He swallowed. "Didn't want to make him suspicious—"

"I don't know why you were so concerned about the Angel," Alison said lightly. "He seemed like a perfect gentleman."

"A gentleman?" Doc suddenly walked over to where Elliot lay, eyeholes gaping, jammed the pistol into his mouth and pulled the trigger. Alison closed her eyes as chunks of Elliot's head blew out across the pillows. Doc wiped the barrel on Elliot's pajamas. "See that?" he said to her. "That was *nothing* to me, but I'm not in the Angel's league. No one is." He lowered his voice. "I took him on anyway. I didn't care about him. All I thought about was you."

Alison checked her manicure. "Well, thinking is easy, isn't it?" she said, not even looking at Doc.

Rain pounded against the roof as the storm raged outside, buffeting the hilltop. Nick stared at her as the thunder rolled around them.

"Move!" Doc jabbed the revolver at Nick, beckoned toward the waterfall. "I'll show you, Alison. You're going to have a front-row seat for this." He nodded at Elliot's body as she passed the round bed. "Elliot was a grubby toad, but hey, he was the one who introduced us. He sold me this tape of you talking to some dumb suburban dad . . ." He licked his dry lips. "Yes, Elliot was useful. Just like Perry." He led them to the edge of the pool surrounding the waterfall. "Take off your clothes, Nick."

"You first."

Doc spun the pistol. "Do it." He watched Nick slowly take off his clothes, eyes black and shiny as beetles in dead wood. "That the dick you used to fuck my girl?"

"You don't have a girl," said Nick. He wasn't cold. His skin was warm and tingling. Is this what it felt like when you knew you were going to die?

"Get into the pool," said Doc.

"You're repeating yourself," said Nick. "This is a rerun of your hot-tub scene with Perry and Sharon."

"It's a little different this time," Doc corrected him. "You're the only one who gets his tootsies wet." He put his hand on Alison, claiming her, then jerked the revolver at Nick. "Into the pool."

Nick jumped in, slipping on the rock-strewn bottom. The water was cool, waist-high. "What did you mean when you said Perry was useful?" The waterfall splashed behind him, spraying his bare back, the mist filming his glasses.

"Are you feeling a little . . . vulnerable, Nick?" inquired Doc. "A little under the gun, maybe?"

"You kill me in here there's going to be questions about the similarities," said Nick. "Cops will start wondering—"

"What are you complaining about?" said Doc, rocking gently on his heels. "You got to try out my girl for the last few weeks. That's what Elliot told me. How was she, Nick?"

Nick looked at Alison. "She's the best."

Doc took a deep breath. "It's okay," he reassured Alison. "I don't blame you. You were just biding your time until something better came along." He caressed her hair. "I know what that's like. I was so bored with this outlaw-biker horseshit, crank and carburetors and Evil Dead forever, blah-blah-blah. I've been starved for conversation for so long, Alison . . . I knew the first time we spoke that you were going to change my life."

"So what took you so long?" Alison smiled. "I was beginning to think I'd lost my touch."

"It's not so easy . . . making changes," Doc said, his gaze drifting off. "I told myself it was just talk between you and me, told myself it didn't mean anything, but I couldn't get you out of my mind. Then . . . it must have been a couple of weeks after our first call, after you told me, be bold, just a couple of weeks later, I was in the men's room of some cycle joint in LaBrea ramrodding this burger queen. She had her hands braced against the sink, a cigarette in the corner of her mouth, while I crammed it in. I looked up and she was watching herself in the mirror, blowing smoke rings in the air, and I knew, I *knew* I was meant for better things."

"We both are," said Alison.

Doc blinked like he was caught in a bright light. "Nine million dollars, Alison. Nine million dollars and no one searching for it. We're free and clear."

"Free and clear?" said Alison. "Stallone got twice that for *Judge Dredd*. Nine million is Demi Moore money."

Doc's mouth hung open.

Alison shrugged. "I guess it's a start."

"It's not just the money," Doc hurried. "Look at the planning required. The subtlety. I had to leave just enough loose ends to pique the Angel's interest, just enough to cast doubt on Ben's story." His face sagged. "I had to leave my favorite bike behind. I *loved* that Indian."

"Why kill Sharon and Perry?" said Nick, inching closer, trying to hold himself steady on the rocks.

"Perry asked me the exact same thing when he was in the hot tub." Doc laughed.

"Was Perry part of this?" said Nick.

"Perry was too stupid to think past his next payday," Doc snorted. "I told him I owed money and needed to disappear; he pissed all over himself he was so eager to help. He was supposed to wait a couple of days after that last call, then bring the tape to the cops with my phone number." He nodded to Alison. "It might have worked, but I was . . . worried about the Angel. Anything too obvious and he's not going to buy it. I didn't anticipate your getting so involved, Nick. Thanks." He picked a speck of lint off his sweater. "I thought the red fiber was a particularly deft touch."

"You were worried about the Angel," Nick said grimly, "but that's not the only reason you killed Perry and Sharon."

Doc beat his chest. "Guilty, guilty, guilty," he mocked. "Perry said you and wifey were going out that night. I expected to find him with Alison. I wanted to fuck him up right in front of her, wanted her to see him beg." Doc spat in the water. "Here we are all over again. I must have wished on a star." He grinned. "On your knees, Nick."

Nick didn't move.

Doc spun the revolver around his forefinger. "I shot out Elliot's eyes from over fifteen feet away," he breezed, "Magooed him so fast he didn't even have time to blink." The pistol whipped back and forth. "Here you are all bare-assed, Nick . . . Where do you want me to start with you?"

Nick looked at Alison as he slowly eased onto his knees. The water was up to his neck now.

"Look at your tough guy now, Alison," said Doc.

Lightning crackled outside, thunder rattling the windows. The lights flickered out. There must have been an auxiliary power source, because the lights immediately came back on, but even more dimly now, the room swimming in green shadows.

"Kind of romantic, isn't it?" Doc crooned to Alison. "We're going to have such a great life together."

"Yes, we will, but let's leave Nicky here," Alison said, the spray from the waterfall running down her leather jacket. Even in the murky light, Nick could see a vein on the side of her neck throbbing.

"Can't do it," said Doc.

"Sure we can," said Alison. "No one will believe him—"

Doc grabbed her by the hair, shoved the revolver into her face. "You think I'm stupid?" he said, gritting his teeth. "Give me some credit. What's so special about *this* guy? After all I've done for you. For us . . . You are breaking my fucking heart."

Nick felt around at the bottom of the pool, found a fist-size rock.

"What's *he* got that I don't?" said Doc. "You can tell me, I won't get mad," he said, forcing her head back with the gun.

Alison's eyes widened but she didn't make a sound.

Doc buried his face in her hair, inhaled her scent. Tears ran down his cheeks. "What do I have to do? Tell me. I did everything you wanted. I put my life on the line for you." His tears dripped into her upturned face, the gun barrel pressed under her chin now. "I love you to *death,*" he said bleakly, pulling back the hammer. "Don't you know that?"

Nick gripped the smooth rock in his hand, holding it so tightly it should have crumbled to powder.

"You don't have to do that, Doc," murmured Alison, her hands at her sides, melting into him.

"I don't want to," sobbed Doc, the pistol still at her throat.

Alison kissed Doc, her lips parted, kissing him deep, eyes closed, her hips rotating slightly.

Nick stared at them, the sound of the waterfall filling the room.

Doc slowly lowered the pistol, kissing her back, still watchful, kneading her ass with his free hand, turning their bodies so that Nick could get a good view.

Alison broke away slightly, coming up for air, then biting his upper lip, moaning softly in the green light, taking his head in her hands. Doc's eyes fluttered shut and in that instant Alison looked directly at Nick.

As Nick surged out of the pool, she hooked Doc's leg with her foot, tripping him. She grabbed for the gun as he fell to the floor.

Gunshot!

Nick hit Doc across the head with the rock as he started to rise. The pistol slid across the floor. Nick hit him again. And again.

"N-N-Nicky?" Alison groaned, the sound so soft that it was impossible to believe it was connected to the shot.

Nick scooted over to her, gingerly touched her side. His fingers were warm with her blood.

"I'm cold, Nicky." She tried to laugh. "Just like in the movies."

He grabbed his clothes from the floor, covered her with his jacket. Déjà vu. He had covered Sharon with the same jacket the night she was murdered. Doc moaned. Nick had to resist the impulse to finish bashing his brains out. Instead he folded his T-shirt and placed it over Alison's wound; he held the makeshift bandage in place with one hand, with the other he fumbled in her purse and pulled out her flip phone. Someone plucked it out of his hand, tossed it aside with a clatter. Nick looked up into the icy blue eyes of the Angel.

"You didn't hear me this time, did you, Nick?" said the Angel. "Perhaps it was the waterfall."

"I need to call 911," Nick said quietly, continuing to apply pressure to Alison's side.

"Soon." The Angel bent over Alison, staring at her eyes. "You're going to be fine," he pronounced, straightening up.

"That's easy for you to say," Alison said weakly.

The Angel smiled at her, then walked over to where Doc was sitting up. "Doc, it's a pleasure to finally meet you."

"Please . . . don't," Doc said, the words oozing out of him.

"I was monitoring Nick's phone, in case you were wondering," the Angel said. "I still had my doubts about Ben being the guilty party, but I have to admit, I thought you were dead." He stood over Doc, grabbed one of his arms, straightening it. "You should have *stayed* dead, Doc."

"P-please . . . I'll tell you where the money—"

There was a wet, popping sound and Doc screamed. Another pop. Doc's shrieking echoed across the room, an undulating, high-pitched wail. The Angel effortlessly scooped Doc up and carried him toward Nick and Alison.

"Put him down," Nick said.

"I can't do that, Nick." The Angel stuffed his handkerchief in Doc's mouth, muffling his cries. Doc seemed unable to resist, his arms hanging limply. "Poor Doc has dislocated both his shoulders," he explained to Nick.

"He's mine." Nick held the T-shirt in place, feeling it warm now with Alison's blood. "You can't have him."

The Angel shook his head. "I appreciate your . . . tenacity, Nick, but Alison needs your attention. Your *touch*. You wouldn't do anything that might jeopardize her." He stared at Nick. "You love her. That makes all the difference."

"Call 911!" said Nick.

The Angel basked in the pale green light, listening to the rain beat against the windows. His expression was dreamy. "People think it's easy to lose themselves, Nick, but it's not. One has to travel light to have any chance at all, light as a feather, light as air, but people are burdened by their habits, their pleasures and love . . . well, *love* is the heaviest burden of all. It's what we love that brings us crashing down to earth." He nodded toward Doc. "You should be flattered, Alison." The Angel watched Nick, his deep blue eyes empty as the sky. "Do you want to know why God is God, Nick? Because he doesn't love anyone or anything."

Nick met the Angel's gaze. "Then I feel sorry for God."

The Angel started to speak but stopped himself.

"Nicky?" Alison looked up at him. "Let the Angel have him."

The Angel waited.

Nick saw Doc struggle against the Angel, frantic now, kicking helplessly. "Go ahead," said Nick. "Take him." He heard Doc scream, heard him through the gag.

The Angel carried Doc in the crook of one arm like a bag of dirty laundry as he called 911.

Nick leaned over Alison, still applying pressure to the wound, silently begging her not to die, please don't die. When he looked up the Angel and Doc were gone. He watched her chest rise and fall, afraid she was going to stop breathing. After a while he heard sirens in the distance. "The ambulance will be right here," he soothed her. "Don't try to move."

"Yeah, Nicky, like I'm going to start tap-dancing . . ."

"Shhhhh." Nick brushed hair away from her face and his hands left blood on the blond strands.

She looked up at him. "For a moment back there . . . when I was going at it with Doc, you almost believed it, didn't you?"

He shook his head.

"Come on, Nicky, you were worried. Just a little."

"Not for a nanosecond."

She smiled, pulled him closer and kissed him, her lips warm and soft. Time slowed as they breathed life into each other. She sighed as they finally parted, nestled against him, her eyes sleepy now.

Nick cocked his head, listening. The sirens sounded like they were right outside. The storm was slacking off too. He was sure of it.

POCKET
B O O K S

This book and other **Simon & Schuster** titles are available from your
book shop or can be ordered direct from the publisher.

0 671 85469 0	**Becker's Ring**	*Steven Martin Cohen*	£5.99
0 671 85503 4	**Absolute Power**	*David Baldacci*	£5.99
0 671 85602 2	**Total Control**	*David Baldacci*	£6.99
0 671 85483 6	**Dead Man's Dance**	*Robert Ferrigno*	£5.99
0 671 85468 2	**Vertical Run**	*Joseph Garber*	£5.99

Please send cheque or postal order for the value of the book, and add the
following for postage and packing: UK inc. BFPO 75p per book; OVER-
SEAS Inc. EIRE £1 per book.
OR: Please debit this amount from my:

VISA/ACCESS/MASTERCARD ....

CARD NO...

EXPIRY DATE..

AMOUNT £...

NAME...

ADDRESS...

....

SIGNATURE...

Send orders to:
Book Service By Post,
PO Box 29, Douglas, Isle of Man, IM99 1BQ
Tel: 01624 675137, Fax 01624 670923
http://www.bookpost.co.uk
e-mail: bookshop@enterprise.net for details

Please allow 28 days for delivery.
Prices and availability subject to change without notice.